MATCH FOR THE BILLIONAIRE

A Boss Romance

Seattle CEO series
Book 1

EVE MADISON

Editing: Shika Tamaklo

Proofing: Gennifer Ulmen

About

MIA

He's making me an offer I can't refuse.

When I'm offered a job—by my most difficult customer at my waitressing gig—as his assistant, I thought it would be simple.

I never expected to agree, to say yes.

But I needed the money.

And I needed the time to work on my art.

What I didn't prepare for was slowly but surely becoming the center of my boss's attention.

He's sexy and strong, but he's insufferable and impatient.

He's gorgeous and cocky and full of himself.

He's always right, even when he's wrong.

But he just might be the one…

DEREK

I'm desperately trying to avoid the worst business decision of my life.

When I ask Mia Kamaka to be my assistant, and she accepts, I'm a little too happy.

She's beautiful.

I want to do a lot for her.

But many burdens lie ahead.

We can't continue on this path.

Well, maybe we can.

But here's the catch: what if there's a better path?

What if she's the one?

Match for the Billionaire is a standalone novel, and a part of the Seattle CEO series. The Seattle CEO series are standalone romances, with no cliffhangers and characters who make cameos in other books of the series.

WARNING: Explicit love scenes and strong language, and adult situations.

This is for the amazing women in my life—women like Becca Syme and Jamie Poole—who taught me that it was okay to start over.

Remember: It's never too early and never too late to begin again.

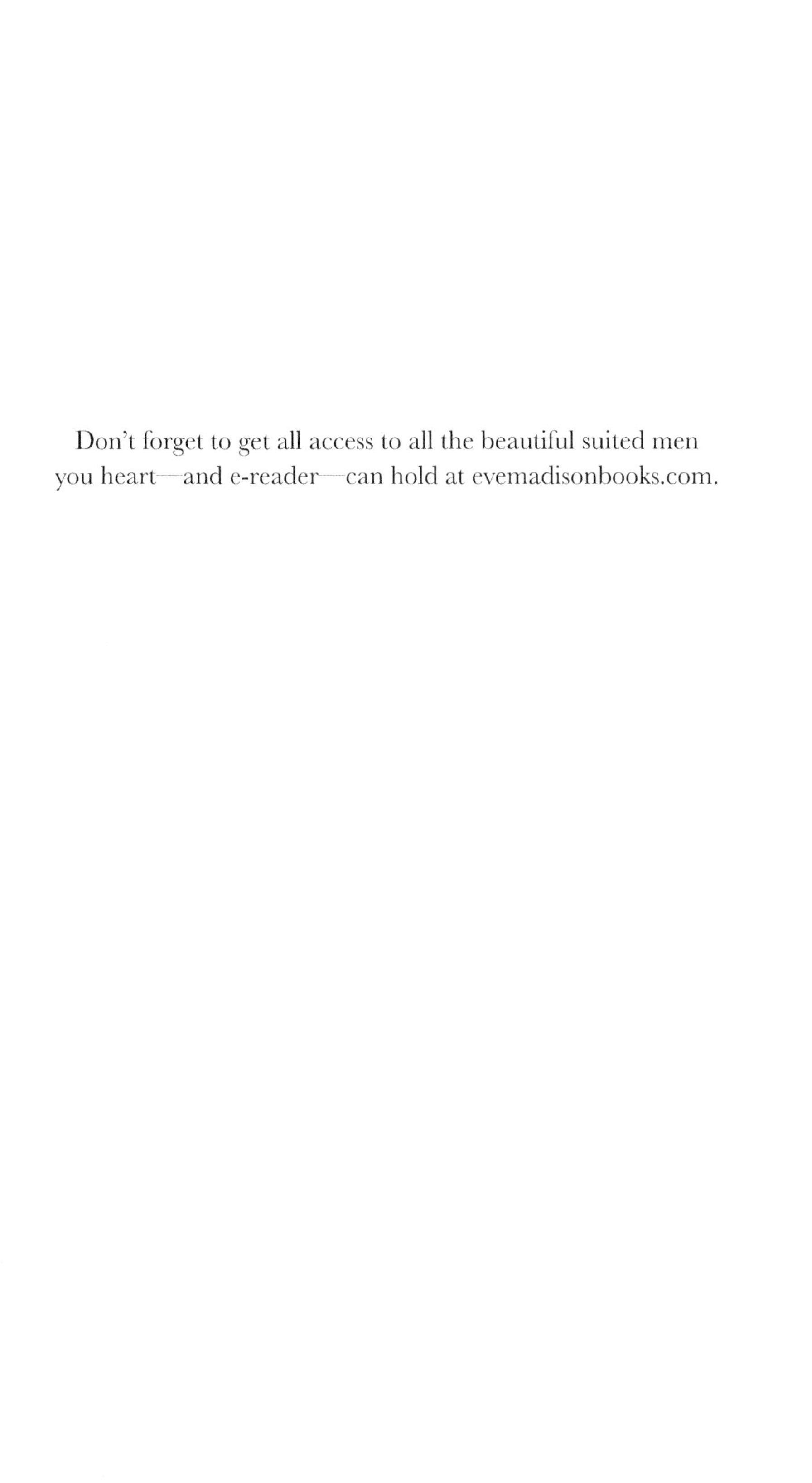

Don't forget to get all access to all the beautiful suited men you heart—and e-reader—can hold at evemadisonbooks.com.

Chapter One

SEATTLE WASHINGTON

MIA

"You're firing me? But I—I just walked in the door two seconds ago."

More like one second ago. But Jerry doesn't seem to give a damn.

I'm sure my restaurant manager here at Sopra doesn't give a damn about many things—unless they have nipples on them, but today, that normally smarmy smile of his is almost sad, his thin lips pressed in a soft frown that lets me know it's exactly as I feared.

I'm being canned. And I don't even know what I've done.

Okay, scratch that. I don't know what I've done lately.

Tempted to fidget with the dark curls piled at the back of my neck, I shift on my black kitten heels in the doorway of the noisy restaurant kitchen, my chest starting to squeeze as I run down a list of the mistakes I've made since I started this waitressing job.

And the list isn't short.

"It's not that I'm firing you, Mia. Because I'm not." He glances at my chest. "With your set of…skills, I'm definitely not. It's just that…we can't have you spilling hot coffee on customers. Especially customers whose business we like to keep." He lowers his voice. "Now, I didn't tell you this, but this guy—the customer you pissed off? He knows the owner. So it wasn't me." He raises his sweaty hands, taking a step back, his brown eyes muted under the dull fluorescent light streaming just two feet away.

Having successfully dodged the blame, he smiles again, and a disgusted shiver crawls down my spine as I wring my waitress apron in my hands.

"So that's it, then? I'm not being fired. But I'm obviously in trouble. So, what is it? What's my situation? Am I still serving customers? Or should I pass that nice lady at table seven without her afternoon coffee?"

Jerry shrugs. "Just think of it as a warning. A strong warning. One more of those, and I think Danny the owner might have another girl auditioning for your wait spot next week…"

"Probably one with even bigger breasts," I mutter, glancing over towards the restaurant's main floor. I plaster on a smile, raising my chin. "You got it, Jer. Won't happen again."

His gaze flickers to my chest again. "Oh I'm sure it won't. I believe in you, Mia. I know you wouldn't do anything to jeopardize this job."

Like hell, I wouldn't.

But I bypass him anyway, slipping into the kitchen, my hands tying my apron around my waist.

I try not to let my fingers shake.

It's been four months that I've been working at Sopra. Four months of making the biggest tips I've ever seen.

Working at one of Seattle's most famous, four-star restaurants has its perks, least of all the customers.

And though I wasn't winning any awards for World's

Greatest Waitress, I had managed not to kill anyone or seriously injure them.

Sure, I'd splashed a little orange juice on a few suits and dropped a few muffins more than once. But serving wasn't rocket science.

Except today, it might as well be as I pick up Table Seven's order, trying to keep my brain focused on making it through the day—just one day without any mishaps—as Jerry's words spin like a record in my mind.

I've just slipped the plate on Seven's table when someone waltzes in step beside me, their footfalls echoing softly over the understated dark marble floor as they whisper near my ear.

I almost jump back.

"Sooo?" Christina hisses inches from my eardrum. "What do you think? You like the new job?"

I keep walking. "Well, I struggle not to coat my customers with one drink or another every time I serve and I'm struggling not to get fired. But so far, so good." I tilt my head, blinking my eyes. "Luckily, I've got a calming crystal in my purse. Which I think is keeping me from eating my own shoe in embarrassment."

Christina nudges me, following me closer to the kitchen, her brown bob swinging in my direction. "You and your crazy crystals. And no, I'm not talking about this job. I'm talking about the 'other' one. The one I got you last week? How was that?"

"The one last week was with a private investigations firm. And I have less than zero interest in what they're asking me to do."

"What? It's extra money. Money for that magazine competition of yours. And it's photography! It's what you've always wanted to do."

"Yeah, Tina." I spin by the bar, keeping my voice low. "Photography. You know… Art. Actual photos. Not snapping away at philandering husbands caught with their pants down."

My closest colleague rolls her eyes. "Beggars can't be choosers."

"And fifty-year-olds with erectile dysfunction shouldn't be cheaters. But here we are."

I grab for another tray from the oak bar, my hands struggling to balance it, and Tina luckily leaves it alone, letting me walk away.

At twenty-six, sometimes I feel too old for the bullshit that comes with serving.

I'm already too amped up to walk straight in my kitten heels. And Tina bringing up last week's embarrassing job interview isn't helping me stay mishap-free…

The bright side is: I'm only two thousand dollars away from my goal.

So far, Table Seven made it without wearing her favorite Americano, but the rest of my customers remain to be seen.

I won't even think about the one customer who ratted me out. I already have a good idea of who it is.

As I load my plate with dishes for Table Twelve, I try not to think about him. About his infuriatingly smug face. His chiseled jaw. Or even those stupid, stunning, blue eyes.

I hit the main floor of the warm, cozy Italian restaurant, counting my steps, praying I don't fall.

Luckily, I make it.

"Here you go," I say to the two businesswomen sipping their Seattle martinis. "The chef's favorite. Buon Appetito."

Only about two more million of those to serve and I can count this day as a success. Another day to put money towards the photography competition hovering over me like a money cloud for months.

Three hours pass and not a drop spilled.

As the cool northwestern day falls into a colder evening, I

glance out the front glass wall of the building, counting down the minutes until the end of my shift.

Only two orders left and then I'm out of here.

With the clock striking six o'clock, I head back to the kitchen in a daze, grabbing the next table's order.

I'm just about to slide it over to the table that ordered it when a strong pair of hands come into sight, whisking the glass of dark whiskey right off my tray.

I look up to find a random customer grabbing the drink.

But not just any customer.

It's him. Asshole of the Month.

A customer whose icy demeanor and smug face has haunted me for the last two months I've worked here—ever since he showed up one day and sat down in front of me at the bar, barely acknowledging my presence.

He doesn't talk to you. He doesn't acknowledge you. He doesn't smile at you.

He most definitely doesn't ask for permission when ordering a drink or a meal. It's as if he demands it first, that way his order is always perfect.

Right now, the way he waltzes the drink into his hand, as if I were a bar stool and not an actual person, tips my core into an even deeper fever. A flash of hot anger blazes my temples.

He passes by me in a blink, slinking into the corner booth. His eyes on his phone, he barely notices me. I stand there, gaping at him from where he sits, when he raises a pair of cool blue eyes, assessing me, his gaze guarded.

Under Sopra's dim gold recessed lighting, his golden-brown hair gleams, the blue-white screen of his cell phone screen making the perfect strands shine.

The device buzzes several times in his hands, signs of incoming texts, and he dismisses me just as coolly as he grabbed the glass from my tray.

"Can I help you with something?"

His gaze stuck on his phone, he pads his thumbs over the small screen in his hand, and I have to struggle not to breathe out fire, I'm so mad.

Instead, I even manage to grit out a few words. Yay me.

"Uh, yeah, I think you can," I respond, at last. "Mind handing me that stolen drink back?"

"I'm sorry?" He doesn't glance up.

"Yeah, the drink. The one in your hand? You mind putting your lips on something that belongs to someone else?"

That gets his attention.

"Unfortunately, this glass has an owner. And she's right over there." I reach over, snatching the thick-plated glass from his hand before I can stop myself. Tension holds my body rigid, brittle enough to break in half. "Maybe you should wait for your waitress to return to your table with your order."

He frowns. "That's not my drink?"

"Well, I do think that me saying so about five times confirms that fact, so yes...that's correct. That was not your drink. You should talk to your waitress."

"I don't have a waitress. Not yet, at least. I ordered a whiskey at the bar, and they promised they'd bring it right over."

"Well, I'm not the 'they' they promised. Good luck with that."

I try to turn away. But his voice stops me, the words as smooth as silk.

"A shame," he says, his head tilting back to the phone. "How much would it take for a man to get a drink around here?"

"Our prices are on the menu. I'm sure you can find out there."

"I mean for that drink. The one I almost put my lips on." He smiles at his phone, but I know it's meant for me. And no, it doesn't make me feel funny things happen in my pants.

And Mr. Perfect keeps talking, not missing a beat—as if he's practiced this.

"I'll pay double the price on the menu, if you sit it back down. No questions asked."

"See, that's the problem." I sway on my feet, gazing at his downturned face, the tray in my hands growing heavy. "If I give you this drink, then the woman who ordered it might have to wait another twenty minutes for another one. As you can see, the bar's kinda full."

"Three times the price," he says, still typing.

"This isn't an auction. You don't have to keep jacking up the price."

"Four times."

"I really don't think you need to—"

"Five times the cost." He finally gazes upwards. "And I'll buy you one, too, Whiskey Police. You look like you could use it."

And I'm not the only one who could. The guy seems busier than a one-man circus show, his typing never stopping, his fingers constantly moving.

He's like a machine.

Completely cold. Totally calculating.

And I don't know why it intrigues me. Why his total nonchalance and dogged focus drive something in me that wants to take a peek behind his perfect curtain.

I decide to give it a try. "Look, you seem like a guy who's used to getting what he wants. So, I'll make it easy for you..." I straighten my shoulders. "This drink does not belong to you. And neither do I. Like I said, I'm not your waitress. Now... I'm sure your actual waiter or waitress will be happy to serve your needs whenever they come. But as for me? I'm already spoken for. Have a nice night. And while you're at it, try not to steal any more drinks. The managers really frown on that kind of thing. And so do the cops, I hear. Good luck with your whiskey."

And with that, I spin away, feeling triumphant, like I won some unspoken contest.

Like I've rightfully pissed him off.

A little payback never felt so good.

That is, until in all my spinning and walking off, I twirl my tray right into a customer standing a few feet away.

The glass goes flying, whiskey spilling everywhere. It sloshes and splashes with a final drenching...right onto the suit of Scott Macpherson—known to everyone in this restaurant as the Big Boss.

The one who writes all the checks.

The owner of Sopra...and, subsequently, of my ass.

And within seconds, after staring in horror at his wet face, I think I know what exactly is going to happen to that ass tonight...

So much for avoiding mishaps.

I swallow thickly, my job and the magazine competition I'd been hoping for flashing before my eyes.

Chapter Two

DEREK

She was right. It's been a long time since I've heard "no."

And her "no" might be the sexiest one I've gotten in some time.

I might be distracted. But I'm not blind.

I like to think of myself as a master of multitasking, and even in my efforts to secure a whiskey, respond to Jen's texts, answer a thousand emails, and finish off this after-hours meeting, I don't neglect to notice that my waitress is goddamned stunning.

One first look is all I need. But the last look confirms what I suspected from the instant I crossed her path…

She doesn't really like me. She wouldn't be the first person in Seattle.

And sexy or not, I'm just about to let her go, let her leave with that sassy attitude and the whiskey I wanted so bad when she collides with some stuffy-shirted dickhead in a polo—some prick that acts like wetting his collared shirt is a cardinal sin.

I watch from where I sit as he wipes rivulets of dark liquor from his face, his bald head gleaming under the gold light.

"Jesus fucking Christ," he curses out loud, drawing attention. "You think you could watch where you're going?"

"I am so sorry, Danny—um, Mr. Macpherson," the formerly slick-tongued waitress stutters. "I could get you a towel—"

"No, leave it. You've done enough already."

But she's already turning, whipping into another waitress. And down waitress number two goes.

Her tray goes flying in the air, sending more liquid splashing all over the place, and if I weren't supposed to be in the middle of the most important meeting of my life right now, I'd laugh.

Instead, I tuck my phone away to avoid the spray, standing to my feet, when I notice that my unwanted waitress is wearing some mystery orange sauce on her uniformed blouse from the small melee.

I try to hide the smile that hits my face.

"Well, at least it's your color," I mutter, taking in the mess.

The brunette glances at me, horror imprinted on her face, not seconds before the man in the polo turns to her, his face turning an unnatural shade of red, his neck strained.

"Could you be any worse at your fucking job?"

He approaches her, still dripping wet.

God fucking help me, I don't know what gets into me. Because instead of calling Simon Disrick and rescheduling our meeting location and getting the hell out of Dodge, I step suddenly into the balding man's path, hands up, my body blocking his path to the cute little server that was just making my life a living hell.

And somehow it feels natural as hell to me.

My fingertips nearly touch his damp chest, I'm so close. I can smell the cigarette smoke on his breath.

"Look, she said she was sorry, guy. Let her get you a towel and someone'll get you another drink. Preferably one you don't have to wear on your shirt. How's about that?"

He goes to say more but a slew of waitstaff come to his aid, whisking him away. And stuck between a wet spot and an angry waitress, I turn to the latter, eyebrows raised at the look of dismay on her face.

She says nothing, quiet for the first time all night. And I break the silence.

"You do have a hell of a way of making friends around here, don't you?"

She shoots me a look, that stubborn gaze of hers wilting by a fraction, and without another word, she takes off towards the back of the restaurant, in what I'm sure is the direction of the restrooms.

And I feel like a fucking tool.

I could go after her.

Sure, I could do that. Or I could sit back in my booth, shoot a text to Mr. Disrick and close this acquisitions deal before the stroke of nine.

Securing his publishing house would be the much-needed cherry on my shit-sundae of a year, and I know if I act now, I can clinch the deal, grab a shot of whiskey or two, and crank my Alice in Chains playlist to ear-splitting levels all the way home.

Yeah, I could do that.

Or I could go after that crazy waitress.

And from the looks of the puddle on the floor, I already know what the better choice is.

But for the first time today, reason doesn't win out. My feet do.

And they drag my unreasonable ass in the direction of the retreating waitress, who, as guessed, hightails it in the women's restroom, the door closing behind her with a dull thwack.

I stand on the other side of the heavy wood, lost for where to even begin. I clear my throat.

"I—uh… Look, that joke was tasteless. I shouldn't have said anything."

Nothing but silence on her end. I keep going.

"Look, don't listen to that walking, talking penis out there, alright? You're not a bad waitress. A mean one, maybe. But not bad. You didn't deserve that."

I wait but still nothing.

Seems like the version of the waitress I first met—the whiskey police—is still here after all.

I run a knuckle along the door. "That offer on the drink still stands, by the way."

I'm just turning away. I have places to be. Places that don't include the inside of a ladies' room. But just as I'm turning to make my escape, the door slides open.

"Really?"

I'm doing my best to rein in the need that's suddenly clogging my throat. She's standing there in the doorway, her thumb and pointer finger holding the door, the rest of her arm red and stained, some of the sauce having found its way onto her skin.

She's still sizing me up. I try not to glare when I can feel my eyebrows rise at their own willing.

"What I mean is, do or don't you want to take that drink?"

Like some kind of idiot, I smile—fully aware that it's probably not something she'd appreciate.

But before I can continue with the gloating, the door slides open some more and I'm face to face with her, the same dark, curly hair peeking out around the edge of the door.

She says nothing, eyeing me up and down like a dirty dish rag that she hasn't decided to rewash yet. Then she sighs.

She's got her hair swept to the side, the end curled under, making it appear shorter, framing her pretty face.

A good look on her.

"I'm sorry," she starts. "For before. For whatever I did back there. I—I don't know why I just did that. It…it wasn't right."

What do I say to that?

Instead of looking in her eyes, I focus on her lips, her knuckles.

“Hey, no worries,” I say. “It was my fault, too. I should’ve stepped in sooner. And I do apologize. I had it coming. Forgot who I was dealing with.”

She stares at me, eyes wide. “Oh.”

"That's my asshole way of saying that you're tough." I snort. "'Tough' is a good thing. It means you can handle yourself and that's an admirable trait to have in Seattle." I pause. "You're not from here, are you?"

Out of nowhere, she raises an eyebrow at me. "No. I'm not."

"So…what are you doing here?"

"I... That's a rather personal question."

"Well, you didn't answer the other one, so I'm asking you again."

She pauses, her heels hitting the ground softly. She glances at her shoes before looking up at me and clearing her throat.

A knot that was dwelling in my stomach unwinds slightly.

"Okay"—my waitress lifts her chin suddenly—"to answer your first question: I think I do want that drink. And to answer the other unspoken question in the air right now: Yes, I haven't stopped thinking that you are still in fact a jerk."

I smirk. "That's good to know."

She blinks hard. And then: "I'm Mia. Mia Kamaka.”

"So it would seem. So, what'll it be?"

"I'm not letting you buy me a drink."

"I thought you said I could buy you a drink."

She scoffs lightly. "I said I'll have a drink with you. I never said you could buy it. I'm not letting a customer spend money after I spilled drinks on him tonight."

"At least they weren't my drinks."

"Still, I'm not letting you buy me a drink."

"Fine. How about a dick shooter?"

"What—" she sputters, momentarily taken aback. "What in the world is a 'dick shooter'?"

I laugh. "A mix of Jack, Jameson, and two types of whiskey. It barely classifies as a drink. It's more engine oil than anything else. I'll mix up a pour for you."

The waitress tries and fails to stifle a smile.

"And don't do that."

"What?" she asks, biting her lip, a move I now know I'm not immune to.

"That thing you're doing with your lip. That says more about you in this moment than whatever words you could possibly say to me. Your lip is saying 'I'm rethinking that drink' and that is cheating. So stop it. And stop saying 'what' after everything I say."

She reaches up and touches her lip lightly, a perplexed look in her eyes. She rests her hand on her chest.

"Fine," she says. "You can buy me a drink. But whatever you're thinking, a 'dick shooter' is not appropriate."

"Fine. Cock shooter."

"I'm not drinking that, either." She huffs, her nose in the air.

"Are you always this difficult?" I ask, my lips in a tight line.

She holds her hands up. "Never."

"Fine. A plus-one shot."

"Less gallant than the cock shooter, right?"

"Something like that. It's a classy drink."

She twists her lips, a lopsided expression. "It's still rude."

"I never claimed to be anything else...Mia. And to extend this rude kick I'm on, let me just tell you this: If that guy out there was your boss, then you're way too good a waitress to be dealing with that," I say, gesturing to the door. "This place needs people like you. Not the other way around, remember that. Keep that in mind...and you just might make it in Seattle after all."

I hold out my hand, making sure it's not just some reflex thing, my eyes on her as I slowly extend my palm.

"But in case you don't make it here—in this restaurant or Seattle at large, at least you can say you've made at least one friend out of a customer...albeit one thieving, whiskey-guzzling one."

Slowly, she takes my offered hand.

"Is that what you're doing here? Making a friend?" she asks, and I look in her eyes, somewhere between skepticism and blankness. And then, I catch a hint of a smile.

"What I'm doing here," I answer, softly, running the pad of my thumb across her knuckles, even as I realize that there's still a small chance I'm blowing Mr. Disrick off, "is making a really big fucking mistake. And I usually don't make those. It's refreshing."

"Ah, I see we have that in common today."

"Yeah?"

She nods once.

I pull my arm back slowly and wait for her to take the bait. Wait for her to tell me no again, wait for her to change her mind.

But she doesn't.

Instead, she looks at me for a long, hard moment, her eyes moving from my eyes to my lips before she brushes past me to walk out the restroom door. I follow, every bit of reason I thought I'd brought here tonight vanishing over the past few minutes as I realize that, despite being on the cusp of securing a new publishing deal and taking my company to a so-called "brand-new level," this is the first time I've been excited about anything in—I don't even know.

Years?

I step out of the door, following her through the restaurant, through the kitchen to the back door, where she throws her coat on, shrugging her shoulders as she puts it on. I wait until she's buttoned her coat and looks up at me.

I'm nervous.

I can't figure out what I should say. What I want to say, how I should set up the next step, what is the right thing to do.

All I know is that I want her.

No matter the cost.

I want this Mia, someone who just cursed me out over whiskey, who looks like she's got the cojones to jaw a guy three tables over and then compete in the Miss America beauty pageant in one night.

An oil-stained waitress just passing through town and a guy like me, who hasn't had a relationship in—when did I have a relationship last?

"So, are you always dressed like you're heading to an important business meeting?" she asks, looking up at me, tilting her head.

I don't hesitate. "Yes. I was born in a suit. This is my natural-born state."

"Hmph. Funny. Because this seems to be mine," she says, gesturing downwards.

I look over at her, my eyes on her stained shirt, low heels, and pressed skirt.

"I have to say"—she talks as she walks—"for a guy who looks like he's never had his khakis wrinkle, you certainly know how to be charming."

"One"—I lift a finger—"I don't wear khakis. Two, I'm not charming. Just saying what's on my mind. It's a gift."

"Packaged in with your many, many lines."

"That a good thing or a bad thing?"

She blinks. Takes a deep breath. "I don't know. Maybe. Definitely. I haven't decided yet."

"Noted."

I gaze out at the evening rain just starting to fall into the streets, the lights of downtown shimmering to the west and my hotel being just to the east, the car I've rented for the night just a few blocks down, parked outside the hotel's front door.

With a glance at the city before us, I almost start to tell Mia that she changed my usual mode of operation tonight.

My monk-like solitude has been rocked by a woman I don't know.

A woman who doesn't particularly like me.

My thoughts never stray from her, from the meeting of our eyes, from the regret in her voice, from the way her lips curled when she told me her name.

Sounds crazy. Maybe it is.

But I don’t have time to figure that out.

Because I just have time enough to catch a whiff of her skin, grin a little too hard, and walk out the back door with her.

Chapter Three

MIA

I must be crazy. I must be insane. I must be getting soft in my old age of twenty-six. Or maybe it's something in the air. And by air, I of course mean whiskey.

Because tonight? Tonight, I've drunk enough of the brown stuff to kill an ox.

And I feel fine.

I feel like I'm fine for at least two hours after Blue Eyes and I leave Sopra. Although, that might be because of all the lovely, lovely whiskey that sang its siren song in my ear until I couldn't possibly resist its call.

All in all, I'm not feeling sorry for how this night has gone for me.

Sure, I lost one of my shoes in a gutter, got kicked out of bar and almost summoned dolphins while off-key singing Backstreet Boys karaoke. But that's okay.

At least I feel totally, utterly and completely desensitized. I'm numb everywhere.

Everywhere but my feet, that is. Because my feet are a hell of a lot sorer than they were back at the diner, when they were stuck in those ugly, uncomfortable but oh so homely black heels.

I giggle at the thought of never having to wear them again now that I'm fired from the only steady job I've had in months. As we walk out of another bar into what I assume is the mainstream of downtown Seattle for the night, I kick at the damp concrete in front of me with more energy than I've had in ages.

The air is chilly in Seattle tonight—cold, wet and icy from today's on-and-off frozen rain.

With a final laugh, I turn to my companion for tonight—Mr. Blue Eyes, ready to laugh some more at my stupid adventures of the night.

But I get no laugh.

I blink a few times, finally noticing the deep furrow on Blue Eyes' face.

He doesn't look like he wants to laugh. In all actuality...he looks mad, his caramel-brown eyebrows knitting together, that full mouth of his grim and cold.

He stares at me, his eyes under the dim lobby lights hunting me down.

"What?" I ask as we face each other.

"You. You're shit-faced drunk."

"And you're very astute. Great powers of observation, Dr. Blue Eyes."

"You said you could handle your whiskey. You've had one and a half drinks...if you count the one you stole from me. Which I don't. Did you take something?" He leans in closer, his large hands supporting my frame. "Any pills, maybe?"

"No, I didn't take anything. I just...-" I start to tell him that I've just never been drunk before. Not like this. Not where I don't really care about these stupid things that really matter to me. "I just needed to forget everything."

“Like?”

“I don’t know. Like everything. For someone out there

who's just a magnetic hardass, you sure don't pick up on things easily, do you?"

"Trust me: It turns out I'm not picking up on a lot of things these days," he says, shaking his head slowly with a smirk that's somehow both knowing and a little bit bitter. "Like the fact that you obviously don't drink."

"How do you know?"

"You mean other than the fact that you're walking like a baby deer fresh out of its mother's womb? I never would've invited you for a drink if I'd known you were this...inexperienced." He crosses his arms, holding me as close as he did on the street back in the bar.

I tip my head back and look up at him, feeling his presence, his magnetic presence that pulls me – no, keeps me – from doing what I'd been trying to do earlier tonight—leave.

"Like you know the first thing about my life."

"I know you're way too drunk to make good decisions right now. And the rest..." He pauses, looking me over. "You can fill in for me later. But first, a word of advice..." He steps closer, towering over me. "You need to be a little more distrustful, Mia. Like letting a stranger—even an entertaining jackass like me in a suit—carry you from bar to bar. You're lucky I'm not some deviant—a man without scruples who...." His stare darkens. "...would've taken advantage of you like this."

He sounds like he's warning me. Warning me from doing something that would get me...in trouble.

I try not to, but I can't stop my body from shuddering lightly at the thought of some mental image Blue Eyes has conjured up.

I'm just not used to anyone—man or Greek God—being nice to me. And I don't know if it's the booze or his crisp, clean smell. But I take a step towards him, my head tilting to the side.

As though he knows what I'm doing, he steps even closer,

his body now shielding mine from the wind and the rain and what's left of downtown Seattle.

I'm not so sure he's really shielding me. More like trapping me.

And I'm not so sure I mind.

"Why are you so concerned about me tonight?" I ask softly, too softly, my words all breathy and strangely out of tune.

"I'm not. I..." He strokes his right hand against my cheek. "Just want us to be responsible here."

I laugh. "Mr. Perfect has rules. Well, how's this for responsible?"

I rise up on my tippy-toes and press a kiss to his mouth. And for the love of whiskey and Backstreet Boys fans everywhere, he actually lets me.

Despite the cool December air, his mouth is warm, full and inviting.

Every inch of my body is on fire as he kisses me back. Slanting his head, he angles his kiss against my lips, sliding and sweeping in broad strokes that leave me panting and wet.

I've been kissed before. But never like this.

So sensual. So raw. So slick with layers of natural power.

Heat rushes through my body, the tingles sneaking in between the slosh of whiskey. His hand cups the back of my head, then traces its way down my arms, pushing them in between us.

"Mia..."

The way he says my name is a warning, a full stop.

I pull away, my mind swimming in whiskey, a blast of fresh, raw and unfamiliar emotions—and a strong desire to feel another kiss, another touch of his hand against my body. Wide-eyed, I wipe the back of my hand against my mouth, as if I can erase what just happened.

"I'm sorry," I blurt out, warmth creeping into the skin of my neck. "I'm not usually like this. Usually..."

"Drunk?" Mr. Perfect cocks one amusing eyebrow. "I know. I can see that, Mia. Which is why I'm not pushing you up against a wall right now and doing things to you that might make us both see God."

Oh my.

I clear my throat. "So, why are we...not?"

"Responsibility," he says, his voice scratchy and still close to me. "Because you needed help and I could give it to you. But I didn't. I need to get you home. To bed."

"To yours, or—"

"To your own. You're way more inebriated than I am, Mia. And I will not take advantage of you. Or this situation. Not my style."

"I see. So, condescension is your style then? Because I'm perfectly capable of making decisions rationally."

"Oh really?"

"Yes."

"And where are we now, then?" He looks up. "Do you know what street we're on? What part of downtown Seattle we're in?"

"I—"

"Because I do. Before you kissed me, we were actually wandering into a sketchier part of town. Normally, I wouldn't mind. I actually know people in this area of town," he says. "But I also know you've had a lot to drink. I can risk my own well-being. I'm not inclined to risk yours."

I try to make eye contact with him, but the fog of whiskey, a ball of emotion and the earnest look in his blue eyes make doing so nearly impossible.

I try to remind myself that I still don't know this man. That no matter how 'White Knight' he may come across, I really do need to get my starry-eyed shit under control.

I've been in this line of restaurant work long enough to know that these men are usually not who they seem. And he is no exception.

Men of a certain social class—men like Scott Macpherson, like my ex-fiancé, like this guy—are all the same.

Sure, the fashionable clothes, the designer suits...the sculpted jaws...the lengthy vacations in exotic locations...are usually enticing in the beginning. But eventually, the shiny veneer that they erect for the world to see fades.

In Blue Eyes' case? The veneer just happens to extremely enticing, which makes me even more wary.

How many men look like this? Have money like this? Smell as unfairly delectable like this?

Even as I drift closer, arms crossed, I can smell his cologne.

Something purely clean and crisp on the nose. Something that reminds me of the Pacific Sound—waves crashing over sharp rocks. Something that sings of deep masculinity and French open-air cafes.

His phone rings in his pants pocket, but after glancing at it, he tucks it back in the pocket.

Turning back to me, he gives me that grin I'm growing to hate less and less by the minute.

My face heats as his stare traces over my face, up to my lips, and finally my eyes. I shift on my feet. "What?"

"You're staring," he says, one eyebrow hooking.

"I'm not staring...Simply looking at your bionic, vibrating slacks. Important call?" I joke in return.

He raises a brow as his phone goes off again, this time he pulls it out, checks it, and then tucks it back in his pocket.

"Nothing important enough," he answers me.

Cocky Blue Eyes walks past, doing more than a few more inches of separation before he turns back, hands folded behind his back as he gazes at me. "So... what kind of work got you into all this? Doing what you do, I mean. Or is waitressing really your calling?"

I roll my eyes, pursing my lips. "It's not that complicated."

"Sounds like it is," his eyes travel down my body, "since you're wearing today's special-order sauce."

I feel my face heat again.

"Well, I'm curious."

I scoff, looking around.

"Mhm." He nods. "Lemme guess: What you did back in the restaurant...is something you've never done before...correct?"

I frown. "What do you mean?"

"I mean," he places his hands in his pants pockets, his head tilted as he gazes at me, "you've never done something like what you just did. Walked out of a shift while in the middle of it. No offense...but you strike me as the kind of woman who tends to play by the rules. Who plays it safe." He steps forward, holding his hand out to touch my cheek. His eyes darken, like the evening. "When my judgment isn't clouded, I'm usually a good judge of character. Or at least I have to be in my line of work. I can see it in your eyes: You're terrified you've fucked up your life tonight. Probably because you don't make many mistakes in your life. You've just walked out on your job, and you're staring at an overdressed bastard like me, wondering if you've made the biggest blunder of your life by following me out those back doors and ultimately heading home." He hesitates. "Am I right?"

My jaw drops, and any snark I have ready to throw his way vanishes in an instant.

Holy Howie Mandel, this guy is blunt. And though it should turn me completely off...all I can do is stare.

His eyes tell me it's the truth. And his words...

They're having an effect on me.

Men in my life don't exactly have a reputation for honesty. And when they were...it was far too late.

I lick my lips, noticing moisture from the rain starting to trickle down my face. "I never said I was going home with you."

He shrugs, a small smile on his chiseled face. "You're not. When I said 'home,' I meant yours." He holds up a phone towards my face. "This is your phone. I swiped it earlier when it was unlocked and texted the person you talk to most, who I presume is someone who lives near you..." He reads from his phone. "Christina King. I've already dropped our location back when you were screeching out the Backstreet Boys in that little karaoke episode at the last bar."

My heart races as I grip my phone from his fingers, my legs shaky.

His eyes turn back to mine, the blue of his irises darkened. "Today wasn't your first really rough day at that job, was it? What happened at the restaurant. Before that. Your boss never came out. I know they had to see what was happening... And yet nobody stopped that guy from yelling at you. And I've seen the work you do. How efficient. How helpful you are. How willing you are to put up with asshole customers like me and still show up for your shifts every week, like clockwork. I know all this. Sopra's my favorite restaurant, I pay attention."

He pauses. My eyes search his. "Maybe you're too nice, Mia. Maybe you underestimate yourself." He says my name like he's trying it for the first of a thousand times. Testing its sound. I blink up at him. "You certainly haven't deserved what just happened. But you know that. You deserve more than this. Running out on your shift like you did...you're not a flake. Or-or a coward. You're a woman with a conscience." He gestures to me with his face tilted slightly. "My guess...is that many people don't appreciate that. But I do." He looks down at his phone. "I left my number in case you need something, Mia. Or if you ever want to...talk. Or-or something," he says the last word like it's a question. "And if you ever want a job, a different one... here's my number, too." He pushes a card into my hand, his fingers lingering for a count of about four before he takes them back.

I am unable to form words.

My mind is blank.

I have no reply, other than a stare.

I shake my head, both in disbelief and at the onslaught of a feeling I can't quite describe.

His words are so sincere. So raw. They make me...uncomfortable.

I'm breathing faster now, his intoxicating scent swirling around me, the words he's saying to me causing my heart to pound, my skin to warm...all the way to my toes.

Blue Eyes smiles, taking a full step so we're nearly nose-to-nose. He leans in, just as I hear the whoosh of a car door opening not far away.

A voice follows. And I jump nearly ten feet into the air, scrambling for space as I hear my name ring out in the alley.

"Mia? There you are! I was looking for you everywhere! You've been gone for a while." Tina gapes from thirty feet away. "I thought you had fallen into one of the bathroom toilets. Or was abducted! Until your friend texted me. Jerry is fucking furious. He was so mad you walked out that he slipped and fell on that perpetual wet spot next to the pick-up section. He's got brown goo dripping down the ass-crack of his pants and you are missing the laugh of a lifetime. The busboys can hardly bus the dishes, they're cracking up so hard." Her grin turns quickly into a frown. "What are you doing out here, anyway?" Tina pauses, putting her hands to her hip. "Are you doing some sort of seance back here with those crystals of yours? Because I don't think you can conjure up any better revenge than the one Jerry's getting right now." She laughs, chucking a thumb over her shoulder.

I give her my full attention, now taking a step in her direction. "Typical, I guess. Jerry's mad? Why? Because I walked out of the job before he could fire me?"

Tina scoffs, her brown bob swishing near her chin. "Complete horseshit. Jerry's not going to fire you. Jerry needs you. The entire management does. The entirety of the Seattle restaurant scene is short-staffed. There's no way Sopra is prepared to lose a pretty face, not to mention the best damn out-of-towner waitress Seattle has ever seen." Tina smiles, staring at me like she's waiting. "So...? What are we standing around out here for? Scott Macpherson left. Jerry's ass is wet. And I found the customer who complained to Jerry about you in the first place. The bartenders already put him out on his ass, and I—What?"

But I don't have words.

I turn towards Blue Eyes, ready to ask him all about this new revelation—considering the fact that I thought he was the one tattle-told in the first place.

But when I spin back to the spot where he stood, he isn't there.

Just a cold wind in the alley, the scent of his skin lingering where his body used to be.

My eyes scan the alleyway, my blood quickening.

"Mia?"

Tina calls, stepping into the alleyway. She scans the space and then she tilts her head, eyes widening. "What's wrong? You look weird."

"Yeah...I was looking for...oh, never mind. Just my keys," I lie, patting the bag on my shoulder, feet moving slowly towards her.

"Okay, well, hurry up. Jerry's probably cleaning himself off as we speak, and I haven't even taken pictures of his wet ass yet." She tucks her black and white polo in, her hand patting her terminally bone-straight hair square back in place. "And the best part?" She blinks sweetly, ushering me in. "That customer with his panties in a bunch left his wallet at the bar. So it's free drinks on him tonight. We'll close up, get out, head back to my apartment to watch The Devil Wears Prada for the fiftieth time and get properly chocolate chip-faced while we're at it. Oh, and apologize to Jerry now, okay? Everyone else already has for laughing right in his face."

I smile at her, but head towards her busted Oldsmobile's car door, stepping across the deserted alley.

I can't help but glance at the place where Blue Eyes stood and think about the last words he said to me.

Phrases like "deserve more than this" and "woman with a conscience" have never been directed towards me. I've been fed a line or ten before, but I've never had a man look me straight in the eye and speak so sincerely.

So boldly. So honestly.

Never before has a man so seductively not come on to me.

And I've never wanted to know a man more.

Behind Tina, I grab for the car door with a shaking hand and let go of a hard breath, realizing that she was right.

After watching The Devil Wears Prada, forgetting the day will be a breeze. But forgetting the man I spent the last few minutes talking to? Forgetting what it feels like to let a complete stranger read me like a poem...?

That'll be the million-dollar question.

I'm usually good at keeping my distance from people, but then, ordinarily, I don't allow complete strangers to just walk me into alleyways and speak to me like they've known me for years.

So, yeah. Maybe Tina's right and I'll wake-up tomorrow with everything forgotten.

Shake the dream. Wipe away the very thought.

But the way he said those words to me.... The way he somehow melted into me and then vanished....

I already know it's a memory I won't let go of easily.

And I don't even know his freaking name...

Chapter Four

EREK

"I need a new assistant."

My secretary Jenny stares at me over her red eyeglasses. "You have a perfectly fine one already in place."

"That's the problem. Maybe she's a little too 'fine'." I lean back in my leather office seat. "At least she thinks she is. She's been in the bathroom outside of her cubicle for over an hour."

"Is she ill?"

"Mentally, yes." I throw down the stack of folders just delivered on my oak desk, blowing out a breath hard enough to ruffle my dark hair. "Somehow, out of all the assistants in the greater Seattle area, I managed to pick up the one who is physically incapable of being on time and uses enough filler in her face alone to keep the Washington plastic surgery industry alive."

Jenny rolls her eyes, clutching the empty file of folders she just pulled from to lay thick papers on my desk. "You're picky."

"I'm particular."

"You've fired five assistants."

"Hmmm, technically, they were on a trial basis. They didn't make it past the trial. I didn't 'fire' anyone."

Jenny sighs, her heels circling my office carpet, red hair gleaming under the Seattle skyline's dull gray light.

"You say you want this acquisition of Bella Publishing to go well. Changing up your employees right before the deal goes down might not help."

"It has to." I stand from the leather office seat, practically leaping onto my brown Ferragamo shoes. "And after this article in the Seattle Post about me, I can't risk any more mishaps. More mistakes. More fuck-ups."

Walking over to the floor-to-ceiling windows overlooking downtown Seattle, I imagine all the people down there, on the street.

All reading about me. All snickering. All laughing about the publishing big-wig whose life was so screwed up he didn't know up from down.

I grit my teeth, placing a forearm on the glass. I look over to Jenny.

"I've already decided, Jen. I need you to tell Alexa. Tell her now. She's officially fired."

Once they're out of my mouth, the words feel good. I should have done this a long time ago.

"What about the files?"

"We'll figure that out." I rub my chin, staring at my office. "And while you're at it, can you re-confirm dinner reservations with Scott Disrick tonight at Sopra?"

"Sure. That is, unless Scott cancels on you...again." She lifts the stack of folders in her arms and shakes her head.

"Last night's standing-up will be the last time. He'll be there. He'd better be." My resolve hardens. "Unless he wants me to sue his ass for breach of contract. And I just wrote a thirty three-million-dollar check for that man."

"Got it. Fire your assistant. Re-confirm dinner. Pray Scott Disrick doesn't bail on you. Would you like me to clean the lobby, too?" Her voice is flat. "Or feed you grapes while you work? Since I see ridiculous requests are on the table today."

"Fuck, Jen, don't do that."

"Do what?"

"Treat me like the jackass, demanding boss I know I am." I open my arms as I walk over to her. "I'm trying here."

She meets me in the middle. Kissing my cheeks, she says, "God, it's scary how you can turn the charm on and off. You're even worse than Ryder these days."

"Damn." I puff out my chest. "Being compared to the brother I swore to never be is the very definition of pressure."

"Well, if the jackass tail fits."

I laugh, snorting at the white staining of the world outside as snow starts to fall. "Shit. Honestly. I'm really trying not to be a jackass...which is why I need that new assistant. I need someone who's more interested in doing a damn good job. And someone who's a lot less interested in...you know...me."

Jen's perfectly shaped eyebrows raise slightly. She hums softly. "Well, I mean...Alexa wasn't the one I picked for you, remember? I told you: Hiring assistants who look at you like they're seconds away from orgasmic bliss from being in the same room isn't going to be the best long-term solution for your professional success."

"I know. You did tell me." I put an arm around her shoulder and walk her to the door of my office. "And you've been saving my ass since it was practically in diapers. And that's the only reason I'm begging you go back to the temp agency and try to get me someone who can actually put up with me. The deal with Disrick is an important box to check off on the road to Hare & Holeton going public. None of us—not a single one of my brothers, the assholes that they are—can afford any more missteps. This deal is everything."

"I have to say. After everything we've been through, I'm surprised you care about this company this much. Just last week, you were cursing your job as CEO and threatening to become an artist instead. That was a short-lived thought."

I nod, smoothing down my ever-present tie. "It's still our baby. The company that has been given my name, my fortune, my blood. We built it together...unfortunately." I laugh bitterly, casting a glance at the rare ice-rain swirling around downtown Seattle. "But we've made it this far. We built it with funding we couldn't afford. And it's time we took advantage of that."

"Oh, I would say your brothers are taking plenty advantage of it, thank you very much. I walked past Ryder's office this morning. Heard him mention that since the weekend alone, he's already been on three different dates with three different women."

"Jenny, I'm going to say this one more time. My brothers...may be dating degenerates. But trust: They want Hare & Holeton to succeed too."

"You may be right. But that doesn't mean their antics are making things a little...bumpy along the way."

"Good. I hope they're enjoying the ride."

"Are you?"

I stare at her, trying to judge her mood.

"Don't worry. I'll get you someone by Monday." As if reassuring me, she twists her fingers into a cross.

"I trust you, Jen. I mean—we're not talking about finding a Betty White-double or some shit. We're talking about someone who can do their job fast, is willing to learn, and doesn't fall apart when I ask them to do anything. I mean, I could go find another Alexa. But I don't think that I should. Gonna need someone who can help me make sure this acquisition goes off without a hitch."

"I know. I just have one more idea, but we'd have to talk about it later."

"Hmmm. And speaking of the degenerates..." My phone makes a new ring in my pocket—my brother Ryder's ringing tone. I pull the phone out, eyeing the screen. "You know, I have a feeling I already know what you're thinking. I'd rather not. Just, please, get me a new assistant that can, you know… fulfill at least eighty-percent of my needs." I stop. "Needs of the non-sexual variety… okay?"

My phone rings again—and again, I glance down at the screen.

"Sure thing. And Derek?" Jen calls out.

"Yeah?"

"Don't send me anything else stupid to file. New assistant or not, someone has to answer your phone when it rings. And it's going to ring after this new article in the Seattle Post. A lot."

I raise an eyebrow at her, nodding in agreement. "It's ringing now. Ryder. Unless you want to hear him talk about the fourth date he's been on this week?"

"Welp. That's my cue to go." Jenny turns, walking out of my office.

"Not a moment too soon." I watch her, letting the door close before surrendering to the ringing phone in my pocket again.

I walk back through the dark office and pick up the phone, just in time.

"Did someone die, Ryder? Seriously. This better not be about whoever's open legs you stumbled into last night. Or the receptionist in the lobby with the brand-new tits. I heard enough about 'em last week."

Ryder chuckles. And it's not hard to picture his boyish smile, white teeth with that metallic hum of his voice at the other end of the line. He snorts. "Who? You mean, Stassia and her new boobs? I have news for you, man. I don't wake up and immediately begin the day with hooters on the brain. Besides..." I can practically hear him salivating over the smirk he's breaking out. "We have a date set up for tonight. Don't need hooters on the brain when you can have them in your hands."

"You already have four dates set up in one week. You realize you're setting some kind of record?"

"I could do it again. If I wanted to."

"Could have fooled me. You sound like all this entertaining is exhausting you already."

"Never. I just like to be in control of the menu."

I hold my laughter in, not wanting him to realize I actually found him funny.

"Don't pretend like you're not jealous."

"Just a little." I scoff, sitting in my chair, resting my head in my hands. "So, what's up? Why'd you call me? You need me to pick something up from the 7-Eleven so you can avoid that cute clerk you slept with?"

"No, no, nothing like that, Needle Dick." Ryder's voice, always playful, a little too carefree and much too amused, fills the line. "I've just been missing our brotherly chats since you got back in town last week. Thought you'd forgotten all about me. You went completely MIA, dude—checked out. It's been a while."

"Uh, yeah." I sigh, trying to play it down. "I've been busy."

"Yeah, busy avoiding me...and everyone else from the way I hear it." He hesitates. "I take it you read the article already?"

I glance down at the article on the edge of my desk, the Post's headline clearly illuminating the white page.

"I did," I say, turning my head to glare at the paper. "And I am starting to regret even giving the interview. Amongst other things."

"C'mon, man, look on the bright side. You're on the front of the Seattle Post. In print. You're world renowned right now. You are a celebrity. An icon."

My teeth clench on their own. "For having a girlfriend that was paid to date me."

"Would be worse if they paid Mandy to leave you and your dick a one-star Yelp review? At least she says you were great in the sack. All over Seattle, panties are falling to the floor to your picture right now. You can't pay for that kind of publicity."

"Yeah, well, our company is going to be the one paying for it...if Disrick bails on our acquisition deal. And then my assistant issue...I'm barely keeping up with emails and calls as it is."

"Still no luck?"

I shake my head. "None. Hard to find people you can...trust these days."

A beat passes. "Trust?"

"Yeah."

He's quiet again—a quality my big-mouthed little brother and Chief Technology Officer isn't exactly known for.

"Ryder," I start, "if you're going to ask me if I've talked to Killian since the article came out, don't. You know I haven't."

"I didn't ask," he says, his tone stiff. "And I wasn't going to. I don't know how those bastards at the Post found out about, um, Mandy and what Killian did. But I do know you, dude. Going to be kinda hard to avoid it for long, seeing as how he is the COO and second only to you—the boss."

"Ah, yes. I haven't forgotten that Killian is the Chief Operations Officer. And since you're the chief technology officer, do you think you can make a call to one of your high-tech buddies and get me an app that could let me send out emails out to the entire Seattle area, so I don't have to resort to meeting and interviewing in-person for a new assistant?"

Ryder pauses, and I know we're both thinking the same thing. I've long avoided this new assistant-hiring process like I've avoided Killian...and him. Like I'm avoiding everyone else from work. And I can't exactly live my life inside my office, though the thought had occurred to me.

Still, Ryder exhales out loud, letting me off the hook. "Sorry, man. Don't think they've built one yet, but I'll do you a solid. I'll talk to my assistant Oliver. He might have some leads for you. But a little heads-up: His leads typically come through the strip clubs...of the male variety."

"Hey, if they can do the job, I'm all ears." I stand and walk to the glass wall of my office, staring out at the work floor of Hare & Holeton, running my hand across the back of my neck, a habit I've had ever since the article was published and people began to look at me differently. "I'm not biased when it comes to gender here. I'll take all the available hands I can get."

"You sure about that?" Ryder stresses meaningfully. "Trust me: Oliver's good. But a male assistant can't give me all the hands I need."

"Maybe that's because the kind of 'hands' you're looking for are more concerned about what's going on in the front half of your trousers."

"Maybe." He laughs. "But hey, that's not my fault. I can't help it that our Anderson family genes gave me these stunning eyes, a chiseled jaw and an ass that won't quit."

"How unfortunate for you."

"Tell me about it: I've been cursed with it my whole life. And it was only one female assistant," he stresses, "that was giving me a, uh, hand with my trousers, alright? But one insane-o assistant is enough to scare me off hiring any more like her. I sure as hell don't need any more stalkers than I already have, thank you very much." He pauses. "Speaking of stalkers...Aren't you tired of being one with Scott Disrick lately?"

"No," I say, holding the phone closer. "The sooner we can get this acquisition deal done, the sooner we can rake in the dough and get our attention back on this IPO at the end of the year."

He's quiet for a beat, before switching into a different tone. "We'll get it done. As for getting you a new assistant, any particular type you're looking for?"

To which I say, "Nope."

"Seriously. Are you looking for someone hot? Someone smart? Or just someone who fits your ridiculous standards of perfection?"

I don't answer right away, my thoughts going to Mia Kamaka. The waitress fits my 'standards of perfection' to a T, with one big exception—the part where I can't have her.

Or have fun with her like I did last time we met. Or kiss her like she kissed me that last time I saw her.

"I don't know," I say, trying to concentrate on the call. "Just send me a good candidate. Prefer someone who can at least do what my former assistants couldn't. You know, stuff like answer phones, reply to emails and take notes."

"Sounds simple enough. And in the meantime, you've got Satan in a skirt as your Chief of Staff." He tuts. "I've never seen what you found so damn endearing about Jenny in the first place. She's fully loaded with crazy, man. I wouldn't trust her as far as I could throw her, which I bet would be about as far as she could throw me."

"Ah, you just don't like the fact that she's been calling you on your bullshit ever since the second grade."

"Okay, fine. I'll admit, she's got a pretty spicy tongue that puts our competition in their place."

"Part of her charm."

"But you can't deny that she's bossy as hell. She likes to get the last word in every conversation. And she's always trying to do my job. Which is cool—as long as I get the opportunity for a last word."

I almost laugh. "She gets results, Ryder."

"So do leeches," he says, before taking a deep breath and snapping back to a different topic: "Anyway, you done with me?"

I'll admit: Ryder's not always happy about his image as the "playboy" of our company. But he's even less happy that Jenny is a woman who knows all his charming tricks. And is able to shut them down at any given time.

"I'm still sussing out candidates for that potential CIO spot on the executive team," he tells me. "I've barely had time to breathe since the beginning of the year, what with the IPO and everything. So, this is where I end my services. You've got my number if you need me."

"Thanks. And I'll owe you big time for this one."

"And about our latest bro chat...Let's have that talk over dinner on Friday night, okay? We can be alone, put these crazy adult careers we've both managed to somehow land out of our minds for a few hours."

I start to nod when I swear I hear a sound outside my office door. I wait but the sound doesn't repeat itself.

I shrug it off. "I think I'd prefer to have your information rather than a chicken sandwich at the Del Fino, if you don't mind."

"Fine by me." He sounds amused. "I'll have the wild salmon and the fettucine al tonno."

"Who the hell orders that?"

"A man who regularly goes on dates with two women in one night. You have to eat light...when you're having two dinners. Good things restaurants are the only place where I 'eat light' if you know what I'm saying..."

"God help me," I groan, "if I ever start sounding like you, Ryder. I'm going to run clear off my sanity."

"You're just too much of a realist, Der. Leave the romance up to me. But if you ever want to, you know, leave that self-imposed monastery you're hiding in, there's always an open invitation from me. Right now, I'm working on an open invitation from Stassia." The sound of his smug laughter fills my ears. "I'll see you on Friday."

"Friday, man," I say, my mind straying back to the sound I imagine I heard earlier. But when my hand knocks against the Seattle Post on my desk, I turn my attention back to the page and ignore my frustration.

Hanging up with Ryder, I can't help but wonder if the

reason I haven't found a replacement assistant might be linked to why I haven't encouraged or invited anyone to dinner in months.

Hell, I can't even find a woman I want in my life just for casual sex.

No wonder Killian hired Mandy to sleep with me, to seduce me, to date me.

I wouldn't have met a woman otherwise with the hours I'd been pulling.

The only times I can get out of the office are my daily walks to get coffee or the lunch breaks I take Sopra. And even now, the waitresses and baristas were tired of my demanding ass, much like my Chief of Staff Jen who's been putting up with my shit (figuratively and literally) since before I was old enough to wipe my ass.

I didn't have time to be charming; I didn't have time to meet anyone outside of a five-minute elevator ride, or a twenty-minute meal, or a few seconds between meetings, the lingering touches and stolen glances that normal people often enjoyed.

Nope. I was the efficient one, the responsible brother.

That was always the deal.

Except it made me fall for a relationship that wasn't real, romancing a woman who was paid to be with me for money.

That, added to my inability to actually be in a relationship where I behaved like a human man...

There you go.

Now I'm no longer even human. I'm having trouble even being rational.

My gaze wanders back to the newspaper in front of me and the words in bold across the page: 'Get Paid to Date One of Seattle's Most Infamous Bachelors: This Woman Did!'

That was one headline that I might want to rewrite or suppress.

I sigh and rub the back of my neck, the action forcing the

tension from my body. Slumping back into my office seat, I snatch the Post off the desk, rip it once more, and toss it in the trash.

I get back to work...on figuring out how I'm going to get through this acquisition deal without fucking (or maiming) anyone like I've done to this article.

First, I'd have to re-schedule a dinner meeting with Scott Disrick. And find a suitable assistant to help me do just that.

I start on a spreadsheet outlining my options.

Chapter Five

DEREK

Two days later, Friday dinner night is not going according to plan. My newly abused liver doesn't get the memo.

The past two days have been busy—restless.

Paying attention to Ryder is harder than normal. And not even a glass of Faustus' finest whiskey can set me straight.

I'm already on my third of the night when I find myself zoning out, my thoughts on Seattle Post headlines and gossip rags, the meetings I've missed and the ones I'm dying to set…

Not to mention one curly-haired waitress who's yet to call me about that job. The one with the backbone of steel, the sense of humor of a comedian, and curves that could go on forever.

"Derek...Yo, Derek." A moment. And then three more. "Needle Dick!"

I jolt, my hand nearly knocking over the dark whiskey on the table in front of me. The amber drops spill over the rim, a sight that would make me swear, if Ryder and I weren't at one of Seattle's swankiest restaurants.

My gaze darts back to my brother. "What's up?"

"Dude, you nearly dropped your phone in your drink. Are you drunk?" Ryder watches, stunned, his long, black hair tousling messily around his wide blue eyes. "I mean, if you are, that's cool. But it's not exactly making you the greatest company to keep. I could've invited a woman out for this Friday night dinner if I'd known I was going to work this hard."

"Who, 'Stassia with the big tits'? The receptionist who couldn't remember her own phone number? Or Janet the bubble-gum sucker, who swallowed her gum after she was done because she was too lazy to throw it in the trash? Yea-huh, I can honestly say my chances are looking pretty great right now, since you've done such a stellar job of picking out the women."

He laughs and wrinkles his brow, eyes darting to the side. "Okay, so I haven't picked the smartest, most sophisticated women. Big whoop. Worst case scenario, I'll meet them somewhere they don't have to open their mouths very long...for talking." He shrugs, letting his blue gaze fall to mine, completely clueless about the visual joke he just made. "In case you haven't noticed, you and I did meet here to talk. And we're not doing a lot of it. I've spoken to Alton, Quentin..." he hesitates, "even Killian about shit in the past couple days."

He pauses, scanning my face, his voice barely audible over the low clank of dish-ware din of the restaurant. Ryder lips his bottom lip. "You've been working yourself past the point of exhaustion. And I worry about you. We all do...whether you know it or not."

I scrub my hand down my forehead, think about pressing him for more information, a thought that shoves my heart into my stomach.

And I do know that Ryder's just concerned about my well-being.

But that doesn't mean Alton, Quentin, or even that

bastard Killian needed to take every opportunity to dig for every morsel, every crumb, about my life.

If it was one thing my family was good at it, it was butting in their noses where they didn't belong.

Alton and Quentin were skirting around the issue of Mandy and the Seattle Post.

As for Killian...

He'd known better than try to reach out now.

In the meantime, I have a job to do first. Keeping up appearances for Scott Disrick, while earning his trust, was the only way to do that.

I flick my gaze back to Ryder.

"I'm a big boy, Ry. I've been wearing my Big Boy overalls since I was nine." I give him a meaningful glare. "Stop worrying about me." I relax back in my seat. "Once the acquisition with Bella Publishing is under our belts, trust me: I'll ease off the pedal I've been pushing. But until then? We all have to play it smart." I straighten in my seat. "So buying into the gossip going around. The press. Their bullshit. We need to take control of our company's narrative." I lift my glass, and we both take a drink. "There's more to business than managing our money. We have to manage perception. The right way. And that...that's what I'm focused on doing."

Ryder nods slowly and doesn't speak for a moment.

His lips pull down at the edges before he speaks. "It'd be a lot easier to control perception if we knew who leaked the information to the press." He licks his lips and meets my eyes. "I'm going to put a team together to look for who sold the story about Mandy. Right now. As soon as we're done here."

I cut my gaze over to him, my tone taking on a harder edge. "Is that what you're concerned about? Some mysterious source leaking information?" I take a tortuously slow breath, reaching for my whiskey. "Sounds like a bit like Alton's paranoia."

I toss back the last couple of drops of the amber liquid in my glass and then slam the crystal to the table.

"Jesus, Der," Ryder hisses. "Are you trying to get the entire restaurant to know what we're talking about? I'm just saying... It does seem like shit timing, right? Just as this deal is getting finalized, we're getting hit with a serious blow."

"You can thank our cousin Killian for that."

"Killian didn't tell on himself to the press, I can assure you that. And if he did, he wouldn't have been stupid enough not to make up a better story."

"You mean showing the world that I'm not sociable enough to find and fuck a woman on my own? Or that I can't tell when a woman's been paid to sleep with me and turn on the charm when it suits her needs? That kind of 'better story'?

"I'm not saying that. I'm not saying that at all. I just—"

"Good," I interrupt. "Because for a minute there, it sounds like you were defending Killian for potentially fucking up our business." My breath leaves me in a low hiss-sigh. "And speaking of business, I'm going to hit the head and then head home." I pull out a couple of bills and lay them on the cloth-covered tabletop. "Thanks for the dinner...and the lecture. But I've got work to do, Ry. Even more now that our company has dug itself into a hole I have to get us the fuck out of."

"Der—"

"Get yourself home safe, you hear. I mean it. Call a cab. You've been drinking."

I hesitate for a fleeting second, then get up from the table without a further word and head for the men's room, straightening my collar and cuffs as I go.

A few people glance up from their phones and tablets to watch me as I pass.

Fuck it. Let them gossip.

For the moment, I'm past caring.

I'm past it all.

Swanky places like this...I'd never been fucking fond of.

This was always Mandy's thing.

The glitz and the glamour.

Me? I was a comfort food kind of guy. I'd visited restaurants with hearty portions and lots of carbs like Sopra when I had a bad week. Or when I was stressed.

I liked to hit the gym. Drink the good whiskey. Bury my head in a bowl of pasta. Sweet and savory. That was more my style.

Or maybe...it was she that was more my style...

The waitress who'd often waited on me.

The pretty damn waitress. All hearty laughs and blushing cheeks and innocent eyes.

Mia.

With her luscious curves and wholesome beauty.

And a laugh that could lure a man into the fires of Hell and keep him there.

I swallow roughly, thinking of that kiss. Her soft hands hanging onto my bicep for balance. The way her tongue skated across my lower lip, into my mouth.

A taste of sweetness that lingered long after her lips left my skin.

With a soft sigh, I finally reach the Men's Room. I grab the bathroom door handle, twist it and push into the room.

The lighting's dim, the color burnt-orange. The decor is bottle-green, black-diamond-patterned walls, and a fat walnut desk situated in the table by the sinks.

The space is small, the air warm. Thick.

It's empty inside when I lock the door behind me, and so is my mind as it goes to Mia once more as I pull my phone from my pocket, searching her username on the screen.

It wasn't hard to find her Instagram after we met. There'd been no struggle, no complex coding to crack. Just one little Google search, and she was there.

I stayed up all night that night, browsing through her

page, letting the small sparks of insight, of that one night with her, burn into my brain.

She shot photos, I could tell that much. And each one was better than the last.

They were perfect, capturing moments of a life that she loved apparently back in Hawaii where she was from.

And what I wanted most was to be able to capture her.

I paged through the comments for hours and hours. I wanted to see what she was shooting.

I admired the high attention to detail, the amazing quality of her photos. Every one was sharp, focused, and seasoned with lines.

She's probably one of the few semi-IG-famous people I know who doesn't worship the details of Photoshop. She can capture a moment, light and shadow so well. She makes things that aren't real, real.

It's one of the reasons why people love her photos.

I'm not surprised by the stream of people commenting on her work.

But I don't pay attention to the number of likes they send her. I pay attention to her work. To her.

To every detail.

To how I want to know even more.

Mia. And that smooth, sultry, whiskey-and-sugar voice that I can still hear in my head.

Mia. With her soft butterscotch skin, her shoulder-length wavy locks, her heart-stopping grin.

I swallow hard, lowering my gaze to the screen as I click through to her page.

I find the newest photo, one that's been on her page since last night, as I stepped into my office, just to find files and folders waiting for me.

I stretch my fingers, so I can pinch the screen between them, the display of her face filling the screen.

Her lips, the soft indent of her canines. And her eyes that are amused. Open, giving a knowing look.

I swallow again.

Then I drag my gaze down, focusing on her neck, her waistline. My fingers on my phone, despite the warmth of the room and the humidity of Seattle's January nights, start to tingle.

My mouth goes dry; my throat aches for a phantom of a taste of her.

I set my phone on the bathroom countertop.

I direct my gaze to the mirror and the reflection of my own face.

I grip the edge of the counter, barely see it.

I'm too deep in thought, too deep into a cloud of Mia fantasies, to even see the burning brightness of my eyes as I reach for my belt buckle.

It's not hard to imagine her here, with me in the bathroom.

In my mind, I picture her curvy frame, the fullness of her perky breasts.

She's in front of me, her lips parting as her hands rise up to her chest.

I push forward, goosebumps now on my neck and skin, as the image of her skin responding to my touch showing up in my head.

"Oh, god," I groan as my fingers try to reach her again.

I ache, my touch begging for a soft, warm touch.

I close my eyes, waiting for a mass of darkness to consume me, but it doesn't.

It's the curve of her back, the flare of her hips, the fullness of her breasts as I picture holding her.

Just one time.

To know her.

To have her.

To pick her curvy body up and feel how soft she is. To

stroke around her generous waist. To feel the ridges of my fingertips stroke the soft smoothness of her back.

I groan again, my fingers moving to the top of my pants. I sink my hand into the waistband and settle there.

I imagine every dip. Every rise of her body as I tap outward, reach up, stroke down and grip right above her hips.

In the bathroom, I groan again, sinking my mouth into my hand to try and muffle the low groan as I flick my fingertips into the top of my own waistband and drag downward.

Any feeling of guilt evaporates beneath my pure need, and I switch my grip, reach down to cup my crotch, groaning as I do it, shuddering as I feel the texture of soft cotton there.

I'm clutching hard, pressing the tips of my fingers against my pants, my thumb rubbing outward, imagining I can feel her soft hand grasping hard, wrapping around my shaft.

These feelings are worse than I expected.

I've only been treated to visions of her.

I haven't had the freedom to taste how damn delicious she must be.

I don't take myself out of my boxers. I can't.

I'll explode all over myself like a teenage boy without training wheels if I do.

"Just one time," I ask the empty space of my bathroom.

I try to drag my mind back to thinking of her lips as I clutch my eyes closed.

I think of my lips on her neck again. Her soft lips still parted as I settle in closer to her.

My fingers drag lower, wrapping around the zipper of her pants.

I hesitate.

Stroke up.

Stroke up.

Stroke up.

Up. Up, up, up and there.

So close.

So easy to tickle the spot that I've wanted to touch since the first time I reached out to shake her hand.

I'm close enough to stroke it, to caress it, to feel her.

Just close enough, so close.

She's right here.

In front of me. In my hand.

I can just—

The sound of a ringing phone makes me jump and jerk back.

My eyes fling open, the blue now sparkling like the fire of hell as they lock onto the mirror right in front of me before swinging to my phone on the counter.

Reaching to fix my pants, I drag my hand from the haze that clouds my mind, the ride of that tingling pleasure through my body with it, just to pick up my phone.

Time stops again as I take in the lack of a name on the display.

It's a private number.

An unknown caller.

My heart stops.

I swallow hard.

If it were anyone else, they'd just call my office or one of my colleagues. If an editor called and I didn't know who they were, I'd have the secretary allow them a moment to explain who they were and what they wanted.

This is different.

I answer quickly, my heart in my throat as I do it, my grip on my phone tight so the groan I let out when I catch the ring can't be heard.

"Derek Anderson speaking."

I waited for the reply, my grip on my phone tightening.

"So, that's your name...Derek Anderson?"

I hear the amusement in the woman's voice. Something inside me told me who it was.

But I didn't believe it.

Not until she spoke.

"Mia," I breathe out, trying to keep my voice level, "It is."

At the sound of her name, the tingling comes back with full force.

My body responds.

My cock presses against the soft fabric of my underwear.

I nod. "I'm glad to hear your voice."

"Thank you," she pauses, "I'm glad to hear yours as well." She hesitates, her words coming out quickly. "So, you know, I've been thinking...About that job you offered..."

"Yes," I reply, my voice laconic. "I remember."

"Well, what's it entail? I mean, what job opening are you offering?"

I shift on my feet, my head going light. "Uh, to be honest? I...I need an assistant." I clear my throat. "Basically...I run a publishing company that's slated to overtake some of the original Big Five publishing companies. I'm looking for a personal assistant who can handle all of that for me."

"Okay, what does that mean for me? If I take the job?"

"To be honest?" I tap my foot, my nerves still shattered at being interrupted. "Spending time with me. Uh...I need someone who can not only take care of my day to day business but can also act as a message runner and gofer. Do you know what that is?"

She stays silent for a moment, so long that I start to think she's hung up.

"I...I think so. It means that, yeah, I know how to word all that. It is all the tasks I was performing back at Sopra. Well, I mean, not all of them, but most of them." She pauses for a moment. "So, let me get this straight, you need me to run around doing errands for you? The same errands your secretary does?"

"I need you to run errands for me. Right now I have a staff of three. A chief of staff, an assistant and a receptionist." I pause. "I was hoping that would be a good starter. If you're interested, I'd be glad to have you back at our East side office, by Monday morning. The basics of the environment are listed on our website, which is www.hareandholeton.com, under the career section. There's a list of expectations and application forms."

Now it's my turn to pause without speaking. I know I'm crossing a dangerous line in telling her so quickly without fully knowing her.

But I need help. And I need it now.

The Scott Disrick-Bella Publishing deal won't wait. And I need an assistant who's not afraid to go through the fires of Hell and take down all the devils in my path.

I need someone with the balls to say no. Someone who can do this well.

Someone like Mia.

I can hear her thinking about it.

"Uh, would I have to have some experience in this sort of thing?" Her voice is small. "I don't have any. I mean, I know that there's a lot of heavy lifting, word processing and stuff...I know how to do some of that. But really? I'm a waitress. I just..." She sighs. "I run around taking orders. I can balance plates on my wrists, arms and the inside of my elbows. I can memorize two dozen people's orders and deliver them like human pacemakers. But that doesn't involve a lot of reporting or anything." She sounds uncertain. "Maybe...maybe I was misinformed about what you were looking for? Because, I mean...that's it. That's all I can do."

"That's what I'm looking for someone to do," I tell her with a smile. "Someone who can balance a lot of things without dropping them...so to speak. And yes," I grin, "you did drop a few plates the last time we met. But I'm no dummy, Mia. I'm observant. I've seen you work at Sopra for weeks. Handle all the books, things, people and laughs. The kind of assistant I need can manage that, do all the stuff no one else can do. Someone who can think for themselves and take on their own direction. A person with balls. And frankly, I think you've got a heavy set of 'em. Bulldozing customers like you do."

"'Bulldozing customers like I do'? And I think that's what...?" She pauses for a moment. "Was that a compliment?"

"If you take the job, I'll make sure you think so. And maybe, I can make it worth your while." My heart is racing again as I say the words. "But if you don't find the job to your liking, please do let me know. I can always offer a higher salary or bonus, once I see what you can do. And I'm open to letting you take your time to consider it."

"Giving me the weekend to decide doesn't feel like a lot of time."

"It's negotiable, confidentially of course. There is a hiring bonus and relocation package involved, too. It's all in the paperwork."

"So, if I do well enough, then you'll want to keep me?"

"Yes." I swallow hard, trying not to glance at my disheveled state in the bathroom mirror. "I'll want to keep you."

There's silence again. So, I run a recap, just to be clear.

"I'm...looking for a person with grit, Mia. Someone who can see what needs to be done, can see it for what it is and take action on it. There's a lot of things I can't do myself. I just don't have the time." I inhale. "Let me tell you what it has the potential to be. What it will be if we're a good fit, if we click and click hard," I respond, slowly, still sounding as though I'm holding my breath. "You'd be a valued member of the Hare and Holeton staff. An integral part of the team. You'd get paid well, a decent living, time off, a good working relationship with some of the most dynamic, innovative men and women in the city. I'd offer you an opportunity to learn, to grow, to take on more responsibility and grow your own career. I'd give you paid holidays and an attractive benefit package."

I bite my lip. "And I'll be there to see it all happen. I'd...let you grow with my name on your back, and on your resume." A slight pause. "What I ask for in return is hard work, service and commitment to success, dedication. I'd see you as a part of my enterprise, as long as you stick around." I inhale one more time. "In your role as my right-hand, my eyes, my ears, my lightening rod...and, most of all, as my closest confidant."

My mind is spinning. I must have said it all wrong, my brain on overdrive with this one woman.

She doesn't respond right away.

"Does that sound like something you can handle?" I ask after a long moment. "Or should I start looking for someone else? I'm sorry, I..."

"No. Uh, no, that sounds exactly like what I needed to hear. I'm just, you know, trying not to throw up from the nerves." She pauses for a long moment. "Uh, Mr. Anderson?"

"Mr. Anderson," I reply, still breathless. "Please, there is no need for that title. Just Derek, by all means. And I understand if you have a way of thinking this is a little over the top for you. I'm perfectly capable of looking for someone else to handle some of what I need, but I'd rather have you around than not. Something in your voice tells me you mean business, Mia."

"I do have a few questions for you. Will it be okay if I ask what you mean by 'service' and how far would I be expected to go?" She pauses again, and the air of mystery and intrigue around my feelings about this woman flares up again.

"It would be a partnership, Mia." My voice is stronger now. Thicker. "Neither of us would want or need anything else."

"All right…"

"Your paycheck would come due every Friday. If you have done your part and done it well, you'll receive a final pay packet of your wages seven days after that date. You'll receive this payment, along with any and all bonuses and payouts. You would also receive the final pay packet on the due date of your contract. You would get paid according to how far along in the process you are at that point."

She's silent, thinking it over. And I'm speaking to her again.

"I wouldn't expect you to work past the time when your pay was due. I am, however, always available to answer questions and check your work."

"Answer questions?"

"Yes. And check your work." The boldness of this woman is ridiculously disarming. "I would expect you to answer your emails and phone calls, be punctual and fulfill most of your responsibilities to me."

"And is it too early to ask you questions now?"

"Not at all. Go ahead. Ask them all if you can."

Her breathing is thick. "If you give me a second to hold back my nervous upchuck reflex, I do have a few that I want to ask right now."

My heart races. Just the thought of hearing her heavy breathing makes the adrenaline spike in my chest. I squeeze my hands around my cell phone. "You may ask your questions. I'm anxious to hear them."

"I know you don't know me from any ole person on the street, but...I want you to be honest with your answer."

"I feel like I'm sitting on the edge of my proverbial seat. Ask away, Mia."

"Okay. I, uh, I'm not sure how to ask this. So, I'm just going to bite the bullet."

Mia clears her throat again before speaking, her voice now soft, aloof and quiet.

She's silent for a long time. I feel like I've been frozen in time. I am silent, my body tense with anticipation.

"Well, uh...I'm...um...Just wanted to know if..." She pauses, her voice shaking. "You're not trying to fuck me, are you? Because if you were...we need to talk. I mean, we really, really need to talk."

Out of all the things I was expecting her to say, this wasn't one of them. I'm caught off-guard. And because I'm whiskey-drunk, because I'm every bit of an asshole that Jen and Ryder think I am, and because fantasizing about a woman I've practically asked to be my assistant breaks every rule of etiquette and sexual protocol I've learned in corporate, I do the worst thing in the world...

I start to laugh.

Chapter Six

MIA

I tense as soon as I hear him laugh, my brown eyes on the slightly smudged bathroom mirror in front of me, clasping my cellphone tightly in my hand.

The bathroom at the downtown Seattle Mexican restaurant El Patio is absolutely abysmal. It sports a rust-and-oil tiled floor and sticky porcelain walls that fit the image of the small eatery.

There's very little privacy in this bathroom and I know it. Two stalls, busy restaurant, shoddy door latch. Exact recipe for a disaster.

But I don't care, because I never thought I'd end up saying what I did to him. And yet here I am, harboring this slightly-growing feeling that regretting is going to take a lot of hard work.

If only that absurd private investigation offer I'd received just a few hours ago wasn't haunting me.

Problem is: The cash is immediate and substantial.

And it's exactly what I need. I'm now fifteen hundred bucks away from buying that Canon EOS that I know I need.

Only the best camera, the right camera, could get me the shot I need to win The Visions Collective photo contest...

And the twenty thousand dollars that would come along with it.

Still, no matter how many fluorite and angelites I pack in my purse, no calming crystal can make up for the fact that this PI photography job is just a pit stop for me on the road to something more. A real job that I can use to get that much closer to my dream.

A professional photography job—one with a national magazine, one that will let me travel, one that will let me...

"Mia?" Derek barks my name. I try to focus. The bathroom suddenly feels damp and musky and sticky.

"Uh...yeah?"

"You alright? You haven't vomited yet, have you?"

“I...No. I'm still good. Both ends are mercifully clogged."

"Are you sure?" His voice is calm, his tone flirtatious and confident.

"I'm sure."

I watch as the phone lights up and vibrates before it lands on the little ledge between the two bathroom stalls. I move myself closer to the toilet, balancing my backpack on my lap as I hold my cell up to my ear.

Is this what I imagined? I don't know. But I'm not in the mood for games.

"Look, um, Derek," I say, my voices bouncing off the walls, a shiver going through my body as I hear his voice over the phone for the first time. "I'm not trying to be Kevin Hart or Robin Williams here…Because I sure as hell don't think this is a joke. I came to you for an opportunity and I'm still listening. But if you're going to laugh...then you can just put down the phone, forget I ever called, and—"

"I don't want to put the phone down."

I'm quiet.

The music from the restaurant makes its way into the bathroom and distracts me from the moment.

"It's just—You have to admit," he replies, his tone smooth and calm, "it's a funny question coming from you."

"And why is that?"

"The way I remember it...You kissed me. Not the other way around."

I bristle. "I was drunk. And thereby vulnerable to bad kissing mistakes."

"Is that what it was? A mistake?"

His question catches me off guard. His casual tone softens my anger, my heart aching from being so frustrated. I'm finding it hard to compete with a man whose voice sounds so hot.

I'm feeling a bit less logical, but I'm playing the game, too.

"I... think we both know that it was." I wait, wondering if that's the right answer.

When I hear nothing, I panic, my brain clicking at the possibility that I just drove him away.

Derek Anderson exhales, long and deep. "Good. I'm glad we both agree. It was. If we're going to work together, any intra-office fraternization has to be strictly professional. I just want to make sure you're okay with that."

My chest tightens at this, but I don't know why. "That's totally fine."

"You have exactly the kind of attitude I need in my office right now, Mia. I need someone that I don't have to constantly monitor. Someone that has the balls to speak up. Someone fearless. Like you."

"I might have a mouth that tends to get away from me sometimes. But I-I wouldn't really call myself fearless."

He snorts softly, his voice going soft. "Vomiting fears aside, I'd say a woman who can step into a karaoke bar and sing Backstreet Boys' 'As Long As You Love Me' at the top of her lungs off-key is pretty damn brave. Nonetheless, bravery is what I'm particularly looking for." He pauses. "D'you know I had five assistants interview for my assistant job in the last six months, and they've all been disastrous?"

"Disastrous? Wait, how?"

"Well, Assistant Number One started a rumor that I was going to fire her every time she made a typo in her notes. Assistant Number Two fainted every time I attempted to talk to her. Assistant Number Three showed up at my apartment in just a bra and panties. Number Four did something that was a remix of what Three did, and my current Five is so scatter-brained that I've been wanting to fire her for months but couldn't find an excuse to." He chuckles softly. "You're different, Mia. I can tell. You're different than all of them."

My heart races within my chest as I listen to him talk. I'm impressed by his honesty, but I'm also feeling a bit intimidated. I mean, less than a month ago I was an unemployed photography grad student making minimum wage slinging sandwiches and cheap coffee to "suits" like Derek.

Except I'm starting to think that there are no suits like Derek...

The man on the other end of the line coughs lightly. "I'm sorry I reacted that way. It's just—You...catch me off-guard. A lot. I mean, that was a blunt ass question to ask a would-be employer. But I get it. I do. It's hard to trust people. Hard to trust that their intentions are good. That they mean what they say. That they're not just trying to use you in business...Or even in other ways." He grows quiet. "It's important to trust, yeah?"

I hold my breath as I listen to him.

He's right. I do.

I want to trust him. It's not until just now that I realize how much I do.

"Listen," he says slowly. "Trust me when I say I'm not looking to hire you for your body. If that was the case, I would have hired the assistant who showed up at my apartment in just a bra and panties." His voice gets hard. "I care about quality of work. I care about desire and ambition. You being a beautiful woman would only overshadow all that if I hired you for those reasons..."

A tingle goes through my body, my nerves getting goosebumps as I hear him speak in his deep rich voice. I have to admit, I like it. I like the way he talks and I like that he can hold so much weight with his words.

He seems powerful and confident, and as I listen to his voice, I imagine him.

Perched against a wall somewhere, in one of his custom-made suits and firm expensive ties, hard eyes glowing into the screen of whatever phone he's using to make this call...

"Mia…Still there?"

My cheeks burn as I realize he's been talking and I've been zoning off. I'm about to apologize for it when I tell myself to save it for another time. I don't know what to think or feel.

I've been tempted by the wrong men before.

But I also keep playing over his words again, and I find myself growing curious about him.

"Yeah," I say, clearing my throat as I try to act like I'm not unsure. I have to admit, I'm not sure if that's a lie. "So when would I need to give you my decision?"

"The moment you want to. I want you to feel free, Mia. I want you to feel free to figure things out. But if you'd like to learn more about what it means to be a part of Hare & Hole-ton, please...drop by this charity event for the Chambers for the Arts we're sponsoring at the Japanese consulate downtown tomorrow night."

"Tomorrow night?"

My throat goes dry.

The Chambers for the Arts is a renowned charity event and includes a number of famous Seattle-area artists. All the best painters, photographers, sculptors and poets are there. I've attended a few art events in the city before and never been able to afford anything, much less give a single donation to the cause...

And here I am, right on the edge of it. And I've heard of some people who have gotten those Chambers tickets for the many thousands.

"Yeah, tomorrow. You can get a feel for our company culture, get an idea of what it's like to be a part of our world, and meet several of our associates. If you're interested, bring your resume and we'll discuss it in more detail then."

The words he says make my head spin. But I know how these things work.

One look, one conversation, at an event like this can make or break a career.

I can do this. I just have to remain cool, sane, and collected.

I'd probably have to swallow one of my calming crystals and a bottle of Pinot Noir that cost me a month's grocery budget, but it would be an expensive remedy perhaps necessary for this pre-interview...

"I'd be happy to," I tell him.

"Good," he answers, his voice resonant and alluring. "I'll tell my Chief of Staff Jen to send you an invite. She'll help you get your ticket...and another for a plus-one. If you're interested, I'll text you and you can email me your resume tomorrow by noon. There's a lot to take in here, so you'll have to be ready."

I take it all in and draw in a deep breath. I don't know about all that, but being here would be great for me. I could use the boost, and this might be the first step to an important career. I might be on to something here. I can feel it.

"I'll be ready." I can sense Derek smiling at my answer.

He shares a few more details on when the event is, and when we wrap up talking, he lets out a sigh, soft and yet somehow full of dominance.

"Thank you." I feel my cheeks burning despite how professional I try to be. I can sense his presence and I feel like burning right through the phone.

"No need to thank me," he says to me. "I'm just doing a service for a good cause. But I do look forward to seeing you, Mia. Upchuck reflex notwithstanding."

He hangs up and I still can't believe it. I listen to the dial tone for a few seconds and then slip my cell back into my purse.

Just as Christina bursts through the bathroom door.

"Oh, Jesus. Here you are. Girl," she shuts the door behind her, exhaling, "am I going to have to put a leash on you or something? Every time I look up, you're disappearing. I'm afraid one of those manifestation crystals of yours has gotten into your bloodstream, and, I don't know, bad spirits are possessing you or something."

I can't help but laugh. Sometimes, Christina's like my mother. Constantly getting into my business and making me do what I don't want to do.

And I allow it. Because it's better to have a wannabe-mother than the one I was born with.

"I just had to go to the bathroom," I tell her.

She gestures for me to come over. "So, you want to tell me why it took so long to use it?"

I regain my cool. And I can't help but smile.

"I just got a job interview," I tell her, trying hard to keep my voice from getting all excited. "I got a job interview. I think it might be real this time...I don't know what happened. But it feels good..."

Tina stops in her tracks. "Wait, what about the job you accepted from Steven earlier? I mean, that's the reason we came to this restaurant, remember? To drink really bad tequila and celebrate the fact that you're moving on from Jerry's over-managing ass and waitressing at Sopra."

I hold up my hands. "I know," I tell her. "I'm just...I'm just not sure private investigative photography is what I wanna do for a career, Teen. I-I need the money. You know I do...But stalking people? Digging into their lives?" I shake my head. "Not really what I want to do with my life long-term." I clasp a hand on Tina's shoulder, squeezing it. "I am blessed to know what I want to do in this life. And I'm starting to realize I want to help people, Tina. I want to help people. I want to make a difference in people's lives, do something that inspires awe in them, make them feel grateful. I want to make a difference."

Tina looks between me and the shitty bathroom walls, and she bites her lip. It's very obvious she wants to say something, I can tell. But she has something on her mind.

And I know what it is. I know what it is right away.

I place my hand on her shoulder. "You're wondering how I can handle taking on two jobs, right?"

She sighs and exhales. "Yeah. I mean, I know that you have the right to do what you have to do. And I'm not trying to be a control freak or anything, but I just don't know how you're going to be able to balance all that...I just want you to make the best decision for yourself. And all this job switching isn't helping your case."

Unconsciously, I find myself reaching inside my purse, fiddling with the nearest fluorite I find inside. The crystal always calms me. And I realize I need it as Tina watches me.

"I know," I reply, feeling lightheaded. "I know that. And maybe I shouldn't have accepted this PI job right away. I mean, maybe I should've had a few days or weeks of thinking and praying about it...But the Visions Collective photography contest is in two weeks. And I need fast money to buy that expensive-ass Canon that's going to help me win the grand prize."

I give her a small smile.

Tina watches me carefully for a moment, her eyes wide and knowing.

"I'm sure you'll do great with any camera you use," she finally says. "You're smart. And talented. And brave...despite

Jason and your family trying to tell you otherwise. And it shows. You just have to figure out what you want to do with your life that makes you happy. That's all I want."

I nod to no one in particular, remaining silent as I look around. A new kind of disquiet settles over me at the mention of my ex-fiancé's name. I finally pull my eyes away from Tina.

"Yes," I say. "That's it...That's all I need to do. Besides, Steven hasn't even officially given me an assignment yet—or a target—so I have time, right? I'm sure it will all work out."

Tina pats me on the back and gives me a big smile. "It sure as shit will," she says. "Now, let's make the most of this horrible back-alley shithouse and go get a drink. A really, really, really good drink."

She throws her purse over her shoulder, and we head out the door. And, as always, I can't help but glance at Christina. Cosmetics free and looking gorgeous in her too-small black pants, she taps her boot on the floor.

"I can't wait for that drink, Teen," I say to her. "And just appreciating the fact that it's not a drink that I have to serve to anyone else."

"You and me both. After we get out of this dump, I promise I'm buying you a shot of my own tequila. Maybe I'll just have a shot and a beer."

I let out a laugh, thinking of the "dick shooter" shot Derek told me about. "I've got just the drink. And it sounds like a great way to celebrate my new PI gig with you. And my other potential new job."

"Hopefully, it all goes smoothly and you have your long-awaited happy ending," Tina adds, resting her hand on my shoulder in a show of support. "You deserve it. You always deserve it."

With that, we head back to the main part of the restaurant to meet up with the rest of our group. But not before I make a mental note to head out of here a little early.

Time to start gathering information for my new PI job.

Time to get paid for my services.

Time to win that damn grand prize.

And, most importantly, it's time to learn a little more about Derek Anderson, my potential new boss, who I'm pretty sure thinks he's God.

My stomach sours again.

I ignore the feeling, realizing I just met the man. And I didn't learn anything about him.

If he's anything like Jason—snappy and sexist and full of himself—then I can't wait to get paid for stomping all over his big ego. Derek does strike me as a man who's capable of making people around him bow down to him. A man who can get anything he wants by using that self-importance of his to his advantage.

Yeah. I'm going to enjoy the hell out of my time with this job.

But not without reinforcements.

"Oh, by the way," I turn to Tina as we slip out of the small, untidy bathroom, "clear your schedule tomorrow night. We're attending one of Seattle's most prestigious art events...and you are going to be my date."

Her brown bob swishes as she whirls on me. "Wait, what?" She stops. "Does Jerry know about this? I have a shift at Sopra tomorrow night!"

I keep walking.

"Hello? Mia? Answer me, Mia! Hello! Mia..."

I walk faster and she gives chase, before giving out a loud sigh that says she knows she's already been bested.

I smile, knowing my own power. A power I hope will be enough to withstand Derek Anderson's charm.

If not…

I don't think I want to know the answer.

On that thought, I bypass our table at the restaurant, heading straight for the bar.

Chapter Seven

DEREK

The evening Seattle skyline outside the floor-to-ceiling windows of my rooftop terrace never ceases to amaze me, and I can't help but stare as it shifts in the wind, soundlessly blending it all into a single, shifting picture.

Without seeing it, I know Mt. Rainier looms in the background of that view, casting a shadow of perfect symmetry, like a huge skyscraper floating in the darkening Washington sky.

The sounds of late-shift traffic are faint as I finish my drink, overlooking the city skyline just close enough to touch, but far enough to escape.

Escape everything but the pure madness that is erupting in my life now that social media has caught wind of the Mandy scandal.

Photographers practically surrounded me as I walked out of work just an hour earlier.

I flashed them a quick smile and continue walking to garage where I left my car, one hand on my cell phone, my fingers automatically dialing the best lawyer in the city.

My brother Alton picked up after only one ring. I slipped

behind the wheel of my red Lambo and slammed the door, dropping my phone to the passenger seat.

"Derek," Alton said. "What do you need?"

I hate that he knows that's why I'm calling. "I need your help."

There is a pause.

"Is there anything we can do to stop this story from continuing to run? Send a cease-and-desist? File suit for defamation?" My voice was a growl as if literal grit was ground into each syllable.

"Derek, calm down."

"Alton, this shit is getting worse. I'm telling you. First it was a few whispers, some errant glances. Now? These blogger fuckers are waiting outside of the building, fucking peppering me with questions." I gripped the steering wheel, my knuckles turning white. "Ryder was right. Someone leaked that Mandy story to the press. I didn't think it would get this bad so fast. I thought they would take days to pick it up and then nothing would come of it."

"I know, Derek. Calm down," Alton answered. I heard him sigh. "I forwarded you the email I received. I have a friend on the inside of the local news station. I'll pass an SOS signal along."

"Thank you." I took a deep breath, feeling the fury drain from me as I considered the situation at hand.

The Chambers of the Arts event was going down tonight. Scott Disrick would be there. The entire artist community of Seattle would be, too.

I didn't need an assistant on Monday.

I needed one now.

"Go home," he ordered. "Pour yourself a drink. Smash the glass when you're done. And then regroup. You'll get dressed. Come down to the CoTA event and show these bastards that nothing fucks with the Anderson family."

"'Smash a glass', huh? Is that what you do to unwind in those oh-so-rare moments you get riled up?"

"I'm a lawyer. We don't get riled up. We just frown occasionally, wish for death and then get back to business."

"Yeah," I sighed. "Anything else you want me to do to relax?"

He paused and then shared with me another secret: "Bring me a bottle of Chopin's Nocturnes when you arrive at CoTA. I could use it."

"You got it."

"And Derek, your whole introverted, Dad-like, surly-workaholic-bastard streak won't work tonight. I'm giving you an order here. Be charming at this event tonight. Be flirty. And be, I don't know, human."

"Says the lawyer."

"I mean it. This is our biggest sponsored event of the year, and it only happens once. Be nice. Invite someone to your table." He redirected as I grunted. "Okay, maybe not that. And I know it's too late for you to get a date now. But maybe you can find a way to make friends."

"And what makes you think I can make friends?"

"Because....you're Derek Anderson. You make friends with everyone. You just don't realize it. If you don't have a date, find an artist that you think is interesting. Bring them to your table." Alton rambled off a list of names. "I know you'll somehow charm the hell out of them."

"I can do that."

"And use it as an icebreaker. Be charming."

"Yes, dear. Daddy Fake-as-Fuck's coming."

"Thank you." I heard Alton sigh. "And you're welcome."

We said goodbye, and I placed my cell on the seat beside me.

I looked out over the changing city, the skyline transforming into a background pattern of blurred white lights. I saw the moon lowering in the evening sky, and I wondered if

I'll even be allowed to see its transformation into a harvest moon from my office anymore.

It didn't take long for those thoughts to turn from the natural beauty of the city to the chaos that my life had devolved into.

At thirty-one, I was older than most of the artists dotting the city tonight, but I was just as hopelessly adrift in my own life.

The press had gotten wind of the Mandy scandal, and that wouldn't be the only story about Hare & Holeton that would run in the upcoming days or weeks, I was sure. Once someone started digging into the company's past, other scandals about our family history would surface as well.

I knew a lot about how to run a company logistically. But running its reputation required a different set of skills.

And I've slowly been losing my grip on the company, my soul.

And after the earlier conversation with Alton, I still felt like I was no closer to getting a handle on either.

"Charm the hell out of them." "Don't be Dad-like."

I shake my head and laugh on my terrace. I'd pay a mint to be anything but "Dad-like," indeed. If only someone could point me in the direction of how not be like my wayward father.

If only...

I toss back another swig of my scotch, reaching inside the pocket of my slacks for my cell. I'm calling her number in seconds.

It rings twice before she finally picks up, her voice breathy as if she's run for the phone.

"Hello?"

"Mia. I'm glad you're there."

"Hello to you too, Derek. I wasn't sure I'd speak to you until the event."

The Chamber of the Arts event doesn't start for another

hour and a half. And I have just enough liquor in me to be charming until then. "Yeah, I know. I just wanted to warn you that things may be a little hectic outside of the event."

She sighs. "I heard. I saw a post today on social about you. I didn't read it. Look, for what it's worth, the news outlets can be shit. I don't want to pretend I know what it's like to be you. But if this were me? I'd tell them all to go fuck themselves. You guys are going to get through this. I think what your company is doing tonight is amazing. A lot of people pretend to support the arts, but really don't give a damn. Don't let the haters get you down. Tell them to choke on a dick. A fat one. A short, fat, uncircumcised wiener."

I laugh.

Christ. I could listen to her cool, strong voice for hours. And it doesn't hurt that she said she didn't read the article. Most people would have.

Every time I find out more about Mia Kamaka, I'm more impressed. The woman was honest in a world that was becoming increasingly less so.

"Yeah," I finally manage, feeling like a dope. "I just wanted to make sure you heard it from me."

"Got it. Watch out for the trolls hanging outside of the CoTA."

"I was also thinking...maybe we could ride to the event together. Go over some of the logistics of the assistant role."

"Logistics," she repeats.

"Yes. Turns out I'm going to need an answer on whether or not you're looking to fill the role sooner than Monday. The new spotlight that's been shining on the company means new responsibility and attention. And I was hoping you'd be up to the challenge."

"Oh. You want me to come as your assistant. Not as a guest, right?"

"Well, that's the gist of it. If you're up to the challenge, I can go ahead and make a few phone calls.... That way we could arrive together. And identify you as my assistant then, get you up to speed on what needs doing instead of waiting until Monday like we discussed earlier."

I take another swig of the scotch and drop the glass on my patio table. The sound is loud, making me wince.

I didn't realize how nervous I was until just now.

Mia's the charm I need tonight. The buffer between me and a billion questions from every Tom, Dick and Harry who would ask if the rumors were true about a sex scandal or if I've had a nervous breakdown or if I've finally gone off my nut over having to work with three equally-nutty brothers and a cousin who'd basically been adopted into the fold.

The drink doesn't help my nerves at all.

Especially as I wait for Mia to answer. Watching the city drone on around me bleeds into the starry sky beyond my patio.

She sighs softly into the receiver. "I'd be happy to be your assistant...Mr. Anderson."

"Derek. First names."

"Gotcha. I'm looking forward to it. I was actually just about to go get my dress for the event. If you're ready, you can—"

"Wait, wait. You don't have an outfit for the event?"

"Um, no, not yet. It's been a busy day for me. Lots of errands to run now that I'm not working at Sopra anymore. And I don't exactly keep formal gowns around the house."

I can feel the anxiety in my stomach tightening up. "Not to worry, I've got this covered. Give me your address. My car and I will be waiting for you out front as fast as we can get there."

She's silent for a few moments. I think I hear her inhale. "What? No. It's fine. I'll get a dress on my own."

"The Hell you will. This is a work event now, Mia. I want to make sure you have what you need. And it just so happens I know the perfect place."

"For a dress emergency? The man who lived on his phone for every meal at Sopra actually knows where to shop?"

I laugh at the last sentence. "Believe it or not, I used to have a public life before I became a work recluse. And now let's get me that address and I'll be waiting for you out front. And no, we're not playing any Backstreet Boys in the car when we get there, so you'd better get your 'I Want It That Way's' out of your system before I show up."

She giggles. Before the line goes silent. "Thank you, Derek. This means a lot to me."

I can tell she means it. And something twists in my gut before heading south, squeezing at my groin.

"Good. See you out front soon. Text me the add. I'll be waiting."

I hang up the phone and slip it into the side pocket of my slacks.

Maybe Alton was right after all...

Maybe I do have a little charm left in me.

I just hope that I'm not using too much of it on my beautiful new assistant.

Chapter Eight

MIA

After hanging up the phone with Derek, my hand is still slightly shaking as it lays across my chest. I almost forget to text him my address, and while the tremors are at bay, I shoot him a quick message before nearly collapsing against the kitchen counter.

My only saving grace right now? I've taken a shower, curled my hair and beat my face for the Gods.

If only it were enough to keep the nausea down.

Placing my phone down on the kitchen counter, I feel like my legs are about to give out. Luckily, there's a chair nearby, and with some quick maneuvering, I'm able to get myself into it.

Just as Christina walks in.

She gapes. "Are you alright? You look like you've seen a ghost. Or swallowed a bad pill. Which is it?"

I exhale. "I'm going to the Chamber of the Arts Event tonight." I raise a finger. "Correction: I'm going to the Chambers of the Arts event tonight with Derek Anderson. And I don't think there are enough pills in the world to make me feel remotely all right."

"Aww. Do you need one of your amulets? Or crystal balls? Or whatever you use usually grab to calm yourself down?"

I laugh. "Jesus, Teen. For the last time...They're calming crystals. Fluorite helps me focus my energy and acts as a conduit for my natural psychic abilities. An entire collection of them is not going to help me calm down this time around. I think I need a glass of water..."

"Or a joint." She pauses, gauging my reaction. "No? Okay, let me get you a glass of water. Just looking at you is making me thirsty and anxious."

I watch her walk across the room and pull out the wine glasses I placed next to the sink earlier in the day. She fills two large glasses of water and comes back.

Setting one on the counter in front of me, she leans against the counter, her brown eyes dancing as she lifts one to her face. "I told you...Keeping up with two jobs is going to be a lot. Not to mention when one of them is with one of the Seattle Andersons." She harrumphs, her short brown hair swaying against her neck. "Just saying..."

I freeze. "Wait. Wh-What do you know about Derek and his company? Is there something I should know that I don't?"

“Oh, not much. Only that the Andersons are some of the richest publishing magnates. In the entire country, might I add." She takes a sip of her water. "I mean, Mia, these guys are loaded and pretty young. And all ridiculously, unfairly handsome. That hot boss of yours is only thirty-one. I saw a picture with one where he was heading to some event and through the tux, you could see the entire outline of his—"

"Tina! Please. Concentrate. Is there something you found out that's bad about the Andersons, I mean. From what I could see online, their company Hare & Holeton is a great company to work for. All the employees' reviews were great. The workers seems to love them. Apparently, there's always snacks in the break rooms, gourmet coffee in the till and enough medical benefits to get my teeth cleaned twice a year."

I shrug, finally sipping my water. "Sounds like a paradise to me."

"Yeah, if you discount the fact that the Andersons' relationship with their parents seemed totally twisted...and that Derek is fond of hiring hookers when it pleases him."

I set my glass on the counter. "Derek what? He's-he hires hookers? Why would he do that...? He's a good-looking guy." My arms run a chill. "Why would a handsome, successful man like him need to do something like that?"

Tina bites her lip. "Because if you're a typical guy, hookers are easy targets. No muss. No fuss. No emotional connection. Just a few holes you can bang before you send them on their way with a bill in hand."

"Thanks, Tina. I really needed the visual of that."

She shrugs. "Just saying...That's probably what all of those rich guys are like. I mean, take Jason. He was the same. Always taking the easy route. With the career he chose. The neighborhood he lived in. The woman he chose to mar—"

I stand. "Okay, yes. I've got the point, Tina. Thanks." I wander over to the fridge, sticking my head in the freezer, my hands moving fast enough to distract myself.

I hear the frown in Tina's voice. "What are you looking for?"

"The tequila. I see water isn't going to cut it tonight." I can't help but look back at her. "Even though what you're saying makes sense, it keeps hitting a little too close to home."

I watch her eyes narrow as she studies me, taking a few steps forward. "Fuck, Mia. I'm sorry. It's just—I had a shit shift at Sopra tonight, and all the bitterness is pouring outta me like a canteen. I'm sorry."

I stare at her a moment longer before sighing and dropping into a chair at the table. "Me too. And I suck at expressing it. I'm not normally this...all over the place. It's just —I used to have a plan. With Jason, at least I knew what to expect. But now? I just have a dream. And I'm using every avenue possible to make it come true."

I look at the hands in my lap. "I'm taking a risk, Tina. Maybe even risks I shouldn't be taking. If things go sideways, I'm not sure what I'll be left with...I hope I'll be left with at least enough. Enough to make a new start here in Seattle. But I'm not really sure about the...I'm not sure about the direction I want to head in."

She reaches for the tequila. "I know which direction you want to head in. It's the same one you've been telling me about since college. The same one that kept you out all night, in UH darkrooms, developing photos of wild mushrooms and whatever else you could scare up. You always wanted to be a photographer. And you still do. Everything else is just a pit stop on the way."

"It's a lot of work, Tina. And it's stressful, too. And it drives me nuts." I frown. "Not that I really have the freedom to do it. I mean, I can. I hope I will. Working for Derek Anderson will definitely help me get somewhere. But it'll also give me exactly what I'm trying to get away from. Rich assholes with more money than God who think they can tell me what to do."

She laughs and pours two shots of the tequila in separate glasses. "You're right. But I mean, c'mon. He is hella good looking. And the least you can do is enjoy the eye-candy. You don't have to like Derek Anderson. You don't even have to respect him much, either. Just get the cash. Take the opportunity. Soon you'll be flown out by the biggest brands in the world to take high-class editorial shots. And men like Derek Anderson will be a distant memory."

Once the shots are in front of us, she pushes mine towards me and sits back. "Besides, Steven at the PI job is not a looker. Like, at all."

I gulp the glass of tequila, wincing. "I know. I stopped by his office earlier today. He gave me some of the details of my first PI photog assignment, and he wants me to look over them tonight. His hands looked like they'd been dipped in frying oil, they were so greasy."

Tina screws up her face, gagging as she reaches for the limes on the counter and cuts one. "I think that's his hair gel that causes it. Guy used to be a regular at Sopra. But handing him dishes was so dangerous. I was always scared a plate was going to slip right out of his hands and land in his lap. Forks, knives, he was like a walking avalanche of ceramic."

I slurp down the second shot, nodding as she hands me a lime slice. I bite into it. "I just hope there's nothing else that's 'greasy' about him. I'll open his greasy file when I'm back from CoTA tonight."

Tina nods at me, just as my phone buzzes on the kitchen counter.

"Grab that for me, will ya?" I ask, pushing away my empty glass.

She moves over to the counter, grabs my phone, her rounded pretty face lighting up as she gazes at whatever's on the screen. She holds the cell up to me.

"Look who it is. It's Eye-Candy himself."

I grab the phone, reading the text from my new boss.

"33rd and Union. Where are you, Ms. Kamaka? I'm downstairs. Waiting on you. Whenever you're ready."

I inhale with an audible hiss. "He's waiting on me—right now, actually. We're going to get me a dress for the event. I mean, he's going to get...We're—" I stop. "I need a dress for tonight's event. And he's here to help."

Tina's eyes sparkle as she sizes me up. "I bet he is. Tell him you need a new pair of shoes while you're at it. He's rich."

I roll my eyes, and Tina takes my glass.

"Remember," she says, "he's just a pit-stop. Nothing more. Nothing less. Once you have a style editor job, it'll be time to find someone else."

I look at her, my lips curling upwards. "Wow. How lucky

am I have to have a therapist-life guru-and-roommate all in one?"

She smiles back. "Hella lucky, my friend. Now get going. Eye-Candy awaits."

She kisses me on the cheek and shoos me out the door.

I'm instantly self-conscious about the sweats I'm wearing, but I tell myself it doesn't matter.

Derek Anderson is nothing but an accessory in my day. Nothing more. Nothing less.

I rush down the stairs, trying to avoid the elevator. It's out of service, anyway. Halfway down the first flight of stairs, I meet Derek Anderson heading up them.

He stops, his shoulders perfectly square in an immaculate three-piece suit as both of us come to a stop on the stairway.

"Ms. Kamaka," he says, looking at me as though he's intensely studying everything about my face, his powder blue eyes scrutinizing my features. "So nice to see you again."

He smiles after a moment, displaying perfectly even and white teeth. And for a second, I almost forget everything Tina just said, and I stand there, staring, my jaw hanging open just slightly.

I nod. "Hello."

But then he does something that just makes the whole situation insane.

He reaches a hand out that I'm sure to shake. But instead of grabbing my hand, he places it on my cheek. And I close my eyes, frozen to the very spot.

Oh shit.

Chapter Nine

DEREK

The instant the black Mercedes door closes behind me, I whirl my head around, scanning the street.

No photographers here.

No strangers with their cameras out, filming.

Nada. Zilch.

Mia's street's in the middle of a residential area, with a few apartments, a few business buildings, and single-family homes. Her neighbors probably don't care what I'm doing. Either that, or they have no clue who I really am.

I exhale, feeling more relaxed and confident that I've made the right choice by coming here tonight.

To escort Ms. Kamaka.

I'm wearing a black business suit. Not my usual tuxedo. But Jen-approved all the same. I pull out my cell and read the text I just got from her, my eyes scanning over the text bubbles.

Be brilliant tonight. Don't take drugs. And have fun! You deserve some ;)

I smile, shaking my head. My Chief of Staff is like surrogate mother I wish I had, though she's even younger than I am. She's ever-protective. Caring. But could be a drill sergeant. But the fact that she called me out on not showing my own personality in the Post article to break the ice with the interviewer shows she cares.

They all do. Quentin. Ryder. Even Alton, in his own robotic way.

My brothers are all I had growing up. My father working all day every day in a fish plant, my mother a housewife bored with her routine life, my grandparents growing old in Fiji and not caring much about what happened to their out-of-touch son's fiercely independent children in America.

So my brothers and I supported each other. The four of us have always been close.

In a way, our cousin Killian became a fifth brother, but that's another story altogether.

Now older, and working in our own separate circles in luxurious offices, the bonds between us were being tested at every turn, every scandal, every business deal, every challenge...and the challenges were only getting stronger as our company grew.

The weight of our current challenge presses on my shoulders as I push the car door handle, as I step over the dewy sidewalk and into Mia's building on this rainy Seattle night.

I'm halfway up the side stairs when I see her coming down.

That shoulder-length dark hair of hers is more tightly curled, and the brown palette of her face is accented by her dark eyes, her full lips, and button nose.

She's even more stunning in person than on the Instagram page of hers that I've been stalking for days.

But those sharp eyes of hers pierce into the core of my soul.

I take a deep breath, telling myself to breathe again. And flashing her the warmest smile I can muster.

She says "hello." And then I see it.

Something on her face, and my hand moves on its own, reaching out to touch her soft skin. My thumb sweeps across her cheekbone, turning that frown into a slightly upturned lip.

She closes her eyes.

An intense aroma fills my head, my senses, and my groin, as I hear the sounds of the street fade away. Alone, in this stairwell with Mia, I think of a million things I want to do with her.

"You...You have something on your face," I manage, my thumb outstretched, touching the tiny fleck on her cheek.

She blinks. I look at her lips. It's almost sinful how they stir me and make me want to taste them. "I do?"

I nod. "Something pale. Fleshy," I say, my thumb still gently sweeping her face. It's as though I've been electrocuted —I can hardly concentrate on what to say.

"Oh," she says as I pull my hand away, showing it to her. "It's lime. I was in a hurry, I forgot to use a napkin before I left."

"Lime?"

"Uh, yeah. Tina and I were taking tequila shots with lime. Sort of...pre-gaming."

"I see. You needed to pre-game before seeing me?"

She gapes. "No. Not it's not like that. I...Well, this is my first work event at Hare & Holeton. Just needed a little...liquid courage, you know."

"Lime shots," I smile, nodding. "And here I thought you weren't big on drinking, Whiskey Police."

Mia shifts on her feet. "I'm not. Tina fills half the tequila bottle up with water so I can drink it."

"Wow. That's the saddest thing I've heard in a while. Water in a tequila bottle. Terrible. Why do that to yourself?"

"Well, we can't all be expert drinkers like you, Mr. Whiskey-Man. How do you prepare before a big work function? Or an award ceremony?"

My eyes dart to her lips. That one earlier still lingers in my mind.

"I'm not preparing. I like my liquor neat. And I pour my own drink to be more precise."

"Precise."

"Mmhmm. And I never take shots of tequila. I mean, I won't take shots of anything. Ever. I learned the hard way."

"That doesn't sound like you, Mr. Anderson. I'm a little surprised that you don't need to warm up with some drinks before a big event."

"I do." I lick my suddenly dry lips. "I pour myself a scotch before every work function. I had other habits to help me prepare until recently. But I've grown out of them."

"Grown out of them?"

"Yes. Some preparations are more...distracting than helpful. I like to keep a relatively clear head on nights like these. And some of my habits, well, they got in the way of some of my responsibilities. I was enjoying myself a little too much, I think."

A long silence stings the air between us. "Well..." Mia says, exhaling. "At least you've given up some of your 'bad' life choices. That's good. I guess."

My eyes narrow. "You sound disappointed, Ms. Kamaka," I say as I take a step up the stairs.

She takes a step back, her hands lifting to her hips. "No. I'm not. It's just a little surprising. By the way, you can continue to call me Mia. If you want."

"Not a fan of 'Ms. Kamaka'?"

"Well, it makes me feel like a teacher. Or someone's boss. Someone whose title mandates respect."

"And you don't think you're deserving of respect?"

"Not really. I mean, no one really is. But if they want to show me some respect, they can do it by calling me Mia. That's less formal."

"Sorry. Old habits just die hard, I guess. I won't make that mistake again. But you are still a lady. And I'm a gentleman...on my better days. Let me help you down the stairs."

"I don't need help. I'm wearing sweats. And Crocs. I don't think anyone that has ever existed has needed help down the stairs while wearing Crocs. The company should advertise that on their product page. Literally the most unsexy shoe alive."

I look her up and down—the thin-strapped "Crocs" on her feet, black athletic pants curling at the ankle, and a loose white shirt underneath a long black coat. "I don't think it's 'unsexy' on you. You look great, Mia...You really do."

She blushes and lowers her head, and I can hear the softest, tiniest of gasps.

"If I didn't know better, I'd say you were flirting," she says, turning herself away from me, taking a step around me.

"I'm merely trying to show you the respect you deserve," I say, now descending the stairs, keeping pace with her. "I think women are often too damn hard on themselves. All the dieting, the exercise, the 'I have to have the perfect body' mentality society puts on them. Me?"

I watch Mia's full, voluptuous figure as she descends the stairs, her hair awash like a tide, two parts of waves falling to the side of her face, obscuring a small part of it from view. "I think women need to be more accepting of their bodies. Accepting that they are beautiful in all the right ways if they just let themselves be. Because I think, along with feeling soft and warm, there is something so beautiful, so sexy, and so appealing about a woman with curves. As athletic as she might be. As thin as she may be." My eyes can't help but follow the curve of her hips as she nears the bottom of the stairs, causing my voice to get quieter, my words tighter and shorter. "I'm a fan of femininity. In all its forms. Slender. Or curvy. Long hair. Short hair. I don't care. It all appeals to me."

Mia is at the bottom of the stairs now and turns to me. "Well, Mr. Anderson, that's very honorable of you, but I do think most men try to act like they're all accepting. And then, when the women really 'let themselves go', they run and hide to save their own butts."

I smile. "I'm not most men, Mia. I thought you would have figured that out by now. If not, then I'll just have to show you." I open the door that leads us outside. "My car's parked right outside. Raul will take us to the dress shop around the corner. We'll find you an outfit and then I'm sure we can find you whatever else you'd like to complement it. Shoes. Jewelry."

She frowns, looking around at me. "Are you sure I shouldn't just-"

"No. I'm sure. We don't have much time. We need to get there early, and it's better to have the least amount of time wasted."

A small smile graces her lips. "I guess you're right."

I open a side door next to the stairs and let her slip through. By the time I get outside, Mia is already seated in my car. In the back seat. On the far side.

I can tell she probably did it so that I wouldn't open the door for her, show her too much "respect" as she put it.

I take the seat beside her, sliding in the back before telling Raul to drive. I close the door behind me.

It's not too long before we're slowing to a stop in front of Aimee's Formal Wear: a tiny boutique, tucked away around the corner from the salon.

Aimee herself greets us at the front door. She's in her late thirties and is short, petite, naturally pretty. High heels clacking on the old wooden floor, she walks forward with a big smile as we walk inside.

"Derek! What a nice surprise. It's been a while."

"It has," I say. "Aimee..." I motion to the woman beside me. "Meet Mia Kamaka. She's my new assistant at Hare & Holeton."

"Hi," Mia says, then smiles as we shake hands all around.

I tell Aimee we need formal wear for Mia tonight, and the

boutique owner looks at me with an arched brow, her gaze showing a mischief she usually reserves.

"Oh," she says. "Is this a special occasion?"

I interject, "It's a work event tonight for the arts council." The event starts at 8. I picked Mia up at 7:30, but these events are known to last all evening, extending well past midnight.

. "I see," Aimee says. "But of course. And I'm guessing you're in charge of all that razzle, Derek, since you have no choice but to actually be there yourself."

"Pretty much."

"All right then." She smiles at Mia. "Yes, indeed. You're in luck, Mia," Aimee says. "Derek here has the best taste in town. The best taste in all of Seattle, in fact. I have any dress you might need right near the dressing rooms. I'll just get them for you, if you'll follow me."

I take a seat in a rear corner of the store so that Mia can get dressed. I feel a little guilty watching her, knowing I shouldn't, knowing I'm a man that probably should control himself more. But I can't help it.

She's utterly beautiful.

Surprisingly, I find myself quite content with keeping my distance. Observing Mia from afar is like a forbidden pleasure. Something I can partake in with all the messy parts removed.

She dresses in one of the closest dressing rooms behind me, the door already cracked so I can see her silhouette and her frame. I see what she pulls from the rack, sweeping it over her body.

Aimee brings over a handful of things and Mia puts them on. A simple black dress, a tight-fitting cocktail dress, a flowing skirt, a pair of slacks.

They all pour over her curves like water. And with every outfit change, every pair of shoes she puts on, my pants grow tighter, my smile grows smaller.

"You like the black dress?" Mia asks, turning around, obviously a little self-conscious.

I nod. "I do."

"And these? Do they..."

"They all look great, Mia. Really. I swear," I interrupt. "Now, let's hurry up and get this over with."

"Fine," she says. "I'll wrap it up." She disappears behind the curtain once more, closing it all the way this time, and I almost groan out loud, the pulse in my pants throbbing harder than I can ever remember.

After about twenty minutes, Aimee brings Mia a final outfit. I stand to my feet, ready to give my final verdict before we leave.

But unfortunately I find myself stopping breathing.

I'm not sure what I was expecting. But it wasn't this...

This...elegance. This perfection.

The dress is classic black satin with jewels encrusted at the neckline. There's a small train attached to the bottom, which allows Mia to glide across the floor. The upper body is heart-shaped, revealing the well-toned swell of her breasts. The sleeves are black lace with white accented threads.

The material glides over her body like a second skin, hugging in all the right spots. And there are many of them to hug.

It's as if they created her dress especially for her.

The dress is lush, rich, glamorous, and decadent. The jewels are sweet yet sultry, everything on the ensemble itself is tasteful yet sensual.

The simplicity of it... The delicacy.

It's Mia in material form.

"What do you think?" she asks, jolting me out of my thoughts.

"It's very pretty," I tell her. "And it looks good on you."

She frowns. "I can't help but feel so… exposed."

I pause. “Can I say something that might ease your worry?”

“You can try. I won’t stop you.”

I step closer. “If it's any consolation, that dress isn't nearly as sexy as you are in it. You look gorgeous. Gorgeous in this dress. You're a knockout, Mia. You really are. And I don't think I've ever seen a more beautiful woman.”

Her eyes go wide with surprise, her mouth gaping just slightly. I reach a hand out to her shoulder, that slight moment when my fingers brush against her skin bringing back an immediate longing I had nearly forgotten.

That pulsing, that deep stab.

A quiet sound of contentment escapes her, the corners of her mouth spreading into a sly smile. She closes the distance between us, then stops before I can reach her, the shock of our usual invasion of space pulling me off-guard.

Our hands are nearly in contact. We're mere inches apart, the height difference between us much closer now that Mia's in a pair of slinky heels. Our eyes clash, aflame.

And the girl I've had flash fire for tonight steps closer to me until our bodies are nearly touching. She tilts her face up so that our lips almost meet.

I can feel her breath across my face.

"You really believe that," she says, her voice a soft rasp.

"I do. You're absolutely stunning in that dress."

Just acknowledging it has my erection reaching for the sky.

She smiles, her eyelids almost fluttering closed, her warm breath still flying across my face. "You're damn right I am. Thank you."

She smirks, just a brief curve of the lips, but it's enough. It's enough to make me take her in my arms.

Her soft, velvet body fits against mine perfectly. Only one more inch, and I'd be pressing my hard cock against the apex of Mia's soft, inviting thighs.

I'd be lost. Lost inside this woman who's bewitched me from the moment we met.

My body sways, begging me press into her.

But a small cough in the room catches my attention first.

Aimee clears her throat, a warning we're being watched, and we both step apart.

"I'm sorry for the interruption," the boutique employee says to Mia. "But is there any other dress you'd like to try on, Mia?"

"Aimee, we'll take the black dress," I answer. "No belt. No extra jewelry." I glance back at Mia. "It doesn't need it."

"Of course."

It takes me a second to shake myself from my trance. But when I do, my eyes meet Mia's. She eagerly meets my gaze, her eyes slick, her cheeks flushed.

Aimee smiles at us, waiting for us to give her the okay to take the fitting room curtain.

Mia smiles back. "We're good."

The curtain goes up, and Mia disappears behind it. As for me, I head directly to the restrooms.

I'm going to need a splash of cold water—and lots of it—if I'm going to make it through the night.

Chapter Ten

MIA

It takes a million years to arrive to the downtown Japanese Consulate. Or at least, that's how long it feels in my head after we leave Aimee's boutique.

The car ride to the event is silent, save the sound of Nirvana playing in the background. Derek could barely look at me.

Adopting that stone-cold demeanor that he'd often kept at Sopra, he'd stayed glued to his phone. I'd decided that was fine and watched the city pass by.

Outside the Mercedes Benz windows, the flashing lights of Seattle dance around us, a twinkling reminder of how new I am to this city, how beautiful it is, and how over my head I just might be.

By the time we reach the Consulate, the tension between Derek and me has turned ice-cold. His voice is ten degrees chillier when we park and he opens my door.

"Hare & Holeton is a sponsor for tonight's event, so it's best that we be on our best behavior," he tells me.

"Got it."

"No harassing the artists. No asking for pictures. No

drinking too much alcohol. I'm going to need you close by, but not to hover, in case I need you to take notes or I'd like to make an introduction."

I smile coldly, pulling my shawl against me. "Great. Is there anything else in the rule book? No talking. No chewing gum. No behaving like a real person. Just an attachment of yours...is that right?"

Derek grins back, but the expression is frosty. "I see you haven't lost your smart mouth since accepting the position."

"You hired me for my smart mouth. I think it's a good idea that you trust that the rest of me is smart, too, Mr. Anderson. I promise I won't embarrass you tonight."

I expect him to agree. But instead, he places a hand gently on my lower back, guiding me inside the consulate building as a gaggle of photographers take pictures from the sidelines.

It's all disorienting. The flashes of cameras. The parade of dresses and suits.

The gorgeous music that is floating on the chilly Seattle wind as we head inside.

The double doors open, and I'm greeted by a medium-sized ballroom, its otherworldly décor displaying rich, enchanting Japanese culture from every corner.

The live arrangement of flowers perched on the wooden columns in the center of the room. The curved, wooden ceiling that looks like something out of an ancient pagoda.

The smell of jasmine is in the air, practically ushering us inside.

The ballroom is warm, filled with art and laughter and champagne trays as far as the eye can see. I'm instantly awed by the event.

Beside me, Derek must pick up on my amazement because that categorical coldness of his begins to drain away. "It's remarkable, isn't it?" he comments.

"It's incredible. Truly breathtaking."

"We're proud to have sponsored this event," he says. "We

almost didn't. Took a little convincing but I finally got my brothers on board."

I turn. "This was your idea?"

He meets my eye. "Yeah. Hare & Holeton is a publishing company. Our writers are artists, first and foremost. I figured supporting an event like this would be more effective than advertising in magazines and other things. Those things don't really change people's minds in the world. But if you can start with the ones who really don't know much about other cultures, you're stirring up belief and acceptance. Seattle is a big city and a mix of so many different ethnicities and values and cultures. The Chamber of the Arts event is just one place that seeks to bring them all together. I grew up in this city. I'm dedicated to it. And it's these kind of events that make me realize how lucky I am to live in a place with such beautiful people."

I almost lose my breath when I hear him.

It's times like these where Derek Anderson and his blatant honesty simply blow me the hell away. I forget that he's a workaholic prick with a mini God-complex and a good suit.

In those brief moments, I see something else behind his shiny veneer. And I like it.

I like it a hell of a lot more than I'd to let on.

I inhale. Hard. Staring at the rest of the room. "You're extremely optimistic, Mr. Anderson."

His grin returns slowly. "Mm. Sometimes. You're going to have to get used to it if you're going to be working with me, Kamaka."

"I'll manage."

"You know this event really is a pleasure to attend. So much art. So many great people. My chief of staff Jenny isn't here tonight, but if you need anything, I'm only a text away. I can always step out, if you need me." He turns towards me. "Remember: Try to stay close. Keep your phone on you. And try not to swing from the chandeliers."

"I'll do my best."

"Other than that, have fun tonight. Mingle. Meet people." His voice softens. "Give people the honor of meeting the best assistant in publishing."

I smile. "That remains to be seen."

"I believe in it. I trust in you. That's all that matters. Are you going to be okay by yourself?"

"I'm good," I answer. "Great, actually." I nod as he catches someone's eye.

He raises a hand to the stranger before turning to me. "Now if you'll excuse me, I need to at least to pretend to be a dutiful CEO. Enjoy yourself here, Mia."

"Same to you, Mr. Anderson."

His blue eyes defrost for a second before he leaves my side and heads off. I watch him every step of the way, feeling the strange mix of emotions that come with being anywhere near the intoxicating presence of a man like Derek Anderson.

My eyes stay fixed on his muscular back moving effortlessly beneath his black suit jacket. I completely miss the fact that I'm no longer alone.

A voice speaks about a foot from my ear. I nearly jump.

"Gorgeous, isn't he?" The masculine tone is warm and honeyed.

I turn and meet the curious green eyes of a blond man standing beside me in a suit. He's not too tall but lean and seems friendly.

I decide to play along, my mouth tweaking upwards into a wary smile. "You think so?"

"Oh, I know so. Derek Anderson is one of the most eligible bachelors in Seattle. And with you as his date, I bet the whole room is drooling on their Pradas."

I raise a hand. "Oh, I'm not his date. I'm just his assistant. I'm brand new. My name is Mia. Mia Kamaka."

I extend a hand and he takes it, shaking it.

"How do you do, Mia Kamaka? I'm Oliver. Oliver Blare.

I'm the assistant for Ryder Anderson. Derek's brother and the Chief Technology Officer at Hare & Holeton."

"Ah, so we're practically family then. From one assistant to another."

"Trust me: I'd like to be 'more' than family with Ryder Anderson. Or any of them for that matter." He sighs, green eyes wistful as they sweep the room. "Unfortunately, Ryder doesn't swing my way." He glances back at me with mirth. "He only hired a male assistant because he doesn't trust himself to keep a female one."

"Difference in values?"

"No, actually. Difference in dick. In that, once the last female assistant had a taste of Ryder's, she went full Fatal Attraction on his well-formed ass." He shrugs. "I'm just here tonight to drink the good booze. And find some dick of my own to enjoy tonight."

I laugh. "Is The Chamber of the Arts event a good place to meet people?"

"Oh, yes. It's the foremost annual gathering of Seattle's art community. And one of the most worthwhile, as far as I'm concerned." Oliver looks me over. "But I don't think you'll need help finding someone tonight. Seems like you've already got someone." His gaze goes to Derek again. "I think you're his type. God knows he needs a good woman after the last turned out to be fraud...with the worst fashion sense I've ever seen. I mean, my God, I thought escorts were supposed to be trained in that stuff. Go figure."

I stiffen, holding onto my shawl. "So, Derek really was dating hookers?"

"Escorts, love," Oliver corrects. "No one calls them 'hookers' anymore. And Mandy was too high-maintenance to be anyone's 'hooker,' trust me." He shifts closer. "She was hired by Derek's cousin Killian Anderson, the COO. Second-in-charge of the entire company. I guess he thought he was doing Derek a favor, since the man is such a loner, so busy with the 'finer points' of the business. It's a pity the favor backfired in his face the way it did."

I stare at him, feeling the urge to escape. But my body won't let me. I admit: I'm dying to know more about Derek, even if it takes gossip to get there. "Favor?"

"Hiring escorts for Derek, my dear. You see, Killian thought maybe Derek would have some fun. Loosen up. He never thought that Derek would actually fall for Mandy, believe their meeting was some karmic fate. Because, well, Derek didn't know Mandy was an escort. He made her his girlfriend. And it lasted a few months, actually. Until the truth finally came out." He exhales soundly. "And now Derek is icier than ever. I think I saw a snowball fall out of his ass when he was walking down the hallway the other day."

"Derek isn't icy," I declare defensively. "He's actually a really nice guy when you get to know him. I swear. He's kind. Charming. Even tender when he wants to be."

Oliver snorts. "Beautiful. But a man of a million masks. A chameleon."

I frown. "It seems you don't like him that much."

His eyes flash. "Come on, Mia. Men like Derek Anderson or Ryder Anderson use people for a living. It's how they're bred. It's how they're built. How all these powerful types are." He shakes his head, his expression soured. "I know from personal experience. I say...If you're going to enjoy Derek Anderson, enjoy him. Have fun on the ride. But don't expect anything else out of a guy like that. Which is why I plan to get my fill of one of those sexy execs fluttering around here tonight and then walk away without any bruises or scratches on my poor heart. These men are only good for a week, tops. My advice?" He reaches for a nearby champagne glass on a passing tray. "Ride the golden dick. Get a great pair of shoes out of the deal. And use those great shoes to walk away when it's time." He raises his glass towards me. "Cheers and ciao, Mia. Don't forget to have some fun."

After Oliver walks away, my eyes swing back to Derek.

I truly believe Oliver Blare is wrong.

It was one thing for me to speak a little harshly about the man I now call 'Boss' when I was alone or when I was venting to my closest friend Tina, but it was an entirely different matter when a complete stranger, who seemed to know little about Derek and his 'true' character, was so scathing in his opinion of the man.

There is something exceptional in Derek. He is fine, there is no doubt. And god help me, the man is built to be the star of women's wet dreams the world over.

But there's a softness in him that he's buttoned up beneath this immaculate suits. I've seen glimpses of it.

As my stare stays on his gorgeous back, I find myself watching him mingle with other guests. His large hands are expressive, his blue eyes focused and confiding. I don't know if he knows it, but he has this natural charm and charisma that effortlessly pulls others in.

I would know. I'm one of them.

Furtively, I take in all his angles: his broad shoulders, his lacquered hair and sinful mouth that very nearly kissed me tonight.

He notices me watching and throws a small smile my way that makes my insides turn to water. I return the smile, glancing away before it can linger too long.

And with as perfect timing as ever, my phone buzzes inside my clutch. I grab it.

Christina's name dots the top of the screen. A text message.

"How's it going? Did you meet any famous artists? Are you famous yet?”

I grin, responding.

“I haven’t mixed and mingled yet. But I’m going to. I’ve been left to my own devices so I figure I’m going to have some fun. And no, I'm not famous yet. But I'll let you know when Kim Kardashian calls."

Tina texts me back. "Good. Tell her her new line of lipsticks really sucks. I want my money back."

Laughing, I place the phone back in my purse and resign myself to actually enjoying my night.

It's not as hard as it looks when I finally get going.

I speak to the artists. I speak to the buyers. Soon, I'm chatting up the writers. Then three scandalous artists, one leading a city-wide chat forum.

I met one of my favorites, photographer Ume Masahige, who actually gave me her business card. Gah!

I gawped at some sexy kimonos, met the Seattle arts elite —artists and collectors and entrepreneurs, and even the tiny man who started the famous ice wine and fine art festivals on Pike Street during summer.

I receive a few introductions from Derek to his colleagues and even fewer text messages about notes he needs to take.

I'm finally believing I can make it through this night in one piece, despite how it started when my phone buzzes again. This time, it's not from Christina.

It's an email instead of a text.

I open to find a message from Steven Mayers. It's an electronic file of the info he handed to me in the folder earlier.

And his apology is swift and sincere.

"I'm sorry I didn't send this over earlier. Sometimes, it's as if I'm not in the digital age. Anyway, here's the e-copies of the info on your newest target.

The investigation begins next Wednesday night at 8pm. Please don't be late. I'll connect you with Blake Haughton, who you'll be working with.

Christina speaks highly of you. I'm confident you'll do a great job.

Happy hunting, Mia."

I smile, scanning Steven's message, ready to let my phone

fall back in my clutch when I decide to open the email's attachments instead.

My heart is racing. In a way, this is exciting. Even if I told Tina that this wasn't exactly my cup of tea.

For a second, when I see the first image, I'm sure I've opened up the wrong email.

But that's not the case.

This is Steven Mayers' message, alright. And there's no mistaking the handsome blue stare or the chiseled jaw that's smiling flirtatiously into my eyes from the small screen.

I recognize his face instantly.

How could I not?

It's the face I've been staring at all night.

The target of my new private investigation gig is none other than Derek Anderson.

The man across the room.

My new boss.

Holy fucking Backstreet shit.

Chapter Eleven

DEREK

Mia catches a ride home from the CoTA event instead of letting me and my driver take her home.

And in a way, I guess I deserve that for the way I acted with her all night.

That near-kiss in Aimee's boutique seriously threw me the hell off. I'd been seconds away from plunging into Mia's mouth, taking her sweet breath and stroking my tongue along hers until she moaned out loud.

And doing so might've been the biggest mistake of my career.

Coming off the Mandy scandal, I have no more room in my life for more bad press. Or drama. No room to risk the company's hard work—my work, my brothers' work—because I can't stop myself from putting my hands on my gorgeous, fiery new assistant.

I got what I wanted out of CoTA. Good press. Another meet-up with Scott Disrick about our acquisition.

And another appointment with him in the books.

Still...freezing Mia out was not the answer.

It takes nothing short of the hand of God to stop me from

texting her all Sunday to check in on how she's doing. How she's feeling. How I've made her feel.

Her reply to my text to see if she made it home Saturday night from CoTA was short. My patience? Even shorter, after not having a chance to see her or talk to her the entire weekend.

So, I wait it out.

And on Monday, when it's time to head in to work at Hare & Holeton, I drive myself, giving my driver Raul the week off so I can rage in peace. Cranking Mother Love Bone to ear-splitting levels in my Lambo as I drive through the Seattle streets, I don't neglect to notice a few furtive paparazzi lingering around the office building to Hare & Holeton when I pull up.

I slip in the back door easily enough, after parking in the private garage with key access only.

Once I'm inside, I'm already shooting off texts to Jenny in double-time. My nerves high, I head for the elevators, only to find that someone else is already inside.

It's the last thing I need. Being distracted, when major drama is swirling like a tornado waiting for the kill.

But it's too late.

I already smell her hair, that warm coconut scent, before she even opens her mouth.

Brown eyes meet mine as I look up from my phone, the air deflating out of my lungs. In a white button-down shirt and simple black skirt, Mia looks like a million bucks filtered through the lens of heaven.

Seeing her here, of all places, is enough to make my heart nearly stop. The blood in my veins thickens as I walk inside the small, isolated car, waiting for the doors to close.

As they do, Mia looks my way.

"Mr. Anderson," she greets me, totally professional.

"Mia," I finally manage to say, giving her a brief nod in

greeting. "Good morning. And happy Monday. Welcome to your first day on the job."

"Thank you. I'm glad to be here."

Her voice is even and smooth—icy.

I answer her with another nod, slipping my phone back into my pocket and pressing the button for the top floor. Hare & Holeton.

Heading into work for the publishing company I built with my own hands usually gives me a rush. But not today.

Today, my pulse is thumping. But for reasons that have nothing to do with being CEO, and everything to do with the woman standing two feet away from me.

She glances at the climbing numbers, as our silver car ascends. And I fight the urge to reach for her. To simply touch her and feel her soft skin.

To try to test to see if it's as soft as I'm remembering it.

Instead, I force myself to cross my arms behind me.

"So, how was the rest of your weekend?" I find myself asking.

"Uh, uneventful...pretty much like most weekends."

Her lips say one thing. But her eyes say another.

"You?" she asks.

"Too eventful, as it were. That Seattle Post article is really picking up steam. The New York Times reached out. The Washington Post. I've been featured in the publications before, but now?" I shake my head, sighing. "It's like a fucking nightmare that keeps slipping from bad into worse."

I watch Mia's lips tighten. "How bad is it?"

I shrug. "Well, it's not exactly a good look for the business itself. Our writers are doing better than ever. Robert Cole's memoir. Elaina Johnson's women's fiction. Even the Harlan family stuff is a hit for the first time in forever. But...it's not what I wanted for Hare & Holeton. To be the subject of scandal. It's not what I want for the reputation of the business. And it's not what I wanted for its future. I wanted..." I stop.

"I'm talking too much. Don't listen to me. It's been a long morning."

I hear Mia sigh beside me. "No, really. It's fine."

I snort. "Bet you thought you left all the drama back at Sopra. And now you're walking into just more of it."

Her eyes light up as I sneak a glance at her. "Very different drama. And Sopra's drama was silly. It was all about what customers were tipping and being assholes, which servers were sleeping together and what new bartender Jerry the manager was hitting on at any given day." Her soft brown eyes narrow as she thinks. "At least here, you guys are doing something. Making a difference. Impacting lives. Feeding artists." She straightens. "I saw what I needed to see at CoTA. Hare & Holeton sounds like the real deal. And like you said, I'm a partner. A part of it. And that means something to me."

I gaze over at her, trying not to stare. "So, you did enjoy yourself at the event?"

"Yes, I did. What makes you think I didn't?"

"I mean, you left as soon as it was over. As soon as I relieved you of any duty."

She turns slightly, eyes snapping to my face, her amber gaze soft. "I did. Was there anything else you needed me from me? Did—did you want me to stay longer?" Her lips part slightly as she puts more weight on them. "Because I could have, if you wanted me to. I just wasn't sure—"

"Wasn't sure of what?" I catch her gaze, holding it hard.

The air inside the small lift seems to sizzle and crack, every nerve in my body standing on end.

I open my mouth to say something else.

But suddenly the elevator stops, the metal doors sliding open to our top floor.

Jenny is already waiting outside of the doors, peering through her regular red glasses at the two of us. "Ah, that's perfect. I found you. Just the two people I was looking for. Great timing."

I can't help but gawk at Mia. "Yeah, great timing, it is." With a nod, I slip out of the elevator into the waiting room. I glance back to Mia who's still in the elevator. "Uh, Mia, Jenny here is my Chief of Staff. She's going to get you started, get you onboarded. You'll probably be with her most of the day."

"Sounds great," Mia replies, a small smile flashing before disappearing. "Will I—" She clears her throat. "Will you and I get a chance to work together at all today, or—?"

"I'm not certain yet," I tell her. "It all depends. I'll be in my office, so I'll be easy to find. Until then, Jenny will show you the ropes. Prepare you for Hare & Holeton's needs." I pause for a second. "For my needs. I'll be with you soon."

There's the briefest look of disappointment on her face before she nods, almost demure-like.

"I'll be fine," she says. "I'm nothing if not ready," she adds, giving me a flash of a grin.

Jesus Christ, that grin.

She steps out of the elevator and near Jenny. The two start talking fast, quickly becoming acquainted as Jenny presents Mia with a battery of forms to fill out, starting with her employee ID badge.

As they disappear down the hallway, I find myself lingering, watching them go.

With a heavy sigh, I turn and head back toward my office at the end of the hallway. I should feel a least little victorious.

I'm still on the Bella Publishing acquisition track. A dinner appointment set with Scott Disrick in two days.

Our path to our much-anticipated IPO is still on track, despite all the issues.

So, why do I still feel like something is terribly missing? And why does that feeling intensify the second Mia leaves my sight?

I try not to dwell on it, despite my body still buzzing.

I enter the office, close the door behind me, and plunge into work.

MIA

Over the next week, Jenny makes sure that I get a lay of the Hare & Holeton office.

I quickly discover that the onboarding process at Derek's company starts off the way any other onboarding would.

Jenny makes sure I'm up to speed on the company's computers system. Online access. Accounting. Project management. Organization design. Auto-dialer training.

Tasks at hand look simple enough, but as my finger hovers over the scan button, I know there's no way I'm leaving here the same way I arrived. Not the same on so many levels.

This is my new job.

It's a dream come true. Or it would be, if Steven Mayers wasn't trying to pay me to spy on my boss.

"Not bad, eh?" Jenny asks at last, having been watching me closely. A set of red-tinged eyebrows raise in my direction.

I nod distractedly, barely listening as I scan the vast array of computer files, settings, and menus.

Trying to understand my new boss.

Trying to figure out who the hell hired a PI on Derek Anderson. And why.

Trying to figure out how I'll report back to Steven. What I'm going to tell him. If I'm going to accept the gig, what he's paying me. The money I need for the Canon of my dreams-a dream that's getting more and more complicated by the minute.

I sigh, looking up at Jenny and smiling. "Is this cubicle where I spend the rest of my day?"

"That depends. You'll probably be in Derek's office a lot. In your assistant position, Derek is going to have to lean on you for a lot of things. All the small details. Production details. Checks. Schedules. Things he can't have his hands in as CEO."

"So, I'm a finger-on-the-pulse kind of employee. Got it."

She nods, her long red hair falling in a curtain around her face. "Yes. And I have every confidence that you'll pick it all up super fast. I mean, you've only been here one week. And yet, you've done more than the last assistant Alexa did in six months."

"Ouch."

She laughs. "Sorry. Not to insult the woman. I get it. It can be hard to work for Derek, if you're not used to it. He can be...demanding, when he wants to be."

"So I've seen."

Jenny continues on, typing into my new computer on my office desk. "He's really not that bad. But his drive can also be overwhelming, if you're new to the job. He'll expect a lot of you, right off the bat. That's just him." She shrugs. "I guess he's really always had to be this way, though. The price of looking after your brothers when your parents have essentially walked out on you... His parents' extramarital affairs kept them busy." She snorts. "Busy with everything but their kids. They were always off, in another town or bedroom, it seemed."

I furrow my eyebrows. "Wow. Really?"

"Yep. We all pretty much grew up around each other. My father told me his parents were always off and having affairs behind each other's backs. And my parents' lives were no less, er, interesting. Derek's parents were actually on a vacation together to reconcile their marriage when something happened. An accident, or a fight...whatever it was, their car went off a bridge and into the river. Somewhere along the Washington coastline. The story was in the paper."

"Oh my God," I gasp.

She nods. "Yeah. " Her face goes dark. "So, we're all very damn careful to avoid getting tangled up in a messy relationship, love or otherwise."

I try to imagine Derek as a kid, a young man going

through this. The thought breaks my heart into pieces. "Growing up together...you all must be pretty close."

"Oh, we are. In some cases, whether we like it or not." She shrugs. "But that's just part of who we are. That's the secret to this company. We're kind of like a gang. A family in arms. And the bigger we grow, the more we need to expand that circle."

I like Jenny already. She pauses, glancing my way, suddenly shy. "So, you can see why all this process stuff, with all its minutia, can be a bit of a trial," she declares.

I nod.

"I know you may feel a little behind. But you'll get the hang of things in a jiffy," she assures. "And if you need anything, I'm always here to help. Or to yell at Derek when he's being a pain in the ass."

"Thanks, Jenny." I smile, and I'm amazed at how naturally it comes to me around the energetic Chief of Staff. When she talks about Derek, she gives off the loving admonishment of a sister. Reassuring and encouraging the same way a sibling would.

I guess that's one of Derek's many strengths. The people around him.

They do seem to adore him, even when he's an ass.

I glance at Jenny's expectant face. "I'm sure I'll be fine. You're right. I'm sure I'll get into this. It seems well-organized here, so that's a plus."

"Ah, sometimes we get a little messy around here, too. But that's probably thanks to the messiest Andersons, Ryder or Quentin, the CTO and the CMO. I'll introduce you to them, and Alton the CFO, when we have some time. Or if you see us on the elevators. Alton's pretty quiet. Doesn't speak to anyone. He just answers with a grunt and a nod. But he's a sweetheart. And Killian..." She exhales, blowing hard. "Well, Killian is just...Killian. You'll get to know him too. He's the

COO. Smart. Reliable. Well-managed. Kinda holds his cards close to his chest."

"In other words, he keeps to himself."

"Exactly. Takes one to know one, right?" Jenny winks, smiling at me.

My cheeks warm with the acknowledgement.

"So now you know the lay of the land. Time to find out what's first on the docket for you with Derek. He'll be expecting you to take over for Alexa."

I nod, turning to her with my eyes wide. "I'll bet."

"And hey, if Derek doesn't keep you burning the midnight oil, come to Happy Hour tomorrow with me and the rest of the gang." She motions over her shoulder. "Couple of us Hare & Holeton servants get together at the Operahouse or The Sprinkler bar for drinks after work. Know where that is?"

"Uh, yeah, I do. It's right by my old server job. Sopra Italian restaurant."

Jenny lights up. "Oh my God. I love that place. It's got the best Italian food in the city."

"With the worst management," I include. "It could really be a gem, if it was run differently."

"You'll have to join the rest of us folks at the bar, then. We're a huge fan of Sopra." She leans in. "But I'm starting to think I'm sure to be a bigger fan of yours."

I can't help but beam. "I will. I'll see you there, tomorrow night. It's a date."

She winks, before she leaves the cubicle area.

"I know you'll like it here," she told me. "I'm sure of it."

I didn't doubt Jenny's words. At all.

What I did doubt...was that I could keep from liking it too much, too fast. Enough to make me lose focus of my own real goals for coming to Seattle.

Paying for the right camera. Winning the Visions Collective photo contest...and twenty thousand dollars. And becoming the professional photographer my family assured me I couldn't be.

Yes, I'd be receiving a paycheck from working at Hare & Holeton...

In another week.

I needed money. Now. I needed time to buy that Canon camera, shoot enough shots and pick the ones that were good enough to enter the photo contest.

Its deadline was a week and a half from now. And I needed fast cash like a blood donor needs plasma.

Not to mention Seattle rent prices were sky-high.

And without the safety net that had always come from being with Jason, I was screwed.

When he was around, I got my needs met. At least in the food, water and roof over my head sense.

He'd been the one with the great job, the degrees, and the promising future in advertising. And I was the dependent fool who'd let myself fall for his charming demeanor and pretty lies. At the time, it had just seemed like a better idea than going back home and dealing with all the "well thought out" ways my family had of showing me what a failure I was, now that the relationship was over.

The thought has small seeds of doubt starting to sow their way into my mind. As usual.

My gaze flicking to other cubicles around me, I let my eyes scan the floor of Hare & Holeton before landing and settling on the wide double doors of the Executive Office of the Anderson Corp.

I don't know how long I sit there, imagining all the reasons why I should just do what Steven Mayers is hiring me to do. To spy on Derek Anderson. To get God-knows-what information on one of Seattle's richest bachelors.

But I do notice when a shift in the air of the room makes me look up.

My heart thumps, skipping a beat when I see the tall,

strong frame of the man I'd been admiring from afar so much just days before.

Derek Anderson.

He stands at the entrance to my cubicle, dressed in an understated, but well-made, gray suit. His golden-brown hair is pushed back, slicked back, and perfect as usual.

He's already looking at me.

His familiar blue eyes roam over me, up and down, like he's taking me in. As if he sees the secrets in my mind.

I sit taller. "Uh, hi, Mr. Anderson," I say, the words coming out with a slight quiver. "Can I help you?"

He doesn't blink. "Have you eaten yet?"

I have to sit on my hand to avoid nervously running it through my hair. “You mean lunch?"

He looks over at the clock and nods, his gaze seemingly pointing out the twelve-thirty time on the hands.

"No," I answer, my voice no louder than a whisper.

"Good. I'm starving. Let's go get some."

"I ... I don't know if—"

"Grab your purse. We're going downstairs. There's an excellent sushi place a couple of blocks away. Good, solid food. Decent prices."

"But..."

"Lead the way." He holds his hand out. "It's not a request. You’ve officially finished your first week on the job, Ms. Kamaka. I'm going to teach you how things work around here. And," he stresses, "we're going to celebrate you joining the Hare & Holeton team. Aren't we?"

The way he says it, so matter-of-fact, makes me feel like I've been reprimanded.

My mouth immediately dries, my heart races.

I don't know how to react.

But I don't want to.

I don't want to feel like this.

I want to feel strong. Independent and capable.

I want to feel secure in my abilities. Secure around him. Secure in my own certainties.

But there's something about Derek Anderson, my curiosity constantly pulling me towards him, even when I want to walk away. A force that causes me to feel a heated, crazy-out-of-controlness every time I see him.

I know there's a danger to that. To yearning for anything and everything about him.

But having him in front of me, my body longing for his touch, is a feeling I can't deny. It's impossible to ignore.

I get up from my office seat, walking towards my cubicle's entrance. "All right. Let's go." I point, my lips quirking up to mirror his. "But you're paying."

A slow, subtle smile crosses his lips, his blue eyes dancing as he pushes back away from the cubicle wall. "I wouldn't have it any other way."

Chapter Twelve

DEREK

Walking into Tamsung Fusion is like walking into the most charming, small hole-in-the-wall you've ever visited.

It's the real Seattle. The real, true, colorful life of the city. In a way the rest of the city's high, narrow, cold office buildings will never be.

It does not hide its passions. It does not cover up its outrage at the normalcy forced on it by the people like me.

It's colorful graffiti. An eclectic collection of music playing on speakers. Rows and rows of traditional Japanese décor. And yet, it's an open-concept restaurant in the middle of the day.

"May I take your coat?"

I looks up at the waitress, whose name tag says "Michaella Xi", and smile. I'm a regular here, and I recognize her.

"I'm fine. I run cold." I motion towards Mia. "But if you'd like to take the lady's coat..."

She steps forward, with a polite smile. Shrugging off her coat, Mia hands it to her.

"This one's a newcomer," I add, "so treat her right."

I watch Mia's eyes roll, even as she tries to keep herself from smirking too much. Without much ado, Michaella laughs, her voice light as she seats us in the intimate corner of the restaurant with its wood-covered walls.

"Well now, Mr. Anderson, I'll certainly do my best to make her feel at home. What would you like?" She turns to me. "We do a wide variety of sushi here. But we also have some unique fusion dishes. Vietnamese. Indonesian. Chinese. Take your pick."

"I'm here to have it all," I answer, adding, looking over to Mia. "Order whatever looks good to you."

"Oh, okay." I watch as Mia brushes a strand of hair from her face, making her look like a schoolgirl. "Umm, I'll start off light, I guess. The prawns?"

Michaella nods, scribbling on her notepad. "Great choice. Anything else?"

"I-Uh, a peach lemonade," Mia replies.

"Peach lemonade. Got it."

I raise two fingers. "Make that two, Michaella. Thanks."

The waitress nods.

"Think you might be interested in something... A bit stronger?" I pause, putting my hand on Mia's thigh, which is on the booth. "You look like you could use a drink. Something sweet."

Mia's amber gaze goes to mine. "What did you have in mind?"

"A glass of wine, perhaps. I think we could both use it today."

She shrugs a little. "I guess. White or red?"

"The choice is yours. Whatever you like."

She turns back to Michaella. "Perhaps a glass of white?"

More scribbles from Michaella. "And how about you, sir?"

"I'll have a sake."

"Coming right up."

"I'll put in the order for your prawns and be right back with your drinks."

Michaella trails down to the restaurant's kitchen. I watch her go before I speak again.

"So ... how *was* your first week at work, Mia?"

At that, she laughs, a breathy, soft sound that makes her chest rise, her breasts come to life under her white shirt.

She raises an eyebrow, the amber of her eyes warm with the muted sunlight that pours in the front of the restaurant, barely reaching us.

"Well," she exhales, "to tell you the truth: It's been...awful. Just horrible. Every second of my time at work has been spent trying to keep from killing people."

"Oh really?" I come back. "That bad, huh?"

"Just terrible. The people...Blech. I don't know how you handle it. It's just..."

"Terrible?" I cut in.

"Yes. I think I may be scarred for life."

I laugh. "If I didn't know any better, I'd almost believe you. You can be pretty convincing when you're trying to be tough."

She smiles at that, and then catches herself. "So, you don't believe me?"

"Not a single word."

"And how do you know my first week hasn't been terrible?"

"By your smile." I lean in, lowering my voice. "And by the fact that you agreed to go lunch with me."

"It's not like you gave me much of a choice now, did you?"

I grin over at her. "Oh, I did. I know no matter what I say to you, you're your own person. Doesn't matter that I'm the 'boss'. Hell, I could be President of the United States, and I'm sure it wouldn't make a difference. You're a woman who makes her own mind up about what she does and who she does it with."

"Yeah?"

"Yeah."

Unspoken questions linger in her gaze, like she's wondering why I find her so fascinating, why I want to share with her things I've never told anyone.

But then the moment is broken. We're interrupted by the sound of Michaella's voice.

"All right, Mr. Anderson! Your sake. Your wine. And your prawns. I'll be back with the peach lemonade and—"

"Thank you, Michaella." I don't mean to be a jackass. But I'm suddenly too eager to have this moment with Mia alone again. I turn to Michaella.

"Thank you."

Michaella nods. "You're all welcome."

I watch her go, while turning my eyes back to Mia. She reaches for her glass of wine, sipping slow and gentle. I reach for my sake. We stay there like that, drinking silently, these two worlds colliding for a moment.

I don't want to look like my comments made her uncomfortable, so I put away my sake, get up, and cross around the booth, bringing myself over next to her.

"Can I ask you something?"

She turns towards me and nods, giving me a curious look.

"How exactly did you get into photography? I overheard you talking to Ume Masahige at the CoTA event. You seem...fluent in areas that most folks don't even know exist."

She chuckles and takes another sip of her wine. "I guess I must have been into it as a hobby. I didn't always have that 'eye'. But I liked taking pictures as a kid. I suppose it's one of the few things I can do well. I like the process of capturing something beautiful, something I never expected, and creating a nice picture. That always fascinated me. And I think there's a... purity to it that, to me, seems very natural, very organic. It's not just 'photography'. It's...well, I don't know, it's a kind of art. I can't explain it. I suppose it's just how I am."

I nod, understanding. "Your portrait photography really is impressive. Not just because, as you said, you can capture an image that you never expected, but it's...the way the images affect the onlooker. The way the viewer is drawn to those shots is..."

She turns, head snapping towards me. "How do you know about that?"

"I found—I mean, my Chief of Staff Jen found your social media. Impressive work...I see."

She scoffs on a small laugh. "Well, I guess that answers the question of whether or not you guys have been stalking me."

"We don't like to think of it as stalking. More like research. We check out all our new employees on social. These days, it's a necessity. You never know who you're dealing with—a potential threat to our company's best interests."

She looks away. But her eyes find mine again. "Threat?"

"You never know. I told you about my other assistants. If I had checked some of their accounts earlier in their employment, I might've been avoided some really bad apples in the beginning."

"'Bad apples'..." She tilts her head, making her shortened silky dark brown hair fall forward. "So, that's to say you're making sure that I'm ripe?"

My grin widens. "Precisely, Ms. Kamaka."

"Glad to see we understand each other," she answers, swallowing hard.

"Your social media. It's nice. Could definitely use some expanding, though. Some more polish. Maybe I could show you how to do that."

"I already know how. My aunt was an artist. She taught me how to set up a portfolio for my work online. How to shoot better photographs and how to edit my images to my liking."

"And is your aunt here to defend her teachings? Because I have a few suggestions I'd care to make."

There's a pause. A beat.

"She passed away recently," she admits. "Since then, I've been doing my own thing, honing what I do. Even if it comes with a bit of a learning curve."

"I'm sorry about your loss. Did she live here? In the Seattle area as well?"

Another beat. Mia exhales quickly. "No, actually, she lived back in Hawaii. Near the rest of my family. That's where I'm from. Hawaii. I went to school in Honolulu at UH. School of Design, Art and Architecture."

"Admirable," I acknowledge. "Very admirable. You'll have to show me your work. I'd love to see it."

She lets out a slight laugh, lifting a hand to push back a stray lock of hair. "I don't think I'll be showing you much of anything, Mr. Anderson."

"First week on the job, and you're already shutting me down like this? I'm surprised. I thought you'd have a much gentler personality when you're in a professional setting."

"I'm not that gentle. Hell, you should know that by now. I've spilled enough coffee and bourbon on you at Sopra by now. And that was just in the last few days."

"And I still plan on sending over a check for my dry cleaning for that one blue suit. I loved that damned suit." I reach for my sake, taking a long, slow drink.

"I'm going in for this photo contest called the Visions Collective, so if I win that—or the lottery—then I might take care of that check. Though I can't promise you anything."

"A man can hope."

Watching me, Mia taps her fingers on the table. "So...how about you? How'd you get started in the publishing business?"

"Funnily enough, it wasn't always my plan. My dream was to be a comic book artist."

"Really?" Her amber eyes go wide. "For sure? I thought comic books were just a passing fad."

She looks at me with such open curiosity, I can't help but smile. "No, it wasn't a passing fad. It's a niche that's really never over. Sometimes, it just takes a break. Cools off. I was always interested in it. I guess Rena—my crush at the time—was into art. I wanted to impress her, at first. It was much easier to get her attention with drawing pictures than trying to...let's say...get her attention in other ways. I read manga instead of eating my lunch when I was in junior high. I painted cover art on my notebook covers."

I shrug, shaking off the memory with another pull of the hot Sake on my tongue. "Anyways, my parents weren't around much. Didn't have a lot of money, so I went to various comic book art conventions, watched other artists sketch, made contacts, and was even able to start selling my work. I met a lot of artists. Quite a few writers. One day, I got a call from a kid out of the Fraser Valley here in Washington. He was looking for work on a freelance basis. Anyone can draw. But this kid...he had a real talent for the written word. He could really weave a compelling tale. I was so impressed, I offered to help him publish his stuff." I shake my head with a laugh. "And that was the beginning. That kid turned out to be my first publication. And from there, my brothers and I built the business into the Hare & Holeton you see today."

Mia settles back a little. Thinking. It's been a while. She sips her wine. "My God. What a story. I never knew that." She pauses, considering, then asks, "Do you publish any comic books now?"

I frown, my gut tightening as I realize the truth. "Actually...we don't. I've tried, of course. But it's a niche that's...hard to break into. It's easier to write a rock opera with a Yo-Yo than to make it big in comics." I raise my glass to her in a salute. "But one can always dream. Isn't that the old saying?"

This time, she places her hand on my knee instead, a show of comfort that I didn't know I needed until this very moment. And there's no jolt, no instant thrill, just the natural warmth of her touch.

I relax against the chair. "You should know. If, and when, I do something, Mia, I don't do it halfway. I go all the way. I only push things that I'm passionate about." Her hand is still there. And the temperature in the room has risen. My pants have definitely grown tighter. "I'm just warning you, if we work together, Mia. I will go all the way with you. I want to be part of work that makes an impact. A difference. That's why I took you on."

Mia purses her lips, looking away. But then, glancing back, she sighs, too.

"Because I'm a charity case?" she asks softly.

I watch her, watching me, listening to her tone. I weigh my words so carefully. "Because you're damned good. Because you're bold. Brave. Fearless. And not just at Sopra. Anyone could see that. You're bold and brave in your photos. Whether they're of family, or friends...or of people who mean nothing to you. You're fearless with your words. You're not afraid to stand out. To scare people. And that...it's a rare thing. Very rare."

With a grin, she reaches for the wine glass, twirling it in her hand. I don't realize my own hand has fallen on her leg until she turns toward me, and I watch as she lifts her eyes with a slow smile.

She leans in, her heavy-lidded eyes on me. "That courage thing? Trust me. It's still a work in progress."

She nudges my glass, urging me to drink with her now. I toast her before taking a giant swig.

"Well, I'm impressed. I want everyone who works with my company to be brave, bold, fearless. That's why I offered you the job."

Her eyes are on me.

Quietly, she whispers, "I'm a little surprised, I admit. You're not that hard to impress."

I squeeze my hand, hanging on to it, just above her knee. Her thigh is almost between my fingers, as I hold her there. "Or," I hear myself say, "maybe you're just that impressive.

Did you ever think of that? That maybe I'm *too* hard to impress and you're just that good?"

She opens her mouth to speak.

I cut her off. "I've never felt the need to show anyone just how much I enjoy talking to them."

She looks down, away from me.

My next words come out hard. "That stems from the fact that I don't find too many people worth talking to. But you're different. You're not just different from the people I usually deal with; you're different from everyone. By a long shot."

She looks back up.

"I'm not…" she starts, then pauses, her voice low. "I'm not like everyone else. I know that sounds cheesy. I wouldn't say I'm…different from everyone else. I'm just not like everyone else. And I don't mean that as a put-down, or as a put-on. I'm just...not some put-together person. I'm not suave or polished. I'm not complicated. Or sophisticated. Honestly? I don't know how I even got here. Where I am today. And I kind of like it. I'm...free."

Her fingers loosen, my hand sliding up to slip through hers. And against my better judgment, I hold her hand there, my thumb covering the tips of hers, turning side over side, gently, my thumb brushing back and forth against her soft skin.

"Enjoy it while you can," I say. "Soak it up. Drown in it. There won't be much time to enjoy it once we get started. I can tell you that from experience."

"I already know. I have no illusions to think that this is anything other than part of a job. I think I understand that. My question is just what I can expect."

"I'm easy to predict. I will expect you to do what you can, and until that isn't good enough. Then, I'll expect you to do more. I will expect you to do everything you can. In ways that will surprise you. And in ways that won't."

Her eyes go wide, her brows shooting up.

"Trust me," I say. "You can't make that mistake. The only way to survive is to anticipate everything."

"Like you?"

I lean in, my mouth closer than I expected to be. "Like me. I'm as predictable as they come. And I want you to be prepared for the worst. And for the best. Don't let your lack of preparation destroy you. Everything that happens, no matter how rough or strong, will be exactly what you put it up to be."

She inhales sharply. "You seem to have a rule for everything, don't you? You know life is nothing like that. I mean, what a world that would be."

"But it could be like that."

"No, it couldn't. It absolutely cannot. You know everything wouldn't be able to be scripted. There's no way that you could predict exactly what's going to happen."

"What if I could?"

"If you could?"

"Yes."

"Then you're not truly free. You're just putting on a puppet show that looks and sounds convincing. But as soon as the cameras go, and the lights go down, they're all going to turn into starving, snarling beasts."

I don't let myself hesitate, despite her words. "Then I'll feed them. I'll keep them on a chain, so it doesn't matter what they do. They won't get out of the script. I'll keep them on a chain, and my finger will always be on the dial."

"You're kidding." She shakes her head, big brown eyes going wide. "You truly think life is better when you can control everything?"

I shrug, watching her intently. "I think life is better when you don't let anything control you."

She presses her lips together. Her thumb abruptly flips over, and she moves our joined hands. "And you have a handle on both?"

I nod. "I have a handle on both."

"You know how you'll react to everything? That you can predict everything?"

"I'm usually prepared for it, yes."

Mia's voice is incredulous. "How?"

"I react to everything. Life doesn't surprise me half as much as I'm prepared to."

I can see her mind working in the way she leans back, cupping my hand in hers on her leg. Her eyes travel down to my fingers, and she twists her hand, her thumb rubbing against mine. My skin feels warm, her thumb and mine rubbing together, in this intense sort of silence.

Her eyes are on me when she breathes out. "Are you so sure you're prepared for everything?" She moves my hand up her thigh, past the hem of her skirt. "Even...this?"

Her hand slides my fingers farther up and underneath the thick fabric, brushing the soft swell of her inner thighs.

I swallow.

Her eyes are wide, holding my gaze captive, waiting. She doesn't so much as blink. I don't move, my hand holding hers there.

The air is heavy.

And I can feel my breath coming out in quick, shallow gasps.

Shit. I was wrong.

I am prepared for lot of things in life. I swear I am.

But Mia Kamaka placing her hand under her skirt in the middle of a of my one of my favorite Asian fusion restaurants is the last thing I'm prepared for.

I lick my lips, feeling my breathing deepening.

Chapter Thirteen

MIA

It's the wine. It's definitely the wine...

That's making me slide my boss's hand up my thigh and under my skirt in the middle of an afternoon lunch.

It has to be.

My eyelids feel heavy and my knees feel weak.

But I don't care. Not really.

I'm riding a wave of a really good, really ripe glass of Pinot Grigio with Mr. Anderson and I have no interest in stopping. None at all.

"Mia..." he starts.

Of course, my boss wants me to be a good employee. To act reasonably, even.

I don't.

It's our first meeting since the 'incident' (if you could call it that) nearly a week ago. That kiss in the alley.

And we have a lot to catch up on since then.

I close my eyes. "Derek, don't... Don't say anything. Don't ruin it. Just...live in the moment. With me."

I can hear him breathing beside me in the booth, his clean laundered scent floating over me. I can feel the heat of his body, he's so close. And any second now, I expect him to pull away.

To bring back his usual control.

To reprimand me. Or stop me.

But he does none of that instead.

His hand stays still under my skirt for a second. Before it moves, his fingers coming alive.

His thumb swipes over my lace underwear, skimming the fabric. I inhale sharply, the rest of my senses going out of focus. I'm frozen to the spot as the rest of Derek Anderson's fingers begin to play.

They place a sweet, sultry melody over my now dripping wet, v-line panties.

The fingertips travel frantically over the fabric, sending darts of arousal in every direction.

The music. The clangs and clatter of dishware. The hushed rumble of customers' voices.

Everything is all fuzzy. All blurry beneath my closed eyelids.

All except one thing. One person.

Derek Anderson.

His dark heat. His clean scent.

"Mia..." he says, as his thumb tugs softly at me through the thin fabric. "Mia, this is wrong."

I sigh, my mouth opening and closing, but no words coming out.

I can't respond. I can't say anything. I don't exist here.

Derek's words say one thing. But his fingers are currently saying another as the magical melody plays again on another level.

His fingers pull the fabric from my body, and my breath seizes as I feel wetness flush my panties.

I can't see.

But I can feel.

And right now, it's all that matters...

Derek's fingers slip. He pushes through the fabric, and they're there.

Between my legs. His fingers sliding and prodding gently, swirling sensuously around my entrance.

I gasp just as his thumb finds my clit and rubs.

"Derek..." I moan softly.

"Mr. Anderson," I hear him correct me. His voice is gruff. "If we're going to play this game, Mia, let's play it all the way...shall we?"

I moan in agreement.

His fingers encircle the length of my pussy. Until at last, he slips a finger inside, making me yelp into the open air.

"Shhhh," he says softly, the word tickling my ear. "Quietly, Ms. Kamaka. Quietly. This is a place of business, you know."

I open my eyes slowly, my half-hooded gaze flickering through Tamsung Fusion's dining room.

No one notices us here in the booth. Can tell or see that one of Seattle's most beautiful billionaire bachelors is finger-fucking me in a dark corner of a crowded restaurant, his breath a deep, rumbling sigh against my ear.

"You like it like this, do you?" he asks, his finger inside me starting to curl.

I bite my lip and resist the urge to groan. I nod, my tongue darting over my lips.

"All you had to do was ask," he says. "At my company, we aim to please, Ms. Kamaka." He adds another finger, and I bite down even harder. "Are you pleased...Ms. Kamaka?"

I shiver at the change, my eyes fluttering open to see him watching me. He's rigid and still, his shoulders proud and strong.

I breathe deeply, feeling his scruffy jaw whispering against my hair. The smell of cotton and his skin washing over me.

His fingers rub and curl, my hips rocking against the rhythm of his touch.

We're alone with no one watching. All the customers are

minding their business with their own meals, their own conversations, their own problems and stories.

With an intense gaze, Derek's sky blue eyes meet with mine. He watches my reaction carefully as I begin to writhe.

"Don't stop," I whisper.

"Mia..."

"Don't stop."

He screws in a third finger, slower and deeper than before, his hand stilling.

I'm breathing hard. My fingers are grasping the tablecloth tightly as my abdomen moves to match the correct strokes.

"Jesus," I breathe.

He chuckles, his smile breaking out. "Never been called that one before."

"I-I can't..."

He pulses his thumb against my clit again, and I cry out in delicious pleasure.

"God, Derek, you—this is...Just...please."

"Please what?"

"Please let me—"

"Let you?" He looks at me, endlessly curious about me in just this one moment. "Or make you?"

I pause by gathering my thoughts to answer. "Make me lose control," I whisper. "I want to lose control. With you, with you, with you."

My words lose all coherence. And Derek grins, leaning in to kiss the top of my shoulder. "Your wish is my command, Ms. Kamaka."

I exhale again, the passion that's building inside me spilling out into my words.

"Take me there," I say in a breathy rush of greedy words. "Derek..."

His fingers start to move again, faster. His thumb moves exactly where I want it to.

"Been waiting for this since the moment I saw you, Mia."

"Wait for what?" I ask in the back of my throat, my eyelids drooping. "Wait for this...or...wait for what happened..."

"This," he laughs, his tone warm and deep. "This happened a long time ago, Mia. The moment I laid eyes on you."

We regard each other for a moment. I stare into the blue depths of his eyes, hunger lifting from my core.

I've never known a feeling like this. A desire, a lust, so strong I fear I might destroy myself by jumping right in.

But I won't.

I'll wait.

Because that's what I need right now.

I move to kiss him. I don't even wait for permission. I just do it.

The world blurs as my lips meet his. A mutual fire flaring.

The shock of feeling his tongue in my mouth sends me over the edge.

I'm melting. I'm here.

I'm here.

And I'm doing this.

My nails digging into his shoulder, his tongue becoming frantic as I climb towards an already-elevating peak that's sure to consume me.

Derek grabs onto my hip, pushing his fingers deeper as he curls all three inside me.

"Oh, God!" I cry out softly, my head falling back, away from his kiss.

I bite my lip. I can't help it.

I don't even try.

I'm lost in a place I've never been before.

A place where nothing exists except this.

His hand moves to my waist, holding me as my orgasm crests, every nerve ending in my body on fire...

...Burning through me.

I breathe hard, my skin all slick and vulnerable.

I can't speak. I can't make sense of this moment. I can barely breathe.

The lust, the need, the primal joy and longing...they consume all the uncertainty and fear in my heart.

Derek sits back. His breathing is heavy, but that doesn't stop him from intently watching me. Waiting for me. His hand remains between my legs, gently stroking, bringing me down gently from an impossible high I know I'll never reach again with anyone but him.

Within seconds, ever so slowly, he removes his hand, smiling at me. His face is pure, lusty evil as he brings his fingers to his mouth.

His tongue dangles over his lips, rubbing them gleefully.

I drink in the sight of his handsome face. I let my gaze lower, following his hand as he removes his fingers from his mouth.

He smiles then. A playful smirk that would only be matched by a wolf.

A wolf that devours a young, naive fawn...

...And devours it whole.

I gasp slightly, a hot flush overtaking me again.

He's got me.

And I want it all.

I can feel my heart beating and my chest rising and falling.

"You don't play fair, do you?" I breathe.

"I told you..." His blue eyes burn playfully at me. "That this place has some of the best eats in the city, Ms. Kamaka." He gestures for me to look around at the restaurant. "And everything here is on me, too."

I grin, feeling the first real gush of pleasure at that.

"Without exception?" I ask, biting my lip.

He nods, his eyes never leaving mine. "Without exception."

"Fair enough."

His smile widens, growing. "I think you'll agree, this was worth the wait. Right?"

"I think I might be...happy about the wait..."

"Good," he says, a note of smugness to his voice. "You earned it."

We're both silent for a moment. We don't need words to speak our own silent, yet simultaneous excitement.

I need to sit here for a moment. Just let it settle, everything I've been feeling, and everything I've been thinking about this man.

Derek Anderson.

Billionaire bachelor. Famous Seattle figure.

My boss.

I swallow. Just as our waitress Michaella comes back with my peach lemonade and our food.

She gives us a look, her eyes narrowing in on Derek sitting next to me.

I can't help but see the wicked smile that dances across her face, directed at Derek and then at me.

I'm sure my orgasm blush is still freshly imprinted on my face for everyone to see.

I got what I secretly wanted. What my body had been silently begging for…

But what the hell am I going to do now?

DEREK

I don't remember much of the meal after Michaella returns with our food.

It's honestly hard to remember anything when the taste and smell of Mia's pussy is still on my tongue.

Escorting Mia back to the Hare & Holeton building is a blur. So is my response when she kisses me on the cheek in the elevator, scurrying off to her cubicle with me watching after her.

I brought us to Tamsung Fusion so I could avoid more drama, dining at a low-key place where customers were much less likely to approach me with copies of the Seattle Post and my picture in it.

But now I've just landed in much more of it.

An even bigger drama...because Mia Kamaka isn't just a beautiful local photographer who I just made come on my hand during lunch hour.

She's also my new assistant.

As if my luck with women couldn't get any worse.

First, Mandy. Now, this.

My losing streak could be a Guinness World Record, for all I know.

There was no denying the raw attraction, the chemistry, between me and Mia now. The only question is what the hell am I going to do about it.

For now, I decide the best decision is to ignore it. Ignore it until I think of a way to get it out of my head. Maybe I'll take up jogging. Maybe I'll take up a course in metalwork.

I mean, I could do that, right?

I spend the next few hours, my head buried in work, when I receive a quick knock on my office door.

I glance up.

"Mr. Anderson."

My gaze finds a green one. "Oliver."

My brother Ryder's assistant flashes a big smile at me. "You wanted to see me, sir?"

I glance at my desk, at the mountain of work piled there. "Yes. Have you seen Ryder today? I called his office phone earlier. No response."

"I-Um, I'm pretty sure Mr. Anderson took an extended lunch, sir."

I raise a brow. "Extended lunch?"

"Yes, sir. He's, um, working."

"Working? Ryder?" I laugh. "On what, might I ask?"

Oliver's gaze darts around the office. "A special project."

"Special project..." I pause. "This special project wouldn't happen to be trying to find the 'leak' for that Seattle Post article, would it?"

Oliver shifts on his feet, and I press him. "Oliver?"

"Well...maybe, sir."

"I thought so." I sigh and rub my temples. "I'd hoped he'd been looking for a second in command, an equal. A Chief Information Officer to help him out, but of course not. That's not Ryder. Little Bro never could keep his nose out of others' business. Amongst other body parts..." I push out of my office chair, moving to stand. "Well, I guess I know where he is."

His eyes dart to me. "Sir, Mr. Anderson is—"

"Not in his office," I finish Oliver's sentence. "And I have my hunches as to where he is. If you'll excuse me."

Before Oliver can say another word, I'm out of my office and marching towards the same dark-paneled door that I haven't approached in weeks. Not since the news of the impending Seattle Post article came my way.

I place my hand on the cold doorknob.

But before I can twist and open it, Jenny's voice sounds out. "Derek?"

I turn, my eyes locking on hers. "Yes, Ms. Forde?"

Her gaze darts around the hallway, focusing on the same little dark-paneled door that I'm trying to get to. She steps closer, her red eyeglasses sliding further down her nose.

"Do you think that's the greatest idea right now?"

I release the doorknob. "What do you mean?"

She reaches out, grabbing my arm and tugging. "You...Confronting Killian."

My pulse picks up. "I'm not."

Her ginger eyebrows quirk. "You're not?"

"No, actually. Just looking for Ryder. Wanted to give my little brother a message about interfering in my affairs."

She huffs, leading me away. I let her. "I don't particularly think that's the best idea right now."

I laugh. "What do you mean, exactly?"

"I don't know. But you're...a bit tense these days with the new article, and all the big hoopla surrounding it. You might not be in the best frame of mind right now to just march in there, guns blazing, so to speak. Maybe give it a day, go at him in a more de-escalated manner?"

I stare at her. "Are you...joking?"

She shrugs, her austere blouse wrinkling. "Not entirely." She turns and leads me off, down the hallway. "I just want your focus back on the things that matter. I wanted to go over a few things with you anyhow."

I follow her, my mind turning over her words. "Things? What kinda things?"

She sighs, her hold tightening. "Things like the fact that we need a CIO to handle our IT costs, which are quickly getting out of hand. Things like your brother Ryder being the reason that those IT costs are out of hand in the first place. Things...like Scott Disrick rescheduling your Wednesday dinner for tonight..."

I stop. "Tonight?"

"Yes. Tonight. Six o'clock." She glances at her watch. "Which is in less than two hours."

"That's not much time..."

"I know." Jenny's hazel eyes roll, and she waves me off. "Apparently, he has some family to-do he has to attend to on Wednesday, so he wants to push the dinner up. Said he'd have us over for cocktails and dinner, but his attitude changed once he found out about this maddening article. Now, we can barely agree to get him to meet for appetizers. I had to do something." She gives me a pained expression. "Urgently. But...I'll call his assistant to postpone, if you want."

I wave her off. "No."

"Derek? You sure? Saying yes...This is important."

I nod. "I'm well aware of that, Jenny. Why don't you join us? You might as well keep me company. There's no way the fucker is easing his way out of anything—contracts or otherwise—with you there."

She nods, following me at a slow walk back to my office. "He better not. Besides, I'm sure you'll find a way to use tonight to your advantage." She throws me a customary elbow the way she used to when we were in fourth grade and fighting over toys. "And you know I can't make it tonight. I have a dinner date."

I give my Chief of Staff a knowing glance as she enters my office.

"Okay, so it's not so much 'dinner' as it is a family-sized spaghetti bolognese to share with my knitting group." She sighs. "I'm not fooling myself. This is how I like to spend my Monday evenings, okay, Derek? I'm not going to let this..." She shakes her head. "Never mind. I'm very happy with my Monday nights as is, thank you very much."

"For the knitting, or the bolognese?" I ask.

She smirks. "The bolognese." She takes in a deep breath and leans forward, her voice dropping to a near whisper. "I'm fine, Derek. Don't overthink this. So, I'm not a big dater." She walks a few steps. "I'm perfectly fine with being single."

"That Bajan attitude of yours...it's just one of your special kinds of charming."

She rolls her eyes. "Hurry up and get your mind off the personal...problems and focus on the business one. You made a good suggestion. I think it is a great idea to bring someone to the dinner with Scott." She hesitates. "He's bringing a date himself, it seems."

"Really?"

"Yes. That's what he said. I think they may have worked together."

"Interesting."

Jenny eyes me, flinging red hair from the top of her glasses. "Do you have someone you can bring?

"Um, I—"

"Scratch that," she interrupts. "I already know the answer to that. It's no." She blinks fast. "Why don't you bring Mia along? She's easy to get along with, right? She'll wow Scott."

I face Jenny, frowning. "Will she?"

"Yes!" she says, a little too quickly. "Yes, she will. Trust me. I've spent the better part of today with her, and she's beautiful. Smart. Funny. And she'll really get along with Scott."

As I think about it, she may be right. Mia would be a perfect companion for Scott at dinner.

She really is easy to get along with—witty, unlike most of the women he surrounded himself with—and she's the kind of woman that would immediately draw him in and keep him around the entire night. The type to get him to smile.

The way she does me...

"Yeah. I don't know..."

Jenny crosses her arms. "What do you mean, 'don't know?' Hare & Holeton's going public within the year, D. Do you want this acquisition of Bella Publishing to go smoothly or no? Which is it? Yes or no?"

She's right, of course. But she doesn't understand how difficult this may be...inviting Mia to dinner.

"I think it's a great idea, Derek," she says softly, gently. "It'll be fine. Trust me. Mia's a good girl."

"I know."

She points an eyebrow at me. "Better than your usual, that is."

I nod. "I guess so."

She moves to leave. "I'll spread the word to the team about rescheduling the Wednesday dinner for tonight. Have Mia merge the calendars. And have her set up a few extra calls that you've neglected. Oh, and I'll invite her to your dinner with Scott… since you won't."

I stare at her. She leaves the office without another glance back.

Once she's gone, I turn to my desk, my eyes zeroing in on the Seattle skyline in the distance.

Thinking about her.

Mia.

How did I get myself into this?

I feel a searing need to see her again. To know her, to talk to her and coax her back into my arms, into my hands, beneath my fingers. I need to feel her skin, her lips, her even vaguely mussed hair pressed against my face—the way she sounded, the way she came.

I need to know that she's okay, that she's well. Unlike me.

Taking Jenny's advice feels wrong...but the idea of seriously ignoring my growing feelings towards Mia feels even more wrong.

Hare & Holeton's future depends on what we do now. We're really going public by the end of the year…

A bolt of awareness runs through me.

Sliding over to my desk, my fingers damn near shaking, I start to dial Mia's cell number.

Chapter Fourteen

MIA

The clock is ticking. Not just the one against the Hare & Holeton wall, but the one in my hand.

Steven Mayers from the PI gig needs an answer on my assignment.

And I have none to give him.

Most of everyone has already cleared out of the cubicles, and yet I'm still here staring at the blank screen.

The word "yes" is stuck in my throat as well as my fingers. I can't seem to get them to type.

To accept this latest assignment would mean tailing Derek, following his life, inserting myself into personal affairs for God-knows-what reason. To betray his trust.

To not accept would be to say bye-bye to the Visions Collective photo contest, the springboard I know I need in Seattle to get my photos published in a national magazine, even abroad.

I want to win. I want to be published. Not for a place in a museum gallery. Not for a plaque in a book. Not for a grant or a fellowship.

For me.

For my own damn shot at the new life I want so badly.

I shut my eyes tight, my head pounding. It's the same feeling I got back in Hawaii.

When I left Jason. When I abandoned the life my family wanted for me.

It feels like I've been torn in half again.

I wrap my fingers around the words I've been rejecting for nearly ninety minutes now: the words I have no choice but to type. I'm just here to do a job, I tell myself. No harm to anyone...no one gets hurt.

It's just business.

Just business that makes a difference in my life. In this particular case.

Just business.

Finally taking a deep breath, I slowly open my eyes and begin the email to Steven.

I barely hear the footsteps outside of my cubicle, coming closer. And when I do, it's too late.

I gasp when I turn my head to my right, Derek standing there.

With a sorrowful expression that's foreign to his face.

I scoot back in my office chair, heart pounding.

"Derek."

"Mia. I'm sorry. I didn't mean to scare you."

I swallow hard. "I should have been paying more attention. I'm sorry, too."

"No, I don't think you are." His smile is small. "I'm beginning to know you better than that." He looks around his own office, then back at me. "What are you still doing here?"

"I was just sitting in here, wrapping up some final onboarding items."

"Like what? What could possibly be left to do? HR overtraining you on the company policies already?"

My hands begin to shake. I clasp them tightly to my lap.

I shrug. "Just getting familiar with the system and my

post." I feel a renewed sense of guilt driving into me like a rogue wave. "Things like that. I'll be done in half an hour or so."

I sense his curiosity, realize he's scrutinizing every move I make, watching me. He leans against the top of the cubicle wall, his gray suit jacket open, his tie a little loose.

"I was actually trying to reach you," he says when my hands stop shaking. "I called your office phone, but it went to voicemail. Two times.'

"Uh, yeah. I tried to set up my own voice message, and I think I flubbed it. Not a very good sign for day one on the job."

He grins, eyes still wary. "I'm sure you'll make a smooth transition."

"Thanks. I hope so."

To my surprise, he moves from the cubicle wall until he's standing at its entrance, his tousled toffee-brown hair catching the light.

"Mia. There's something we need to talk about."

A cold tingle snakes through my veins.

I nod. "Okay. Shoot."

He shakes his head, a weary smile curling his lips. "I hate to ask you to do extra work. Again. I really do. But I really need a big favor from you right now." He takes a small step closer to me. "Do you have space in your schedule to have dinner with me tonight?"

A lump forms in my throat, deep and thick. My entire body seems to be having a spasm, its limbs unable to move on their own accord.

What did he say?

He said...he said..."dinner."

Even though I barely ate any lunch, I realize I'm suddenly starving. Starving for a human connection. For a connection with him. I can practically see it, this invisible thing that's tying me to him.

Because I want it to be.

Want it.

Want him.

It's the only thing I can be sure of.

The very thought of having to sit down with him, in his presence, makes my heart pound. I feel lightheaded, my pulse quickening.

This is why I can't...can't...

But he keeps looking at me with that weary look. The look that says he is suffering. That he is even now wishing he could turn back time, undo the damage.

I take a deep breath, my knuckles rapping against my desk. I'm aware of a few employees in the hallway. Chatter. Muffled laughter.

Derek's gaze is unreadable, his blue eyes boring into me. I can tell he is having a hard time suppressing his smile, his attempt to mask his hopes and desires.

"Dinner?" I finally ask him.

"Yes," he says, his voice low. "A business dinner. With Scott Disrick." He clears his throat. "Unfortunately, the CEO of the company we're acquiring, Bella Publishing, appreciates the company of beautiful women more than he cares to meet with the CEO of the business that's actually buying his. Go figure." He snorts. "Guy has been like this for a while. I need someone to come with me who will know how to handle someone like Scott. Someone who can help me make him comfortable. Someone warm." He smiles at me, but I don't feel warm about it. In fact, I feel cold. "Someone like you, Mia. You have natural, easy charm. And you'll disarm him, make him feel at ease. Make him open up."

I swallow hard. "And you think I can..."

He takes another step closer to me. "I know you can. You obviously have a gift for putting people at ease." He smiles. "Other than when you're spilling drinks and sauce on them, I think you're an excellent representative for a business."

I feel like I've just been tossed a gift, and I have no idea what to do with it.

I feel paralyzed by his confidence in me. It warms me from the inside out, my body melting, my heart exploding with unfiltered feelings.

"I...I don't know," I stutter when he lingers, waiting for my answer. "Maybe..."

Derek puts one hand on the cubicle wall, his brows beseeching me. "Please, Mia." He licks his upper lip. "I don't have anyone else to ask. I need you for this This is a pretty big deal for me, Mia. And for the company." His voice is low, almost a whisper.

I feel an unspoken undertone of desperation, snapping away at me. And it's all I can do to nod.

"Yes. Of course." I stand up resolutely. "I'm...I'm honored you asked me. It's just...I'm not...I'm not sure I'm very good at handling executives. It's not something I've tried before. And with everything that's happened here today..."

"I know. I know." He looks away, and I can tell he's struggling with his composure. "I probably look like a raving lunatic. And I would never want to upset you. Or make you feel uncomfortable in any way." He takes another step closer. "I promise. I'll be the perfect gentleman tonight. The meal will be at this restaurant, Fellows. They have the best Creole food anywhere. I'll send a car for you. The company will get you a hotel, so that you don't have to drink and drive. All expenses paid. Overtime, everything."

"That's very, very generous of you."

"It's not generosity, Mia. I need you. I need your help on this one." He takes another step towards me. "I can't do this on my own. I need someone who knows what it's like to grace the same dinner table as that guy. And matches his...endowments." He tilts his head to me. "I'm sure you can make him feel at ease."

I want him. I want this.

But I'm not sure I'm capable of being that person. A person who's double-dealing in front of people's faces.

I can't be.

But I can't stop now.

I have to see both of my jobs through. At least, for the time-being. Until I figure out what I want to do.

I nod in Derek's direction, flashing a tiny smile. "I'll go," I say. "I'll be your date...or company rep or whatever it is I'll be."

"Thank you, Mia." He grins. "You won't regret this."

I don't know about that. I don't know about that at all.

I have a feeling I'm going to be regretting a lot more than having dinner with my boss and his biggest acquisition tonight.

"We should get started." He looks around my office. "The car will be here any minute."

I wrinkle my nose. "I'm not dressed for something like this."

Derek looks me over, his eyes roaming up and down. I feel his gaze land in the middle of my thighs, and I squeeze them shut, feeling a rush of embarrassment.

"No," he says. "You're not." His face is soft, his blue eyes kind. "Dinner is not the place to wear a pencil skirt. You'll have something better. I promise. Just leave it to me."

He doesn't give me a choice. He's already moved out of the cubicle, and I'm left alone with my thoughts.

There's not a doubt in my mind. Not even a minute one. Even though with everything that's happened — I'm thinking this is a terrible idea.

My best friend Christina has a way of saying it the only way it could be said. "You know it when you're making a huge mistake."

It's been Christina's way of saying this for years. And there's no way I'm not getting her thoughts on this.

I know it.

But I'm going anyway.

And I feel like I'm making a big mistake. Like I'll regret this. Like what I want with Derek will never work out.

But I've spent the past few days thinking of him. Dreaming of him. Already feeling...

I shake my head. No use thinking about that.

I have work to do.

I have to be professional. Provide the help he needs.

And I also have to be crafty. Hell, I'm going to have to be downright devious.

And I have to be prepared...

If only I knew how to do exactly that.

I stand from my desk, closing the draft of the email meant for Steven Mayers, determined to figure it out.

I'M SHAKING as I put on my make-up, my hands clumsy.

I stay close to the mirror, my eyes avoiding the person—or thing—staring back at me.

This make-up is nothing. It's...fake. It's make-up for a life I don't live. This woman I'm pretending to be.

And no matter how gorgeous the mirror is in my hotel room at the Four Seasons Seattle, I see the guilt in my eyes. The haunted look of someone who knows she's going to regret this.

I stare deep into the mirror, hard and focused. I try to remind myself of why I'm here. What I'm going to do.

Derek said he needed help.

And for once, I need to help someone else.

I swallow and move the curls from my face, the blusher from my cheeks. I blend my bronzer.

I can do this. I can.

I have to do this. I have to.

For my sake. For Derek's. For my job. For my future.

No matter what happens tonight.

I figure if I say it loud enough in my head, I'll believe it. Unfortunately, my ringing cell phone keeps interrupting my thoughts of my mantra.

I answer fast, a makeup brush still clutched in my hand.

"Hello?"

"Mia-bia, where the hell are you? Did you lose your way back to the apartment from work? Or did you drink too many cold ones and run away with that hottie boss of yours?"

It's Christina. I have to remember she's my roommate, former colleague. And my best friend.

Because she sounds anything but friendly.

I exhale out loud. "I did not lose my way back to the apartment nor did I drink too many 'cold ones', for your information. I'm at the Four Seasons downtown right now. But I am, in fact, going out tonight for dinner. For work."

"...and where are you going?"

"Fellows. A Creole spot. For dinner. That's it."

"...and with who?" she stresses, as if she already knows the answer.

"With Derek Anderson."

There's a gasp coming from the other end of the line. "Ah-ha! Caught you. You ditched me for your boss."

"That's not...Hey, it's a long story."

A long story I don't want to tell. But I try to anyway, applying more blush.

"Teen, it's not a date," I declare. "Trust me. It's a business dinner. Nothing more. Nothing less."

"Uh huh. Sure it is. Only a dinner with a billionaire with more money than God and an ass that could stir up a tsunami. I mean, have you seen the paparazzi pics of him on the beach? Dude is fit. And he has a ridiculous amount of cash. A dangerous combination. Especially for someone like you."

Especially for someone like me.

Dangerous.

Probably true. But I'm hoping Christina won't see what's going on.

I bite my tongue. "Look, it's not a date. It's a dinner. With a client. So, yes, Derek and I will be together tonight. At the same place. At the same time. But that's it."

I can hear her drawing breath into her chest. "Isn't that how it started with Jason? A dinner date here? A lunch date there? Next thing you know you were engaged, Mia. Engaged. Fresh out of college. With the world's biggest douche. Remember that? 'Cause I sure as hell do. The asshole."

I bite my tongue again. I don't want to talk about it. Christina's bringing back old memories.

I've heard it all before.

The past—and the future—of a relationship long gone. Jason and I started out well, but we got too close too fast. Too invested. Too quickly.

He was everything I thought I wanted in a man.

Cute. Charming. Ambitious.

And he made me feel like I'd never felt before. Like he loved me. Like he was my everything. As if we were meant for each other.

And I was ready to pledge everything I had to him.

That was the mistake. Beneath the charm was an underlying darkness to him. An anger and jealousy I'd seen from Day One, but chosen to ignore.

The rest is history.

I can't believe I'm thinking about this all over again.

I sigh. "This is different. Jason and Derek are different."

Christina harrumphs. "I'll say they are, for sure. Jason is a Big Law attorney, marrying a woman who's made it her life mission to look like a human copy of a Barbie doll. And Derek is a billionaire entrepreneur with a big dick and bunch of women trying to get at it."

My cheeks heat.

I don't want to think about it.

It's true.

And just because I let Derek make me feel sexy, desirable, and beautiful doesn't change those facts.

Still. I try to normalize the encounter. I'm a professional. I can do this.

Exhaling, I compose myself. "Really. It's business. And as for comparing the two, Jason is not Derek Anderson. Not even on his best day. I mean, come on...you remember how Jason was. Can you remember a time when you ever saw him stick up for me? Defend me? Comfort me when I needed it? He always derided my career. My dreams... I've never once heard him say that he believes in my talent, as opposed to Derek who has ever since the day we officially met." I stroke my cheek with more blush. "Jason has never made me feel like more than just a pretty face. I'll admit: Derek might be difficult...but he's not a douche. And the hooker story isn't true...Well, in a way, it is. But not the way you thought. He didn't hire any hookers. He sort of...inadvertently ended up with one."

"Okay, there's obviously a whole backstory there that I'm dying to hear about when you have a chance." She laughs. "And by 'chance,' I mean when we both have a whole bunch of alcohol inside us, and you're ready to share all the dirty details. Until then... all I'll say is be careful. Jason was all about himself. If he wasn't getting what he wanted, he'd move on to the next thing. Derek better come correct or not at all, 'cause there's only one Mia Kamaka. And she's not up for cheap grabs." She pauses for a beat. Then two. "So, are you going to spill the beans on what's going on between the two of you right now?"

"I'm not telling you. Not now." And definitely not unless I feel it's the right time. "Not yet, anyway. It's complicated. Really, really complicated. And I need to figure out some things first."

"And yet, you're going out to dinner with him."

I roll my eyes. "And yet I'm going out to dinner with him. But don't worry. It's work. And we will be on our best behavior. I've got it under control."

A knock sounds at my door.

"Oh, gross. Who's that now?" She sighs. "I know you're probably anxious to get out of here, so remember: Be careful. As we saw with Jason...A wedding's just a dinner and a ring away! We'll talk when you get home."

"Okay."

I hang up and head toward the door. I open it cautiously and peer through the gap.

Derek Anderson is standing in my doorway.

And he's looking at me like he wants to devour me. His blue eyes complementing the navy color of his suit.

His tall, lanky form towering above my five-foot, eight-inch frame.

He looks...sinfully gorgeous.

And intoxicatingly powerful.

And all I can do is stare.

Chapter Fifteen

EREK

I knock on Mia's door.

Midtown hotel room. Midtown view. Midtown nerves.

Being in this part of the city always gets my anxiety going.

So far from the parts of the city I grew up in.

And left behind long ago.

And yet I always feel the need to remind myself that thought I'm not physically far from that place — the place I grew up — I'm certainly psychologically far from it.

Hell, I live in a different world from the world I used to live in. A world where it's okay to make mistakes and have fun.

A world where it's okay to take a risk.

A world where I'm free.

I no longer have my father's insults to put up with, or my mother's poor-me-I'm-a-single-mother-of-four voice in my ear, or the feeling that all I need to do is fit in and be the best version of myself.

I don't have to fit in anymore. I don't need to be the best version of myself. I don't need to do an inventory of what everyone will think of me.

I am Derek Anderson. Powerful business man. Billionaire publisher.

Except...

I take a deep breath as I raise my fist again.

Except when I'm in front of this girl. This woman…

Mia.

This woman who has me tied in knots and begging.

This woman who has me feeling things I've never felt before.

This woman I want more of.

This woman I still have yet to figure out.

She swings the door open, and her lips part slightly in surprise.

Little by little, her gaze moves over my suit, which for this dinner is a simple, navy business suit, unbuttoned at the top, my grey shirt and business tie loosened or unknotted entirely.

Unlike her.

She's in nothing but a white hotel robe, which leaves little to my imagination. The robe is only loosely tied, letting the top of her tanned breasts peek through.

She takes a step forward into the hallway, and my chest immediately warms.

The gesture is not how I was imagining this to go.

"You know," she says, and I hear the mischievousness lacing her tone. "I'd expected you to wear something flashy. Something that would be in line with the image you're trying to paint of yourself as a boastful and careless playboy. Something that would make me want to run away as fast as possible." Her eyes rake over my body.

Her gaze moves down over my belt. And I hope to God she can't see how insanely turned on I am by her right now. By how damp she still is from a shower. By how desperate I am to have more of her.

Desperate to know if she finds me as desirable as I do her.

That she feels the same way I do.

"Looks like I was wrong." Her tone is playful. Unsure. Uncertain.

Her eyes flick up to mine.

And my voice is embarrassingly raspy when I respond. "You are. I said it in my text message. The restaurant Fellows has a dress code. I apparently forgot to mention that it's pretty strict. So it's kind of hard for me to take you out in just a t-shirt and sweatpants."

The corner of her mouth turns up.

The way it used to. Before we dropped all pretense and became...ourselves.

"I knew it. You're about as spontaneous and frisky as an old man whose wife wasn't his first." She juts her head to the side. "Not that I'm judging." Her tone is mocking.

I shake my head and laugh. "I try to be." I look at her. "But it's not always easy. And I'm not that much of a playboy anymore. Mandy. My ex. She, uh...liked to go to these fancy places, so I'm familiar with how most of them roll." I shake my head. "I hate that word. Ex. She's as much an ex as I am a playboy. I'm too busy to be a playboy. I'm busy staying on top of my game. It takes a lot out of me. And that's why I need things to be more casual. Like this."

Her eyes shift to the side for a second. Then back to me. "I...I get that. I...apologize, then."

"You don't have anything to apologize for. I'm just trying to say...it's nice to be around someone I don't have to put on a mask for. I...I'm used to hiding myself around a lot of people." I shake my head slowly. "It's nice to be around people who are comfortable enough to let go."

"You're not used to this kind of casualness, are you?"

"In the business world? Not often. I'm the CEO of Hare & Holeton. Everything I do is about the next deal or the next project. And before today, that had been most of my life. My business life. And I'm...I'm not really that natural at it."

Mia chuckles. "That's interesting."

"You think?"

She eyes me up and down. "Let's just say it explains a lot." She nods, before finally noticing the several hangers in my hand. She points. "Are those for me?"

I look down at the outfit choices for her. For tonight. "Yes, they are. Courtesy of Aimee's boutique." I lift them a little higher. "I had Aimee choose some of the options you tried on for the CoTA event. The ones we ruled out. There were plenty of great pieces. You looked...amazing in them." I nod, before handing them to her. "I thought you could wear something from Aimee's boutique. To the restaurant."

She can tell where I'm going with this.

She shakes her head. "I can't. I—"

"My treat."

"It won't be the same if—"

"It doesn't have to be."

She shakes her head, her lips pushed together.

She wants to say no.

I can see why Mia wouldn't want to be a part of my world. I barely want to be a part of it.

The pressure. It can be immense.

But there's something about her.

She's so...alive. So...full of life. Of fire. Of this insane aura that makes me want to walk through fire to be near her.

Alive.

And I'm caught up in it.

"I insist." I smile.

"You know, it's really hard to turn down an offer from you when you turn on that secret charm."

I smile harder. "I know. That's why I'm trying to use it. Trying to be nice. Come on. Indulge me. You know how hard it is for me."

"Oh yes. I remember distinctly from Sopra. That moody, brooding prick-ish act you put on for the entire restaurant was such a treat."

"You say it like it's a bad thing."

"I think it is. I'm glad you decided to change it up. This Derek that you're being right now, I like him a lot better." She pauses. "And I'd like him even better than that, if he came inside to help me pick an outfit for the restaurant. For dinner. Or..." She tilts her head and brushes her hand through her long lashes. "...for somewhere else. I need a second opinion on which one."

I can tell she's got a bit of a pout on her face.

Which is amusing.

I could easily say something else. Something out of embarrassment.

But I don't.

Instead, I let out a sigh.

Something that sounds realistic.

Something that speaks of how hard it's been for me to be here. It's more real than I thought it would sound.

"Okay. Fine." I take a breath, before continuing. "I'll help you pick something out. On two conditions."

"And what might those two conditions be?" She's smiling smugly at me. Her lips wrapping around those words. The way that I want them to wrap around my—

My eyes flick up to hers and I shake my head.

"You look like you want to say something." She bites her bottom lip.

"Me? No, not at all." I step forward, close to her, her hand still on the doorknob. "But we've got to move fast, before I forget how to form complete sentences. I don't want to...change my mind."

I see the coy smile on her face, before she pushes the door open a bit more.

I HELP her pick out a breathtaking dress.

A dress that turns heads.

A dress that has the men eyeing her hot and bothered, even though we're in a restaurant and she's sitting at a table, drinking a delicious white wine as we wait for Scott Disrick to arrive.

He's late. Again. No shocker there.

I'm used to it.

And it gives me more time to hang out alone with Mia.

She's indulging me in a few glasses of wine and fantastic conversation, with this exquisite dress on her sultry body. The kind of dress that you can't help but stare at.

The kind of dress that you want to look at more than once.

A dress that I desperately want her to take off.

"Have you ever dated a writer?" Mia asks as she takes another sip of her wine. Her eyes are locked with mine, the way her hair is, the way her dress sways from side to side.

I shake my head. "Not really. Has that ever occurred to you?"

She gives me a smirk, then takes another sip of her wine. "Well, I have. Not often. As a photographer, I feel that I'm an artist myself, so I've never really bought into the whole 'artist mystique' thing. So...I have no idea how that would even work."

"I've dated a few artists."

"Yes, but you're a businessman. There's a very...distinct difference."

"Are you trying to call me uncreative? Because I have a side passion for spoken word. Spoken word that comes out...well. It comes out on a stage. In front of a large number of people."

"Okay, I see it now. This is something I never knew about you."

"I don't reveal it to a lot of people. It's not...something I'm proud of. I found it doesn't help me in business."

"Oh." She nods, laughing. "So, you're not very good at it?"

I snort. "I'm awful at it. Horribly so."

"Maybe it's a fear thing. You're afraid you'll be taken seriously. I don't know. I've heard a few stories of actors playing roles they don't normally play. Well, you know what I mean. Not being taken seriously. So, in the end, I wonder if you're afraid that it will happen to you."

"I couldn't say. I just don't think myself good enough. It's considered uncouth, you know. To go on stage. When people are watching. The stage, the lights, books, a microphone. That's not what I do."

"Well, maybe that's not the right way to go about it. You know, maybe voice lessons would help. Or something like that."

"I'll take your advice under advisement." I smile at her. "I'm just not certain that it's my cup of tea. Business takes up enough time as it is."

"If you ever wanted any pointers, I'd be happy to give them." She giggles. "I'd even volunteer my time, if it meant seeing you on stage. Seeing your words come to life like that. It would be...something."

"Yeah. That would be something."

"You just have to open yourself up to it. That's all."

"I don't know if I want to do that."

"Everyone has to do it. We all have to open ourselves up. We all have to try new things. It doesn't matter how often or how little. It's all a part of life."

I can tell by how she's looking at me that she really means it.

I could use that kind of help.

That kind of closeness.

"I never really thought about it like that." I shake my head. "I mean, I always thought of it more as a hobby. A passion. A way to explore things. And...well...a way for me to express myself and express what I feel. You know, it's not really a way for me to make a living."

"Doesn't have to be," she adds. "It could be something you do just because you enjoy it. Like your comic book art. Stuff like that. It's not your day job, but the passion is still there."

"Yeah. I guess so." I tilt my wine glass stem on the table and take a drink, thinking over her words. "Maybe you're right. Maybe I am a little afraid to open myself up to new experiences."

"That's understandable. I mean, you're a smart man, Derek Anderson. Your dedication to your work is very real. And that's what a successful man looks like. Not someone who's afraid to try new things. And...well, I want to ask you something."

"What is it?"

"I know that you're not very social, or extroverted, or whatever." She takes a gulp of her wine. "But...I've noticed that you seem to be very passionate about your hobbies. About a lot of things, in fact."

I clamp my lips together, mulling over her words. "You're observant," I concede. "I don't think I'm very social. But that's not because I'm not social. I just...what do you say? I don't know how to be. I'm not very good at it."

"Don't sell yourself short, Derek Anderson. I'm sure that you're a fun guy. You're smart, too. You just need to...well, that's a bit tricky."

"I don't mind. I like jumping around, saying stupid things. It makes me feel...better." I squeeze her thigh, making her jump. "But this evening is about you. I'll let you be the one to talk about yourself. I just...I'd rather you not talk about me. Strictly self-promotion."

"Okay." She nods. "Fair enough. But let me ask a question first."

"Be my guest."

She takes a deep breath and asks, "So, why do you care

about impressing this Scott Disrick guy so much? It's not like he's your boss or anything. You're already your own boss. Why not just be you, in front of him?"

I shake my head. "It's...well...it's not that he makes me feel like I have to impress him. It's more like..."

I sigh.

"It's a perception thing." I take a sip of my wine. "Our company Hare & Holeton's going public in a little under a year from now. Disrick happened to be an early-on supporter of the company. We've known the guy since high school. He likes doing business with us. He's been a great help to us as well. We owe it to him to be the best we can be when we go out there. We owe it to the investors we have. And showing him that we're ready, that we are the company he's going to invest in, is kind of important."

"That makes sense. So, you're using him as an example...your good example...of how great the company stock is going to be when you go public. You're showing him that you're prepared to give him a great return he deserves."

"Yeah. Something like that." I nod. "Looking at it that way makes it easier."

"Interesting. Even scarier when you look at it that way." She rests her fingertips on her lips, frowning thoughtfully. "You're afraid to give it your all in front of him."

"I know." I swallow a sip of wine. "That's what I told the others, too. I mean, we have to control the narrative of the company we've built. Tell it how we want it told. Use the people we want to use. Get them to believe in the story we're telling. Otherwise, how can we expect anyone to believe it? Once a story starts spreading, it takes on a life of its own." I tap my glass, my frustration seeping out. "I mean, take a look around us. At all the people staring. People who've read that Post article, no doubt. What we do here in public is just as important as what we do behind the scenes."

With a furtive glance, Mia takes a look around the restaurant. "Jesus. You're right. You are...People are actually staring at us. At you."

The words make me frown. "Yeah, they've been staring at us since we walked in. Now, this crowd is a little too high-brow to pull out their phones and try to sneak pictures, but..." I point to a group of people sitting at one of the tables close to us with their noses pressed together. "...some of them might try to do that in the next few minutes. You never know."

"How sad." Mia puts her hand across her heart, a fake smile on her lips. "Poor Derek Anderson..."

"Yeah. Don't do that." I chuckle at her dripping sarcasm. "You're definitely not getting free drinks tonight."

She laughs, warm and loud, her silver earrings glistening. "I'm just saying...Things could be worse."

"Yeah. But so much could be better," I snap in a desperate attempt to lighten the mood and sounds of everyone around us buzzing with excitement sneaking the air with nervousness. "Have you noticed...?"

"What?" she asks, looking over her shoulder.

"We're the only ones with the least expensive wine on our table. And we're just celebrating a normal, mid-week date..." I shake my head, trying to stop myself from going overboard. "Just saying, it's weird that we're the only ones ordering wine. Everyone else at the tables around us is drinking some fine-ass vintage champagne."

She takes a sip of wine, then lowers it back to the table. "You're right. That's weird." She furrows her eyebrows and scans the room, then presses herself closer. "Can you believe it? We're the least pretentious people here. And that's hard to be...when you're in the room."

"Hardy-har-har. You're absolutely hilarious."

She scoffs on a light laugh. "I am. And I have to say that I'm learning a lot about you tonight. Or, at least, I'm learning things about you that I didn't know. Before today, it was just believed that you were unfriendly and narcissistic. And an over-dresser."

"Ha! I'm glad you think I'm a nice guy then."

Her lips are dry again, thirsty and parched. She takes another sip of her wine, not caring to savor it. "You are."

I give her a look. "Thanks."

"No problem." She smiles. "I've seen pictures of this Scott guy."

"So, how do you feel about him?"

"Well, he's a playboy, right?" She gives me a sideways glance.

"Yes. Well... He thinks he's a playboy. At least, he tries to be. I mean, Scotty was sort of a four-eyed nerd when we were in high school. He and my brother Quentin actually dated the same girl. Or, rather, Quentin stole her from him."

"Your brother dated Scott Disrick's ex-girlfriend?"

"Yeah." I nod. "She met him at the debutante party of some girl he was supposedly pining for. Dated him for a week or two. Then, Quentin came along, charming the hell out of her, and Scotty was gone." I huff out a small laugh. "I never told Scotty this. But I always thought it was kind of weird. I mean, Quentin went from zero girls to tons of them in the blink of an eye."

"Your brother had some serious game," she breathes.

"Yeah. Even at that age, Quentin was a smooth operator." I take a breath. "You couldn't get a word in edgewise. The girls were always on him. I mean..."

"What?" she asks, her eyes sparkling with curiosity.

"It's not a big deal. Just...Girls never even looked my way. I didn't have a girlfriend until I was a senior in high school. No one would even talk to me. Apparently, I was too mean-looking, too serious-minded. I only found out that's what people thought about me because I overheard my brothers talking about it one day."

A shadow of sympathy washes over her face. "That's

awful. I can't believe the others didn't tell you the truth. You must have been devastated when you found out."

"I wasn't devastated. It actually made a lot of sense." I shrug, trying to squelch a sudden wave of resentment. "Because, I mean, I've always been kind of a loner. I'm the second oldest out of our family behind Alton. I was always in a million clubs in school, and I would spend most of my time lost in my mind."

She frowns. "No, I would have been devastated. You're so much harder to tell. You're so quiet."

"Is that right?"

"You are." Her eyes rake me over. "But since I've been with you, I've seen a bit more of you. You're a little uptight. Sometimes, you're too serious. But I think that's because you're smart and obsessive. I guess, in a lot of ways, you're exactly what I thought you'd be like. But...You don't talk about your family. Not a single word." She holds up her wineglass and takes another sip. "What about them? Do you talk about them?"

"Not that I remember. Not anything interesting anyway."

"You must talk about them with your friends. Your brothers all look quite a little bit like you. Only...different. Other than the way you all seem to hold yourselves, at least in pictures, you all look the same. You've all got that same cocky, pretty boy look happening."

"We're a close family. We talk about each other a lot." I pause and rake my voice over her face, then I lower my eyes to the table. "My younger brothers are twins. Fraternal ones. Quentin and Ryder. Both of them are more focused on getting dates than they are on deals. My brother Alton is the oldest and the most anal. He works with Finance and Legal. And Killian...Well, Killian's our cousin and kind of adopted into the fam. He's the COO, so basically he's my second in command. If something were to happen to me, he'd take over. If something were to happen to him, then Alton would take over. My other brothers..."

"Don't tell me you have more of them," she says, her voice thick with disbelief. "God, how many beautiful men can one family have? How fast has your family spread?"

"That's a good question. But no, it's just the four of us. Five, if you include Killian."

"I get the feeling you don't. Include Killian, I mean."

I smile and hold back a hint of irritation. Aimed at Killian, not her. "We're very close."

"But?" she asks, her lips pulling into a teasing smile.

"But Killian has always been on the outskirts. His parents were both single parents. He lived with his mother, and his father was always out of town on business. It wasn't a good situation. But we helped him. It's something we always did. We took care of each other. That's ancient history, though. None of it's important."

Mia gapes at me. "It is important. You're important." Her voice is instantly alive with life. Passion. "You are important, Derek. You're important to me." She blinks. "I hope you know that."

My heart squeezes in my chest. I blink. "I guess I do now."

I open my mouth to confide more to her, tell her about my parents and how much their lives affected us all. I'm a little bit uncomfortable talking about it, because they died so young.

When I was sixteen. I feel guilty when I talk about it.

Because I should have done more.

But the moment is broken, shattered to smithereens at the booming voice of Scott Disrick. I turn to see him strutting up to our table like he owns the place. He's got a tone, a crinkling arrogance in his expression that I hate. It's something he's carried with him since high school.

He has a girl on his arm. But I'm sure she's not much more than an ornament.

Her nearly-black hair is pulled up in a tight, high ponytail.

Her breasts are practically falling out of her dress, but at least she's not showing nipple.

His last date was.

I stand to my feet, greeting Scott, wishing I could dial back time. Un-invite him.

To spend more time with the woman sitting beside me that's made me feel more alive than I ever have before.

Chapter Sixteen

MIA

Scott Disrick is an asshole. One with too much cologne and ill-placed hair-plugs. That much is clear.

And I'm still not sure how I'm going to make it through the rest of this minute, let alone this dinner, sitting at his table.

Derek does his best to mitigate the published head's raging assholery. But I can tell it's hard.

That scruffed jaw of his continues to tick. But he tries to grin at me instead. I can tell it's an effort.

"This is the best meal I've had in Seattle," Scott shouts over the quiet hum of the restaurant.

"I think it's because you ate in a morgue last week," Derek comments. "Or was it a funeral home? I can't remember."

"It was an ancient Egyptian burial ground," Scott exclaims. "Gotta keep things exciting, Derek, don't you think?"

Derek agrees reluctantly. "I think so. Though, desecrating a burial site isn't really my style."

Scott shrugs. "That's what makes life interesting."

I look at Scott, trying not to wince in disgust. "You were having a meal inside a tomb?"

Scott laughs. "Of course not. No, I was merely having a

snack. And I needed a place to do it in. There aren't a lot of places on those tours that allow you to eat while you make out with a girl. But if there are, they don't have 'em on Yelp." Scott turns to his date. "So, I might have used one of the caskets as a table. So what? I mean, those dead kings should be lucky that Chelsie even sat her beautiful ass on their old bones, let alone anything else."

He lifts her wrist and kisses it.

Derek gives me a sideways glance and shakes his head. I try to reel it in—my disgust. But I can't recapture it.

I try to channel my inner Susan Sarandon for a flash moment.

To tell myself that Scott is not the star of my movie. He's not a bad guy. He's just not a good guy. And he's not affecting my life.

"What about you, Derek?" Scott asks, turning his sights on the CEO beside me. "What scandalous behavior have you gotten yourself into lately?"

Derek's jaw tightens, and he shakes his head, his smile clearly strained. "You already know my scandalous behavior, Scott, I'm sure. Anyway, the Seattle Post likes to exaggerate. Anything to sell more issues."

Scott laughs. "Yeah, they needed something to print on their front page. I'm sure it's always a party where you are."

Derek moves his eyes to mine and winks. "Actually, things are fairly tame at the Hare & Holeton headquarters these days. You know the IPO is coming up soon, so we're just finalizing the last-minute details before the stock starts trading." Derek nods his head in the direction of the waiter who's approaching us with a steaming platter of seafood. "Our analytics report is coming in on schedule. The first-quarter launch party is not far off. So we're looking forward to—"

"Blah! Blah! Blah!" Scott raises his arms in the air, briefly silencing Derek. "Spare me the business jargon, Derek. I mean, your business plan is, for all intents and purposes, dry."

Derek sighs and lets out a small grunt as the waiter places glistening oysters and clams, crab and shrimp and a variety of other delicacies that my stomach desperately needs on the table.

Scott chortles. "You never were much of a showman, Derek." He smirks. "But you're doing well, man. Congratulations. It's all happening for you. I'm glad." His voice drops to a more serious tone. "I just wish you would loosen up a bit. Enjoy life. You've worked a long time and got what you wanted. You should celebrate, man. What's the point of wealth if you can't at least rock out with your cock out?"

Derek turns to face Scott, his eyes glowing like blue fire. "We'll need to all be responsible adults a bit longer, Scott. If we want our stock prices to stay IPO-ready. I'd suggest you study up on that."

"Right, I forgot. You're the man with the plan, eh, Derek? The guy who's got it all figured out? You're the sharpest tool in the shed. Everything has to be R-O-A-D, you'll make sure of it."

Derek smiles, but his jaw is starting to get tight again. I place my hand on him and squeeze.

I can't believe we're in this situation. Scott Disrick, the CEO of the company that Hare & Holeton is buying, is a cruel, money-glorifying man, taking every opportunity to make fun of Derek's more responsible, anti-Fyre Festival lifestyle choices.

I can't help but wonder about Scott's position at the company. If it's worth some of the purchase price or if he's just sitting on the board to offset some of his travel expenses.

And I wish he would say something else. Anything else.

I'm not sure how much longer I can sit here. Letting Derek fend for himself.

How can Scott not see the way he's disrespecting him?

His business strategy? His rules? His worldview?

Scott takes a sip from his wine glass and turns to me.

"Maybe you could get him to loosen up a bit," he says. "If you know what I mean."

I look at Derek, whose face is twisted in expression. Like the way it was when he was finger-fucking me at lunch earlier today.

It's a look of confusing sentiments battling behind those mesmerizing eyes of his.

"Mia is my assistant. Just my assistant," Derek says through his gritted teeth. "And I don't mix business with pleasure. It's not the best policy."

"Right," Scott replies. "Well, maybe your business strategy wouldn't be so lame, if you did." He winks at me. I glare at him. "Oh, I'm sorry. I didn't mean to exclude you, Miss Mia." He turns back to Derek, directing his attention to me. "I'm just saying maybe we can loosen Derek up for his own benefit, you know? Get him out of his shell. He's so uptight all the time. The man needs a little experience before he's good for anything else." He chuckles and pours himself more wine. "But maybe that's why he's hiring hookers. Less liability."

My heart lurches. "What?"

Crap.

Scott's smile is blinding as he turns to me. "Derek's into hookers, huh? The more free-range he gets the better, right?" He nods his head in Derek's direction. "I'm just saying, you've got beautiful women in the office already, apparently. No need to go looking for outside help. I mean, if I knew Mia was looking for work, I'd hire her instead. Why pay for ass when you've got your own sexy, caramel-skinned one in-house, am I right?"

My heart is pounding. I don't know how to respond.

But I don't have to.

Because Derek is already up and off his feet.

Before I can process what's going on, all I see is Scott's red face laughing hard in the midst of Derek's dark glare.

Mere seconds before Derek's fist connects with his face.

I can only try to look down at the table, hiding my face as a gaggle of businessmen and businessmen's wives rush to the scene.

I don't want to look up. I don't want to see what's going on.

But I can't help it.

Because I see two things.

Derek raising his arm again, his fist cocked and tightly clenched.

And Scott's date, Chelsie, screaming as he does.

DEREK

It doesn't take long for Fellows' security to move in to try to kick us out. All of us. For causing a scene and making a commotion.

The commotion that started the second Scott called Mia out her name, insulting her, making no attempt to hide his insulting words.

I stand, scanning the room for Mia but can't find her. My heart sinks as it sinks for the second time tonight into my stomach. I feel sick.

I am sick.

Sick because I've definitely ruined the Bella Publishing deal now.

Sick because I should have punched Scott Disrick sooner. Sick because I should have grabbed Mia's hand and dragged her out of here a long time ago.

But I am sicker to my stomach for the way I haven't handled the situation.

The way I haven't handled Mia.

I look around the room.

My heart is still racing. My pulse is pounding through my

whole body, my fingers still stinging from the contact of the punch as I think of what I did.

I see Scott wiping his mouth, his thin lip bleeding.

I see his date, Chelsie, crying.

But I don't see Mia. I dial Raul my driver as fast as my fingers can move, my head still on a swivel as I search for her pretty face.

Raul picks up after one ring. "Yes, sir?"

"Raul," I breathe. "Fellows restaurant. Come pick up me and Mia. Now. We need to leave. Now."

"Yes, sir."

I hear him hang up. It feels like a lifetime before I finally spot her shoulder near the corner of the room. She's bent over the back of a chair, her hands over her mouth.

"Hey," I call to her, just as a security guard moves in to block my path, his wide stance in front of me like a protective fence.

We're almost the same height. Six foot-three inches of rage on both sides.

He eyes me suspiciously, as if I am a renegade who could suddenly explode at any time. "Sir, you're going to have to leave the premises. Right now."

"I know that. But I'm here with someone—"

"Sir! Leave. Right now!"

It's been a long time since I've had to really fight a man. But I know how to.

Growing up with three brothers and a male cousin meant I learned a thing or two about fighting.

Whether it's my fists, my feet, or my piece, I've always been good at holding my own.

"I said, leave! Now!"

"I'm not going anywhere," I say. "Not until I find my date, and I know she's—"

"I'm alright," Mia says—or tries to say—from behind my tall adversary. I turn in time to see her standing.

She looks up, her eyes as wide and as buttery-brown as a Hershey bar.

I look at her face and cannot find the words. She nods, her eyes glassy and full of tears unshed.

"I'm sorry," she declares, her voice small and timid. "I just needed a minute."

I rush over to her quickly, cradling her face, my eyes full of questions. Worried, I try to read her mind. "Are you okay?" I ask her.

She nods. "I'm fine. Really, I'm good," she answers, looking anxiously up at the security guard still watching.

I don't know who he is, but I can tell he's not happy with having me and Mia both on the premises.

With this crowd of exclusive patrons, I'd forget, believe me.

"It's okay, I'll take her out of here," I say to the guard.

He steps aside, and I turn to Scott, my eyes holding his hostage.

"We're done," I tell him. "We're done once and for all."

Scott looks down, and I can see his eyes grow wet. He's teetering on the edge.

He'll either agree, or he'll fight, which would be his second biggest mistake.

Surprisingly, the man is smarter than he looks. "Fine," he says. "Anything to get out of this place."

I look at him and raise an eyebrow as he backs away.

Taking Mia by the hand, I hurry her out of the door. I'm not exactly eager for her to see her date about to be led away into the air-conditioned safety of Fellows' private security room.

She doesn't look back. But I do.

I watch Scott's expression from behind us.

I see his drunk, red face.

I see his hysterical, dark-haired date.

I see the Bella Publishing acquisition going up in flames.

I turn back around to the street.

Luckily, Raul is already pulling up, sliding the big black Mercedes truck up near us. Mia gets in the back seat first, her body seeming to buckle from the nerves, from the shock. I'm right behind her, sliding in alongside her.

Raul casts a glance at me in the rear-view mirror. A big man, he looks almost minuscule in the gigantic driver's seat. But he's a polished, professional gentleman. Just the kind of driver I need tonight.

"Sir?" he says, his voice carefully neutral.

"Just drive, please, Raul," I tell him. I turn to Mia. "Mia, honey?"

She looks over at me. Her eyes are full of life. Full of so much.

"I'm alright," she answers my unspoken question. "Just startled, I guess." She searches my face quickly, her brown eyes almost catching fire. She has her own share of questions to express.

But she doesn't.

I think she holds some of those answers inside.

"I'm sorry," I rasp to her. "I should have stepped in sooner. But I didn't want to fight at all. I feel like a fool." I raise the sound-proof partition separating us from Raul with a tiny wave to my driver.

"I didn't want to be that macho jerk that needs to use his fists to prove a point," I say to Mia. "That's not who I am and that's not how I want to act at all. That's something my father would have done. And he's the last person I want to be." I inhale. "I wanted tonight to be about the project and about the business, but I wanted it to continue to be about you. I wanted it to be about—"

"Us," she declares, her brown eyes wide, her tongue searching for the words.

I nod, licking my lips. "Mia, well—"

"No more apologies. You didn't plan what went on here

tonight. You were doing what you thought was best. Maybe not the right way at the right time, but still. Trust me..." She pauses, looking down at my hands, noticing the way I ball my fists up into tight, hard knots. "You were doing what you thought was right. You were doing what you thought was best. You have nothing to be sorry for."

I nod once, then again, my throat feeling tight.

She's strong.

So strong. Stronger than me in so many ways.

Because at least she knows what she wants. And she goes for it.

Unlike I've been able to do when it comes to her.

I lean over to her. "Mia," I whisper, my voice barely audible above the city's traffic. "I was afraid I was getting in over my head here. I wasn't sure I was ready for something so... intense."

She nods, her eyes holding mine.

"That's the weird thing about whatever's happening between us, you know," I tell her my voice nearly hitching. "With you, I always get it wrong. It's like a snowball rolling down a hill at high speeds. Getting bigger and bigger and bigger. And I'm afraid of it all. So I try to push it off the hill, down into the ditch. But it keeps getting bigger."

I lean over, my face closer to hers.

"But I'm realizing—you're right. And I'm wrong. I'm sorry I have to keep apologizing to you, but what's happened tonight has helped me understand that...shit, maybe I'm not going to have control over every little aspect of my life after all. It's just not possible. Some things are just simply out of our control."

My voice loses momentum, and I swallow. I take in a breath. "Like you. And I'm beginning to understand that when it comes to you, I don't want to have control over everything. I don't want to be in control of everything at all."

She smiles, her eyes tearing up. Her lips part. But before

she can answer, I'm already leaning in again. Sliding closer, our faces almost touching, her lips right there. I close my eyes as I lean in, breathing her in, taking in that signature honeyed coconut scent of hers.

Mia.

Her.

Just her.

I lean in, just a little bit further, closer, closer still. And then our lips touch.

Chapter Seventeen

DEREK

A jolt of electricity. Pure, unadulterated, earth-shattering power courses through my body. Muscles tense and react. Desire floods me and everything becomes so much clearer.

I slide my lips across hers, kissing Mia with everything I have.

And it's not enough. Not nearly enough.

I slide my tongue into her mouth, feeling it part her lips and feeling her tongue meet mine. I slide my strong hands onto her hips, pulling her closer to me until she's straddling one of my legs with her body and our lips find each other again.

We kiss deeper, harder, more urgently. I want this. I want this so much.

I slide my hands up her sides, feeling her skin, her softness even through her thin dress.

I pull away and Mia looks at me, her lips swollen and red, a light blush staining her cheeks.

Her gaze goes to my mouth. "You're very good at that, you know."

"Good at what?"

"Good at the kissing." She laughs. "You're good at the punching, too."

I lean in, close to her ear. "I'm much better at other activities." I make my voice low and throaty. "And I much prefer to use my hands for other things."

I slide my hands up her sides, making her jump as I feel goose-bumps appear on her body. She's trembling, and I feel it through my touch.

"So am I," she says, her voice low and hot, her body leaning into mine, trusting me. "Would you like to see?"

She reaches between us. And suddenly her hands are on my thighs, sliding up my pants and over my crotch.

Her touch makes me gasp, and I groan, inhaling and exhaling in a hard breath. I'm already rock hard, and her touch is only making me harder.

"You're right," I breathe. "I do want to see." I reach for her hands and pull them over to my lap. I kiss her again and slide her hands off my lap onto her own lap and her thigh.

I grab her hips, squeezing enough to make her look at me.

"Show me," I say, reaching for her lower back to lay her down along the SUV's gigantic backseat. Her brows knit together in confusion as she watches my face. "Show me how you like to be touched, Mia." I kiss her upward, her lips parted and wanting, her eyes dark and impassioned.

She shifts, letting me guide her back onto the long leather seat.

She arches slightly and I'm immediately focused on her long, slender neck and the delicate skin that I want to touch and scratch. Her hair now laid across the back of the seat, I tilt toward her hipbones, breathing her in.

Her ass is still in my lap as she lays across me, facing upwards with her back along the leather. I slide my hands up the skirt of her dress, feeling across the fabric of her already damp underwear.

She jerks, her breath escaping in a huff.

"Touch yourself, Mia. I want to watch it. I want to see. Show me how you want it," I whisper.

"How I want it from you?" she asks, her breathing still rushed and fast, her voice strained with the anticipation of it.

I peer down her body, seeing the swell of her breasts and the desire in her eyes. "You know how you want it from me, Mia," I say, not questioning it, only claiming it. "You want it all from me. Don't you?"

"Derek, please."

She leans up on her elbows, looking down her body at me. Her eyes are so soft, so trusting as she looks back at me.

Mine, I know, are dark and full of desire for her. And I want to be what she wants.

I slide my hands beneath her dress, feeling her stockings beneath her soft skin, my lips on her inner thigh as I slide her underwear down her legs from underneath her dress, baring her to me.

She arches slightly as I slide it off. Taking her hands in mine, I move them. Until her own fingers are pressed up against her bare sex, which lies untouched in my lap.

She inhales and exhales sharply again.

And I repeat myself. "Touch yourself, Mia. For me. Right now."

She looks down and my eyes follow, unable to look away as she begins to rub her clit, her fingers moving in slow, gentle movements. I smile and bite my lip.

My fingers slide up her bare thighs, my breath catching in my throat as I listen to her moan and whimper, softly at first, then louder.

My fingers slide farther up her waist and under, feeling the skin of her lower back. Everything about my girl is hot, hotter than the fire in my hands as I run them up and down her arms, the bare skin of her back and her neck.

With the lower half of her naked and exposed to me, I can

feel her shudder, the vulnerability of the position now sending shockwaves through her body, which only makes me move faster and harder.

"You're beautiful. So beautiful," I whisper as her hands continue to move. "Is this what you want?" My fingers move lower, mimicking hers, right over her clit. "You like it slow, don't you?"

"Derek, please," she gasps, and I feel her shudder in my hands on her hips.

"You like it slow to start, don't you?"

Her fingers slow and then pause. A few digits slide down over the sparse silky hair there.

"Derek, I don't know..."

"You do know. Don't be afraid, baby You're gorgeous." I glance at her face and she's watching me. "Just like this."

Her eyes burn into mine. And her fingers move faster. One hand stays rubbing against her clit, and the other delves even deeper, two fingers sliding between her slick folds until she lets out a moan.

"I can hear you," I say.

"I can feel you," she whispers back.

I smile and lean forward, kissing her right where her hands press, my fingers moving up and down, mimicking her motions and adding my own.

Rubbing faster, Mia closes her eyes, her mouth opening with a soft, loud gasp. I flick my tongue against her, and she groans, her soft voice rumbling in the secluded back seat.

"Don't stop," I warn her. "Don't stop."

"I'm not. I won't," she breathes as I put my fingers over hers, my tongue moving back and forth faster, both of us nearly panting, our combined breath echoing in the closed car.

"Look at me," I whisper, my lips against her skin, her fingers still moving. "Look at me, Mia."

Her eyes open, and her mouth goes open, caught between breaths, as she peers over my way.

"You want me to make you come, don't you?" I say, the words causing a soft moan from her lips, her fingers moving even faster.

"Derek, please," she begs now. "Please kiss me."

Her pussy lips are parted, wet and soft and swollen from her desire.

My tongue moves against her wetness, our lips pressed together in a silent clash, her legs opening for me as we continue our delicate dance.

I take my fingers off her, letting her use her own, still holding her close to my mouth as my tongue moves lower, my lips against hers, so soft yet urgent.

"Please?" she whispers.

"Please what?"

There's a brief hesitation, and then her head tilts back against the seat. "Please, kiss me like you mean it."

I push her dress up under by her waist, feeling the skin of her bare back, which I want to touch and kiss with much more passion. "You make me mean it. You make it yours, Mia. Everything about you...I've never wanted anything more than I want you."

"And I want you..."

"I know," I whisper, moving my tongue over her again, feeling her tense as I move her fingers aside and spread her warmth, my mouth moving against her opening. I want to taste it all or I will die. My heart screams for her.

"Oh God. Oh my God, Derek..."

"It's all you, Mia. All yours," I breathe, my body tight against her, her fingers beginning to grip into the soft leather seat.

"Oh, God. It's all you. All yours..." she murmurs. "I need you."

"You have me," I assure her, now putting my lips over her, my tongue lapping at her wetness.

"I have you," she repeats. "I have you. I have you."

I kiss the lips between her legs softly, feeling the wet heat on my tongue and cheeks.

"Am I yours...?" she whispers.

I nod. "Always."

She closes her eyes and shudders, her hips thrusting against my face, her fingers clamped over my hair.

Cupping her delectable ass in my hands, I feel her body in the most perfect way under the hard shell I am now. I feel the motion of her breath and my own, the heat from her own body, so close to mine, the smell of her sex and all the other smells that fill the car with the scent of soap mingling with the honey-coconut fragrance of her skin.

And that's when I decide to push her.

I reposition, closing my mouth around her clit and sucking gently, the agile tip of my tongue moving over her. And she shudders again, her back arching, her hands grasping at my hair, her mouth open.

She comes with a shout that fills the car, her back arching, the shockwaves moving through her body, her fingers tightening around mine.

I push my fingers deeper, holding on to her. She gasps and exhales, her hand squeezing my hair with each long, slow wave that explodes from her body.

I stay put until her body stops moving, her breath slowing, deeper, calmer. Until the scent of her skin and the taste of her sex overpowers every other sense and thought and emotion. Until I can breathe again and I know another wave isn't coming.

And then her fingers slide back down over my lips, down my cheek and neck, her touch lingering longer, almost reverent.

I feel her touch and taste her skin. I feel her heartbeat and inhale the scent of her. I feel her fingers, still moving across my mouth, my jaw.

"Derek," she whispers.

"Shh," I say, placing my finger over her pretty pussy gently. "We're here." I take my finger from between her legs and put it in my mouth, sucking on it. Her eyes widen for a second, each brown iris watery as it looks up at me.

"Mmmmm...okay," she says.

I slide my finger out of my mouth. "We better go."

"You're right."

Sliding Mia's dress down her legs, I pick up her underwear and slide into my pocket as she straightens her clothes. I glance over at her, running one hand gently over her chin. "You alright?"

"Yeah. I'm—I'm great."

She doesn't look okay. She looks beautiful, of course, but I can't help but notice how flushed and bright she looks.

"It'll pass. It's just the excitement," I say with a smile.

She smiles back and reaches over, tucking some of my hair behind my ear. "Too bad you can't hold that over me forever."

"I'm cute and you're having trouble keeping your hands off me. I'm completely going to hold it over you."

"Uh-huh," she says, softly. "Well, here we are, Derek."

I look out the window as I realize Raul is coming to a stop. "Uh-huh. May I assist?" I ask, hopping out of the SUV and extending a hand for her.

She smiles and takes it, slipping out and smoothing her hair.

I hold the back of our truck door open for her, a smile on my face as I watch her moving away from me, her hips swaying as she opens the door and then walks through the entrance and into the lobby of the Four Seasons.

I turn to Raul, who is driving the truck. "Try to stay close, Raul. I might need you on hand."

"Yes, Mr. Anderson."

He drives off, and I walk through the lobby, smiling at the people sitting in the lobby, and then I am stepping into the elevator alongside Mia.

I can see a few heads turning toward me. The interior of the elevator is full, so I press the button for her floor. We wait a second before the doors slide shut.

I hear the ding when we reach her floor and we exit before the elevator starts to move again. And behind me, there are cheers, a few girls giddy with excitement.

More and more, I'm getting recognized from that article in the Post. And more and more, it makes me paranoid.

Especially when I just stepped into a hotel hallway. Alone. With my assistant.

I feel my chest tighten a little more.

This is what I do. I feel this way.

That shard of responsibility that's always sticking in my chest finally ends up sticking in my throat. I swallow, hard, my throat tight.

As the elevator takes off behind us, I walk Mia down the hallway to her room, annoyance at myself and the absurdity of the situation settling in with each second that passes by.

When we stop at the door to her room, she turns with a smile to glance at me. The expression quickly dissolves.

"What's the matter?" she asks, her tone soft and quiet, the uneasiness palpable.

"Nothing," I assure her.

"Is something wrong?" A frown takes shape on her pretty face. "Derek? What's wrong?"

I take a deep breath. "Nothing...And everything." I shake my head, trying to clear the thought. I walk towards her as she steps forward with me. "I guess I'm just realizing how much I've fucked up. Again."

"I...I don't...I don't understand."

I reach out and put a warm, comforting hand on her waist. "I'm sorry I didn't tell you, didn't warn you more about

Scott. I'm sorry that I didn't make you feel safe. That working together is making it harder...That I don't even know what I'm doing. That I've made a mess of everything and..."

I shake my head, exhaling hard and fighting the uneasiness about what I'm about to say. "And that I...I can't stay with you tonight."

Mia blinks, her face going slack. "What?"

"I can't stay with you tonight."

"Why?"

I kiss her again, softly, and tilt my head down to stare at her gorgeous face. "Because I can't be with you. Not tonight. Not with...this. I punched Scott Disrick. Probably got us banned for life from Fellows. And those—those girls in the elevator just recognized me, and..." I pause, my chest tightening again. I take another deep breath and lick my lips, my throat suddenly dry. "And I just need to get out of here. Away from all of this. Away...from you."

"You need to get away from…me?"

"Just for now. I promise. I just...can't. I can't just be around you like this. When I want you so damned bad, I can't see straight. Because if I go inside this room with you, Mia...I am absolutely going to fuck you like you've never been fucked in your life." I blink. "And neither one of us will be able to walk away unscathed. I'm doing all of us a favor."

Kissing her forehead, I release her. "Just...trust me. I'll call you tomorrow." I turn and walk quickly to the staircase.

I take two steps before a ball of sorrow hits me in the chest.

Chapter Eighteen

MIA

I don't see Derek the next morning at work. I don't see him during the afternoon, either.

Jenny, his Chief of Staff, calls me to let me know that he's having a lot of meetings, and I can't help but feel like he's avoiding me. That he doesn't want to speak to me, that he thinks he's doing me a favor by not being with me.

I shake my head. No.

That's not—

I swallow, hard.

That's not true. I know that. I just...it's hard not to feel as if I've been placed on a back-burner for him.

I take a deep breath and force myself to move to push through the Hare & Holeton training exercises while Jenny checks in with me.

I smile at her and nod along, but I can't help but feel like I'm going to snap any moment.

Concentrate, Mia. It's going to be fine. You have to concentrate on the task at hand.

"I know you wanted to probably wanted to work more with Derek today," she says, "but he's just been so busy. He doesn't want to leave you high and dry." She gives me a sympathetic smile. "He just needs to focus on getting through this madness."

"Of course." I nod my head. "How is he holding up?"

Jenny frowns. "He's...afraid. He's never been in this position before, where he's been so on the spot, so public. I'm sure you can understand."

I nod again. I do understand.

And I'm so proud of him. The way he handled Scott Disrick.

And I am so thankful that he is handling a lot of this fallout. Even though it is my fault that he got into this position in the first place.

Maybe if I had shut down Scott sooner. Or refused Derek's invitation to the dinner...

With a shiver, I take a deep breath, needing to fight the rising panic in my chest. I adjust the buttons on my blouse for the fortieth time.

"Mia?"

"Yeah?"

"You're doing great. I know it's not easy. It's not your fault Scott Disrick is an asshole."

I smile, grateful for Jen. "Thank you. And thank you for the work. I really appreciate it."

"Of course." The intercom buzzes. She turns and pauses. "Oh, that's Derek's office. He's calling for me now." She places a hand on my shoulder, her red glasses glinting in the light. "Look, that Happy Hour invitation is still on the table tonight. Just let me know and we'll go. Derek will be in meetings all night, and I have to go put in my time as well, but after 5 o'clock, you'll be off the clock for the night."

"Okay, thanks. I'll let you know. Let me know if there's anything that I can do to help with any of the...reports and phone calls."

"Will do."

I nod and place my hand over hers on my shoulder. "Thanks."

She gives me a genuine smile. "You're welcome, Mia. See you at five."

"Five it is." I nod and get back to work. But not before another email from Steven Mayers comes in.

Hey Mia,

Just checking in. What's the verdict on the Anderson gig? Are you going to take it?

We need your decision as soon as possible because if you don't take it, Geoff is going to hire someone else.

Our client needs an answer. And so do we.

Can you please get back to me?

Sincerely,

Steven Mayers

—

"Mia?" Shelly, one of the junior staff, stops in front of me. I glance up to find her brown eyes bright. "Can you do me a favor?"

I smile. "Yes."

"Really?"

I nod.

She smiles back. "Okay. I heard from around the office that you were a really good photographer..." She pauses. "Is that right?"

I turn. "Well, I'm a photographer. Not sure about the 'really good' part. But yes, I take pictures."

She grins. "Well, I'm applying for this spot on the communications committee for the Puget Sound Priority. And I need some professional photos. I was hoping maybe you could take headshots and profile shots for my portfolio." Her rounded eyes are pleading, and one of her hands wrings the fabric of her red skirt as she speaks. "It's really a small portfolio...but I need help with it. Would you mind?"

I blink, at a loss for words. "Wow, um...Sure. Let's see it."

Her grin widens and she nods, taking out a binder from under her jacket. "Here it is." Her voice grows wistful. "It's not that great...just my resume, my social media stuff, and a little love note about my husband. It's a lot of photos, but none of them are really quality..." I watch as she shuffles through to the attached photos and takes out her printed resume. "I was thinking...maybe I could turn this into something pretty." Her voice grows soft. "You know, show some of my passion for Seattle, for the city, for the environment."

I nod, taking the thick binder from her hands, and glance inside. Flipping through the pages, I find a neat, well-ordered layout. Some of the pictures are of beaches and forest preserves and mudflats. Others are of seals off the shoreline and muddy streams and storms. And then I find the photo of Shelly and her husband. They are smiling broadly in their wedding attire, his arms around her and her hands on her stomach.

I turn and look at her before closing the portfolio and putting it down on the desk. A small knot of emotion twirls in my stomach. "I think this is amazing. Especially that one with you and your husband." I turn. "He's very handsome."

She gives me a genuine smile, the joy clear in her face. "Yes, he is. He was so worried about grad school, and I was pregnant, and then he got that job opportunity right before we found out our baby was due...but I knew he would make it." She winks. "He's so dedicated to his job. Thinks everything through, and he just knows what to do." A proud smile comes to her lips. "But if I get this position, I think we'll be able to start making plans of actually planning now." She takes a deep breath. "And at the end of the day, I can always run home to him."

My mind drifts, and my brain conjures up another picture to add to the ones she's already included. She's standing under a tree in the center of a green field. It's late in the day. A rich sunset settles behind her. She's looking at the camera, smiling and all of her teeth are showing.

Suddenly, I can see the photos I want to take for her, for her portfolio. I would focus somewhere around twilight. I would use a wide angle and light. I would switch to black and white. I would use low, rich lights to highlight the colors of the wall around her...the rich greens and golds streaking the sky and lighting up her face and dress.

I clear my throat. "Well, this is wonderful."

She beams. "Thanks. You're sure it's not bad?"

"Not at all. I think it's great." I pick up a memo before adding. "And given how much is in here, it's going to take some time to get it done."

Her face falls. "But I am in a hurry...I want to get it done before the end of the month...I heard you're also going to be super busy with Derek's stuff though, so I'll understand if you can't. It's just that I, I really need someone to take the photos and-"

"No worries at all, Shelly. I've got you. I'll get onto it this week." I offer her a tentative smile. "I promise that I'll do my best."

"Oh, thank you so, so much! I promise I won't let you down."

"Just stop by my desk and I'll get started right away." I turn to leave, looking back to see her fixing her skirt with both hands. I motion to the skylight picture in her folder, and she finally looks up. "I really like that photo. I'm going to try and recreate some of those pictures as a part of your portfolio. The evening light is perfect. I think it'll make great pictures."

She nods, her eyes still sparkling. "Thanks, Mia."

"No worries."

She smiles and rushes off, leaving me with a bunch of tasks in my queue and as I'm pressing them away, I can't help but think of the joy on Shelly's face just now.

The excitement she felt. The thrill.

It's the reason I got into photography in the first place.

That thrill, that excitement.

The taste of creating something beautiful, something lasting. Something that couldn't just pack up its bags and walk away like most of the world. Something that would be on the wall of a home, in someone's kitchen, over someone's garden, on a desk, or even above a dreaming child's bed.

I sigh and head over to my inbox, peering at the texts and emails.

Reading over Steven Mayers' message one more time, I exit out of the window and move to the right hand of my monitor.

I know I need more time to think about Steven's gig—the entire tailing Derek situation.

I know.

But I don't have the luxury of sitting here needlessly, or of arguing with myself.

I'll respond when I get home.

I tear the message out of my inbox and move over to the recycling bin, where I toss it in.

Right now, I've got Hare & Holeton work to do, but, moreover, I've also got a new photography client.

I need to get to work.

And, aside from the time I've spent alone with Derek, the thought makes me smile harder than I've smiled all week.

BY THE TIME five o'clock rolls around, I'm exhausted, every task I had been assigned completed.

I've made necessary changes to Derek's schedules based on the many meetings he's got coming up and I've even brainstormed more ideas for Shelly's portfolio.

Just as I'm leaning into my chair and stretching my aching back, I hear someone call my name. I straighten up, my eyes on my computer, and hear a masculine voice approach.

"Hey."

I turn in my semi-comfy office chair to find Oliver Blare, Ryder's assistant whom I met at the CoTA event.

"Hey," I greet as he walks over. "What's up?"

He pulls up a seat. "So...? You heading to Happy Hour today with us, or what?"

I've thought about it all day since Jenny invited me, and with still no word from Derek since he dropped me off at the Four Seasons hotel room, I've decided. "Yep. When?"

He grins. "Five minutes ago, dude."

I nod, getting up and fishing in my bag for my cellphone and keys before grabbing my purse.

"Let's go, Oliver."

Closing my workstation down, I push to my feet, nearly linking arms with Oliver as we push through the maze of cubicles and out the door, hauling it together.

"What about the interns?" I ask.

"They've left. They're fine. It's mostly just us over-worked assistants at these things anyway. We need some fun around here. It's been a busy week."

“Busy isn’t the word for it.”

I allow Oliver to guide me down the elevators from Hare & Holeton and out of the glass building's front doors, pushing our way into the icy January air.

The Seattle streets are crowded with downtown workers, making their way to and from bars, coffee shops, coffee chains, and fast-food restaurants.

I shiver and tug my coat tighter around me as we head down the sidewalk.

Oliver notices my hunch and snorts. "Not that cold, dude."

"It is. They sure as hell didn't make the weather like this back home."

His blond hair, short and combed to the side, glints from the specks of ice falling in it. He looks perfectly at home and cozy, dressed in a slick brown suit, trench and a Fred Perry polo.

"Where were you from again?"

"Hawaii. Born and mostly raised. I went to the University of Hawaii for college." I manage a weak laugh, steeling myself for the mix of excitement and horror that I know is coming.

"Nice. So, what do you do when you're not being chained to your desk here at Hare & Holeton, Mia?"

"I'm a photographer." I lift a hand and motion at the gray skies. "I'm looking for a spot for a portrait session. If you know of one, or something like that, I'd be grateful. I'm also working on a special project."

"Hmm...let me think. I got it."

I smile. "What have you got?"

"Hey, I know the perfect place."

"Oh, really?" I flash a smile. "Then you're going to have to tell me now, Oliver."

He nods and turns to face me as he looks up and down the street, his gaze resting for a few steps before he looks back to me, his smile sly.

"It's gonna cost you, though. Maybe a nice dinner?"

I laugh and hold up a palm, dismissing the idea. "Sorry, Oliver. Maybe next time. All I'm looking for is an opportunity to do some work. Nothing else."

"Honey." He holds onto my arm snugly as we walk. "I'm not bi. I'm as gay as a pair of pink, fur-lined top hats. I just want to have some fun picking what I know is that beautiful big brain of yours."

I laugh and shake my head as he pulls me along. "Well, whaddya know? I must be really into pink fur-lined top hats." I smile up at him. "It's a deal."

Smiling at the freezing rain drops that, like him, are now glistening on his hair, I look at my brand-new friend.

He grins, letting go of my arm. "The first shot's on me."

"No, no." I shake my head as he motions towards the fast-approaching bar, a spot called 'The Sprinkler'. "You can buy me a coffee or a hot chocolate. A shot of anything would be a nice treat, but I've had my fair share of those in the last few weeks."

He grins and opens the door for me, taking my arm and leading me inside. "Why don't you have a seat and I'll be right back."

I smile, my ears warm against the boom of the music playing out of the overhead speakers, and take a seat at a back table, my back to the wall and my eyes on the entrance.

As the sounds of some melancholy Seattle grunge band plays in the background, I hear Oliver ask the bartender for two cups of something with cinnamon and I look up just in time to see Shelly and Jenny heading my way.

Ginger eyebrows lifting skyward, Jenny raises her hands. "Mia! Girl! You made it! Just in time to have some fun at a safe locale."

Shelly turns just as Oliver makes his way back. He wraps a leather glove around his fingers and hugs her, giving her a small kiss as he does.

Jenny stops in front of me and smiles. "I'm glad you made it, Mia. I wanted to apologize more for what happened at dinner with Scott Disrick, but we were in the office, and I didn’t want to say too much. I'm so sorry about what happened."

"It's fine." I wave her off. "Everything's fine. It ended as soon as Derek and I left. I just want to forget it. How we recover after is all I'm concerned about."

She nods. "I agree."

I grin. Just as Oliver hands me a hot cinnamon-scented cup of something.

He steps forward. "And speaking of 'fine', I don't know how you did it, girl. All that sweaty, sexy testosterone in one room? The buttoned-up, beautiful Mr. Derek Anderson actually throwing a punch at a man? Whew. I wouldn't have believed it was possible."

I swirl my drink, avoiding Oliver's eye. "I think it was just adrenaline."

"Whatever it was, it sounds like something's changed in our Mister CEO. I've never heard of him acting so...so raw."

Jenny smiles and slides onto the end of the seat next to me. "You've got a point. I've known Derek since we were kids, but he's always been a bit like a polite shark. If you're not part of the pack, he doesn't bother with you. Lately, though..."

I glance at Oliver and sense his sudden urge to search the room. I ignore it as Shelly pipes in.

"He just seems to be a bit more...animated than usual."

"Maybe...he's just having a rough time. What with the papers reporting on him and the IPO. Everyone's on edge." Jenny turns to me and shrugs. She nods to Oliver and I hear her drop her voice to a quiet tone of surprise. "I wish he would come to Happy Hour, sometime. He could use a drink. I mean, I told him the gang's all here. He would know everyone."

Oliver's eyes peruse the room once more. "Well...the gang's not all exactly here."

Jenny frowns. "What do you mean?"

Oliver shifts uncomfortably but Jenny continues to stare at him, her eyes hardening.

I can see Oliver thinking, deciding, and then opting to speak. "I, uh, kinda inadvertently invited someone else to join us."

Shelly leans forward, attempting to be heard over the loudspeakers. "Who?"

Suddenly, I hear a pair of clicking heels approaching across the tile floor behind me.

Jenny turns before I can and what she sees makes her stop. "Huh. Well, I'll be damned..."

Spinning around, I find myself face to face with a beautiful strawberry blonde woman maybe my age, but with the look of a longtime Seattle native. Her blue eyes, powdered in black from the lashes to the actual eyelid, nearly match the black sweater she's wearing, but her face is hauntingly beautiful. Dressed in black, with a pair of knee-high boots and a big, loose collar shirt-jacket combo, it's nothing short of stunning.

Her smile, perfect and white, would be charming...if it weren't so ice-cold.

She takes a seat at the table next to Oliver, her eyes never leaving my face.

Oliver clears his throat. "Ahem. Uh, Mia, I should introduce you to Alexa Bullock. She agreed to join us tonight. Alexa, this is Mia Kamaka."

The blonde extends her hand. "Nice to meet you, Mia. I'm Alexa."

I smile, slowly, taking her hand, but being suspicious. "Hi."

Alexa's smile grows even chillier. "I'm the assistant Derek Anderson fired to hire you."

Chapter Nineteen

DEREK

The craving in my body just won't go away.

As I slowly pack up my desk for the day—a day filled with finicky meetings with my financially-anxious brother Alton about money and the SEC—I find my mind constantly wandering back to the way Mia looked at me when I threw that punch at Scott.

I remember the look of surprise I saw. The look of quiet, sharp judgement that followed. The look of...respect. And then the look of ecstasy on her face when I leaned over in the vehicle, pressing my lips to hers.

I remember the way her mouth tasted, the heat of her body, the way her curves pressed into me.

And it's all making me break out into a sweat.

I should be more concerned with the Bella Publishing deal potentially falling through because I punched its CEO, Scott Disrick.

Really, I should be more concerned with the IPO deal. If a publisher like Bella has its doubts about joining the Hare & Holeton team, then it's likely a whole slew of other companies do, too.

So, why am I not more concerned?

Because I can't stop thinking about Mia.

After I dropped her off at her hotel room, I spent the better part of last night, reliving every touch, every taste, every lick of ours in the backseat of the car. I got even more turned on by the thought that she was fantasizing about me, too.

To think about Mia, alone, in that hotel bed...touching herself at the thought of me...

That's got me aching down low. I want to see that hotel room and I want to see it right now ...just to verify she was really there. I haven't had the guts to call her and ask how it's all going. Yet.

But I know it's not going well. For either of us.

I could barely handle it when I walked her to her door and kissed her goodbye. But the feelings...they're growing stronger.

Every second I spend time with her, that pull, it gets stronger. I'm familiarizing my body with her...as if I already know her. I could kick myself for doing this, because I know it's a losing game.

She works for me.

I'm her boss.

And too many factors are in play regarding my massive IPO plans.

The stakes are rising, but so are my emotions. My feelings are so out of control I'm afraid I'll blow it all with a poor decision if these feelings don't go away.

I want Mia. Bad. That shouldn't matter. This deal is bigger than any one person. That should be more important to me.

But then there's this...

Lord knows, I've tried to distract myself from it. But it won't go away.

Mia.

Her luscious lips. Her curvy body. That fiery attitude.

Last night...

I seriously thought about it all the way home.

I'm still thinking about the way I made Mia come—all the ways I'd make her come—when I hear a knock on my office door and I see my brother, Ryder, perched in the frame of the glass doorway. He lifts his chin.

"Yo! Needle Dick. Got a second?"

I slide a few more folders in my briefcase before exhaling and answering. "Actually, I was on my way out, but I suppose I can help you get a few questions out of your system. What is it?"

He folds his arms over his white button-down shirt, crosses the threshold, and joins me by flopping in one of my lounge chairs. He throws his dark hair back.

"Hmmm, well, not much..." He steeples his fingers in front of him. "If you don't count the fact that I found something very interesting about the Mandy story leak to the Post."

I sigh and close my case. "Are we still on that? I thought your little hunting-and-gathering side quest was over."

Ryder sits up, blue eyes alight. "Are you kidding me? When have you ever known me to back down from a challenge?"

"Uh, the last time you asked Jenny out on a date? Remember that?"

Ryder glares. "We were nine."

"That was the first time she turned you down. The last time was sometime last year...if I recall."

Rolling his eyes, Ryder waves a hand at me. "I have an excuse for that. About three times in her life, Jenny's managed to act like a normal human being. And every time she does, I somehow forget that she's about as warm as a block of ice and is a succubus from the Gates of Hell."

"'Succubus from the Gates of Hell'? That's all?" I can't resist the urge to tease him. "Sounds like something that would be right up your alley."

"Yeah, you'd think. Except..." Ryder flounces forward in

the chair, dark brows contorting together on his face as he realizes what I'm doing. "Hey! Don't get us off track here, you ass. We're not here to talk about me and my love life."

"You don't have a 'love life,' Ryder. You have a sex life. Two very different things."

"Alright, will you shut up and listen already?"

I try to keep a straight face. "Fine. Hit me."

He straightens. "Trust me. You'll thank me later."

"Tell me."

"After the last time we talked, I decided to hire an investigator to dig up any information we could on the leak. I'm not saying that there's anything to it—yet—but..." He holds up a finger. "You'd better brace yourself." He exhales. "My guy took some looks into our servers. And he thinks—we think—the leak about the Mandy story came from someone in the company. Someone sharing info from our servers to someone else's."

I frown. "What does that mean exactly? 'Sharing info to someone else's servers'?"

"Well, it's someone on a Hare & Holeton server messaging someone outside our company—and that someone has specifically downloaded the story to their proprietor's servers. So, to speak."

"Ryder, I'm not following." I put my hand on my neck and make it clear I'm getting hit with a serious case of tension. "Emailing or sending a file to someone is different than sharing it. What if someone on a company computer makes their company files available to a friend or a family member? Or just by accident?"

Ryder pinches the bridge of his nose and exhales. "I know. It's possible but...I don't think that's what happened here."

Rubbing the back of my neck, I take a seat in front of my desk. "Why not?"

"Because whoever did it bothered to try to remove the file

from the harehole.com servers." He leans in. "They botched it, though. It's still up there. So, someone's messed with the information—but didn't remove it." He sits up and flips his hands into the air. "Everyone's talking about the Mandy story being leaked to the Post. Everyone's talking about how it may move the stock prices, too. But think about it, Derek. Just look at the details. The story came out at the perfect time to fire up the market with all kinds of speculation. But more, it's just the darkest, dirtiest story we could have leaked. And one of our first and foremost company policies is to not use company servers or services for personal business. It's a huge security risk."

"I know that policy, Ryder. And so does everyone else in the company."

"Right. Okay. So, then, let's say someone downloads the photos off the company server. For whatever reason. To see them or spread them around, I don't know. But that person does it. And, somehow, because these photos are so explosive, so all-encompassing, so filthy, that person knows that it will cause a dip in our stock price. And let's face it, the company is at a high point right now. Our authors are selling better than ever. But a scandal—any scandal—would lower our stock value for sure. No matter how much the board wants to make money and with our stock price the way it is, this news could throw us into a death spiral."

"Okay, I'm following..." I press my fingertips together, trying to make sense of it all. "But I hope you know what you're suggesting here." My tone is flat and my expression is focused. "This is a major breach of company protocol and you're suggesting that one of our employees leaked this story intentionally...with the intent to cause a stock price drop."

"Yes!" Ryder's hands fall onto the armrests.

My stomach tightens. "Well, let's say we do believe it's legit. What then? We go after it? How do we do that?"

Ryder folds his arms and looks out at the darkened sky. His expression shields him. "I don't want to look at our employees as suspects. But...we need to do something. Because this could ruin everything..."

I swallow, my throat dry. "I know. I hear you. I just...I don't want to go through the inquisition if we're wrong. Can you imagine the rumors? The speculation? The witch hunt that would happen if we erroneously went after one of our own?" I stand and start moving around the room again. "I mean, this is a serious thing."

"I won't do it unless we really have evidence. You know me. I wouldn't do that."

"And if we have to do it, Ryder...you're going to have to call me every morning and let me know where we're going with it. I don't want to be blindsided. Or end up being on the edge of a cliff."

Ryder rolls his eyes and shakes his head before sighing out. "God, Der. You're such a drama queen sometimes."

Flipping him my middle finger, I lean up against my desk. "You have no idea."

My little brother grins, his attitude more relaxed now that the conversation's going more to his liking. "But seriously, maybe we're wrong. But if we are, we'd be better off being dumb with it. Not saying we should let another day go by before we start an investigation. I'm just saying...look, there's no need to get panicky. Not yet. Let the evidence decide."

"And if this turns out to be the real-life answer to the DaVinci Code, what do we do then?"

"Believe it or not, unlike you, I've already thought this through. My guy's tracking the IP address of the originator. We should be able to get to them."

I groan. "Of course. Endless freedom on the Internet...and the freedom to muddy your own name forever by spilling company secrets to a tabloid. Perfect." I turn and look out at the office buildings across the street. "Well, if the smart money's on our employee—or former employees, who knows—having leaked it, I guess we better get ready to show them the door. Whoever they are."

Ryder nods, more time to think. "Yeah." He moves closer, his voice almost a whisper. "I'm going to call my guy in a minute and let him know what we're doing. I just want to see what he says."

"You got it." I tap my fingers on my desk in anticipation. "And Ryder?" I say as my brother stands from his seat.

"Yeah?"

"Thanks."

A sly smile creeps across Ryder's lips. "No problem. What're you thanking me for?"

I straighten, unable to help my grin. "For telling me that...even though you probably didn't want to."

"Oh, by all means, stop thanking me." Ryder raises his hands. "Verbally, I mean. If you really want to thank me, I take payment in cash...and shipments of baby oil, too."

I throw my empty cup of coffee at him just as he darts away.

"Hey!" He raises the back of his chair in front of him. "I'm just trying to save your ass!"

I scoff, shaking my head. "Right. We'll see about that." I flip him off in time for him to see it before he leaves my office.

I reach for my iPad to check the news feed on how Mandy's story is really affecting the finances of my company...and everything else around it. But a spate of messages arrive in my inbox before I have the chance to look.

I click open the last one. Another one from Jenny.

"You sure you not up for Happy Hour? You could use it."

With a deep sigh, I look around at all the walls that remind me of all the dark and dirty things that I could use—things that I want, deep down inside.

After this convo with Ryder and a night of tossing and turning about Mia, I could definitely use a change of scenery. In the form of liquid courage.

Biting the edge of my lip, I tap my response into the text box.

MIA

The sounds of some Seattle grunge band blare throughout the bar where we're having our very "happy" hour. But I barely hear them over the sound of my own voice screaming.

"Another round!" I shout, just as I finish another of those cinnamon drinks Oliver had made for us.

At this point, anything is better than thinking too much about Alexa's stories about Derek. As his ex-assistant, she seemed chockfull of them.

All these tantalizing tales about Derek Anderson and his perfect suits. His perfect hair.

His perfect face.

His desire for perfection in everything...

His house. His clothes. His whiskey.

His women.

Oh good Lord, I'm thinking about it again. I'm thinking about lusting after a guy who's literally my only source of income.

Bleh.

Another shot, please.

According to Alexa, Derek is a hotshot with no time for relationships. Apparently, he's probably got potential personal assistants all over, waiting in the wings at his beck and call, ready to do anything he says...

Because, like me, they can't resist the charms of a man who makes you feel like you're the center of his world...before he ultimately drops you.

It's a story I've lived before.

No, more like a story I've lived every day of my life since I left Hawaii.

But being an apparently perfect man has made me want him even more, hasn't it?

"Another round," I say cockily at Mike the bartender, putting my credit card down on the counter just as Oliver sidles up.

"Okay, princess, that's about enough." The blond assistant's brow smacks the smooth skin on his face. "I'm trying to keep one eye on the clock, you know? This isn't a marathon. No passing out 'cause you got too hammered."

"I'm not passing out, Ol. I'm savoring," I say, giving my chin a salute. "You know I like this place. It's like my happy place."

He sighs and shakes his head. "It's not going to be that happy when your head's in a toilet bowl, you know."

"I know." I glance over at our coworkers Jenny and Shelly on the dance floor. The band on stage changed up and, no surprise, it's an even faster rock song—a Seattle thrash band I'm sure Derek Anderson—Seattle boy that he is—completely lives for. "I'm going to try and keep it on that happy space for as long as possible, okay?"

"Okay. I'm pretty sure that's just not going to happen, though."

"Right." Or not, I think. "But the moment you dump me and the higher-ups think I'm a useless bar slut, I'm out of here. They'll have to pay." I drain the last of my second round. "Or maybe I'll piss in Derek Anderson's coffee pot."

"Ugh." Oliver shakes his head. "If you do that, you really will be useless."

I tilt my chin up. "Probably."

Sighing, Oliver moves in close, sliding one arm around my shoulder. He gives me a quick squeeze. "You know, you can't let what Alexa said get to you, hon. She's just...jealous because you're Derek's assistant now. All that talk about him being 'perfect' is just that...Talk."

It's all I can do to nod my head, because it's true...I can't let the hoarseness in my voice betray me. I'm trying to stay in control every moment here.

It's everything I can do to not let the night's events get the better of me, because the second I become a blabbering idiot, I may as well turn myself in—right to the desk of HR at the company.

That's the last thing I need right now, so I have to fiercely hold it together, no matter how tightly my chest is beginning to constrict.

"Maybe," I concede to Oliver. "But you don't get it." I sigh, shaking my head. "I'm this Little Miss Nobody...at least, where Derek's concerned. And so often, I feel like who I am or what I do doesn't make a difference. And then he...sees me, you know? Like, really sees me. And it's like...in that moment...I'm the only person in the world to him. And now that I have that...I don't want it to go away." I shrug, sighing again. "I'm stuck. Stuck working with the most perfect guy in the world and...the most perfect memories built every day. And all I want to do is tell how much I..."

I stop, my words failing me.

I don't have to tell Oliver.

His face says it all.

Oliver sighs with me, moving his arm to the small of my back, pulling me in close to him.

He gives me a good rub, smiling as he shakes his head adoringly. "Oh, Mia...Hon. You're so talented...you're so smart. So confident. Where did that girl go?"

"She went to the bottom of an empty cinnamon whiskey bottle, that's where." My face goes serious. "Where she'll probably stay for a little while."

Oliver smiles softly "Nah, I don't believe that. Not for one second. I just think you're feeling insecure. And it's understandable. You're...working with the man of your dreams, right? That must put tons of pressure on you. It's understandable that you'd feel a little out of your element. I mean...He's a lot more experienced than you are. More experienced at all of this press and the industry and probably since you've met him? It's not going to feel very easy, is it?"

I nod, not wanting to disagree with him. But right now...

Right now, I'm beginning to think he's absolutely right.

"I mean, he's a billionaire CEO. Stands up to be six foot three, I think. And he's got arms that could probably wrap around me more than once." I hold up my hands, as if to hug an invisible body. "And all I'm this...waitress with hair that won't curl right and thighs that won't separate at all and tits that don't just happen to be the perfect size...I...I am hardly his dream girl."

"Oh, hon." Oliver's face completely changes. He gives me a compassionate smile. "So you think you're not his type?"

"I don't know..." I try to look away, but he catches my eyes.

"No 'buts' about it or 'whatevers', okay?" Oliver's eyes are stern. "Gotta get that thought out of your head right now. Just because he's, you know...super successful...doesn't mean he's God's gift to women, you know?"

I chuckle. "Thanks for the reminder, Ol."

"But that doesn't mean he's immune to the laws of attraction, either. I mean, shit, I date men, and I still know enough about the opposite sex to know that you are a gorgeous, vibrant, intelligent, beautiful bitch. Seriously, I'd want you to be my girl if I wasn't so taken with the likes of Channing Tatum and the guy that plays the hotel manager on the first season of The White Lotus. You. Are. Hot."

"If I wasn't afraid I'd throw up, I'd give you a kiss right now."

Oliver pats my head. "If you want him, go get him, tiger. Unless..."

"Unless what?"

"Unless what you want out of Derek Anderson is something else. Unless you're like...in love with him or something..." He chuckles but loses the expression when he looks down at my face. "Ar-are you in love with him, Mia?"

I lower my eyes, shaking my head. "Oliver, are we in high school? I don't have time for that right now." I'm beginning to desperately need another drink.

"Okay." Oliver gives my hand a squeeze. "Just know that if you are, then I'm here for you. You know that, right?"

"Yeah." I smile weakly. "I know."

"I just want to make sure you know once and for all, you are gorgeous." Oliver gives me another squeeze. "I hope you know that. And maybe it's time we find you a good man to start on. Have you seen any cute guys out tonight?"

"Oh, please." I give him a playful shove.

"I'm serious, Mia. And it's not like I'm not the world's greatest wingman. I will totally find you a good man."

"No. No, you won't." I give him a look. "This isn't some speed dating event. We're here with our coworkers, for God's sake."

Oliver looks disappointed. "Fine, then. What'll we order?"

I just look at Oliver. "Is it really okay with you if I order one more cinnamon whiskey?"

He laughs. "If it's okay with you, it's okay with me, hon. You know that. I've got you tonight...I just hope you don't expect me to hold your hair while you puke it back up at the office tomorrow." His eyes find someone at the end of the bar, and his face brightens in a smile. "Be right back, toots. I'm going to do a little scouting round to help find you your man. And help me find myself one while I'm at it."

As he moves off toward the bar and once I've got my last whiskey in hand, I wander into a booth, taking a deep relaxing breath.

Oliver's gone.

Alexa's gone. Shelly and Jenny are on the dance floor.

So, it's just me—alone with my thoughts. Thoughts of Oliver's reassurances. Thoughts of his questions, one in particular.

"Are you in love with Derek Anderson?"

I tip up the shot.

I'm not in love with him, I tell myself.

It's just...

I shake the memory away.

The whiskey disappears. But the memories won't.

Not of our meeting.

Of the grins, the jokes, the glances. The looks that mean so much.

The sweet moments.

The kisses...so tender, so careful. And the heat, unbridled and all-consuming.

The way Derek Anderson had touched me, kissed me and made it his mission to show me pleasure like I'd never known.

My vision sways, and I rest my head on the booth. My thoughts swirl.

I try to brush them away, but I can't seem to ignore them.

Even when there are questions.

Questions about what he sees in me.

Why he wants me by his side.

Why he seems so into me, makes me his number one priority. And then disappears into the wind.

The thoughts are still there when a bout of nausea hits my stomach, burning my throat like poison.

Stumbling out of the booth, my hands clutch my stomach. I walk on shaking legs to the bathroom.

I have to get there before it's too late.

But I can't.

My feet won't seem to work right. Going too fast, I almost lose my balance and fall.

Until someone's arms catch me.
And then it's all falling up, vomiting.
Strong arms rock me, my body convulses.
And then everything goes dark.

Chapter Twenty

MIA

The sound of a faucet turning off. The rustle of clothing.

A door opening and closing.

Footsteps.

All noises that stir in my subconscious not a moment before my eyes finally open.

I see a dark silhouette, standing at the foot of my bed. And then I see the backlit face of a man.

I quickly raise myself up, sitting straight up in bed.

My heart beats a crazy rhythm as the voice belonging to the silhouette finally speaks.

"Good…You're alive. Good morning, Ms. Kamaka."

The sound of Derek Anderson's voice startles me.

I look over to the bedside clock next to my head.

It's six fifty-four.

And I'm being woken up by my billionaire boss—a realization that even the fact that my head feels like it's been on a carousel all night can't diminish.

"Derek," I reply weakly, scarcely finding the nerve to speak. "What...what are you doing here?"

"Interesting question to ask..." He blinks. "Especially since I live here."

He leans against the wall and runs a hand through his chestnut hair before his eyes meet mine. My gaze flits around the room and lands on the double doors that lead to the bathroom, an elegant dressing room, and mammoth closet.

So I'm in his bedroom.

Alone with him.

And then, before I can stop myself, I start to remember everything.

Oh God.

I wipe my fingers across my eyelids, as if I can wipe away the images of last night.

Nausea hits my stomach.

My tongue feels dry.

"You okay?" he asks.

"Yeah." I look up at him, taking a deep breath. "I think the Sahara Desert crawled into my mouth last night, but I'm okay...I think."

He points. "Thirsty? There's a bottle of water on the nightstand. A couple of aspirin are next to it. Some ginger ale. You can refill it whenever you are ready to eat."

"Thanks. I'm good. Just...just a little out of it at the moment."

He watches me. "You look okay. I'm assuming you slept well?"

For a split second, my mind forms an image of him in bed.

A full out, taken-charge ache hits me, and I quiver, a deep breath escaping my lips before I can contain it.

I didn't realize...

Not until just now, that Derek Anderson, Seattle CEO, is standing in nothing but a towel.

His feet are bare, his golden-brown hair wet. A day's worth of sexy stubble sits on his face and jawline.

He's literally half-naked.

And when I look down, I realize I am, too.

In a white robe with nothing on underneath.

My dry tongue can barely make out the words as I say them. "Um, is there a reason you're mostly naked?"

"You threw up on me last night. I had to take off everything."

"Oh. And is there a reason I'm mostly naked?"

"You threw up on you, too." He smirks. "I got you cleaned up and changed. The blouse and skirt you wore took a hit, but will survive. Sadly, my gray suit didn't suffer the same fate."

"Oh God." I cough. "I'm sorry. That's...embarrassing."

"Don't worry about it. No harm, no foul. You need to eat something. Maybe even get a little more rest. You've had a long night. We both have. I'm just waiting for the coffee to finish up."

I shift on the bed. With the way Derek's looking at me, I feel suddenly very exposed.

Like any moment the full extent of my mortification is going to display on a projector screen above my head.

Still...

My stomach swirls. "Coffee sounds great. I think I could use a whole pot."

"I know the feeling. I mean, you are looking pretty refreshed, though...considering you were flat on your butt at one point last night."

"Flat on my butt? Me?"

"I caught you right as you fell over at the bar." He shrugs, shifting. "That's when the bulk of the vomiting happened."

"Gee, thanks. I didn't think I could be any more mortified. But I was clearly wrong."

Derek's lips bend into a grin. "I told you: Don't worry about it. I'm just having fun with you, is all." He heads to the bathroom, filling a glass with water. "It's not a big deal. If you need anything—a shower, toothbrush, clothes—there are some spares in the linen closet. Just grab what you need. I'll be in the kitchen."

Turning, he takes off down a long hall. And I focus on not dying of embarrassment as I get out of bed and make my way for Derek's bathroom.

Coffee.

That's what I need this morning.

To rinse off my face. To grab caffeine. And then to forget last night.

I certainly don't need to be reminded of my attempt at guzzling cinnamon whiskey, followed by an epic public puking incident at the single-most embarrassing moment of my life.

A mental picture of the man—my boss—and how he looked when I watched him walk down the hall in nothing but a towel a moment ago does its darnedest not to ignite a blaze.

Inside his palatial bathroom—stark marble and artwork that must cost small fortune—I pause.

The mirror in Derek's bathroom reflects a woman who looks like death.

I run the water quickly, squirting some mouthwash into my mouth and gargling around it.

Finding the linen closet, I grab a towel and washcloth. Turning to the faucet in the massive glass shower, I let the hot water run, stripping and folding my robe into a pile on the marble countertop, just as the steam from the streams start to build around me.

I let the cloud of condensation envelope me, hoping it might also erase the past twelve hours from my mind.

Especially Derek Anderson's perfection.

Waking up to him—

Just the thought of it brings my memory back to our backseat dalliance.

My dress ruffled up near my waist. Derek's icy blue eyes. His full lips.

The memory is enough to awaken every half-hungover cell

in my body, and as I enter the shower stall, it's all I can do not to hunch over and brace myself against the wall.

The scent of leather and my arousal in the air.

His voice washing over me.

"So gorgeous," he whispered in my ear. I turn on the water and let the blast hit me square in the chest, hard. So hard, I'm surprised it doesn't actually hurt my ribs.

The memory is just a little too much for me to handle at six-something in the morning.

I can barely breathe right now.

I blink, letting the hot water cascade over my face.

Okay, Mia.

Try to calm down.

Just...push forward. Pretend it never happened. Pretend that the beautiful man with the beautiful mouth didn't make you come harder than you have in your life.

Shit.

A half-pouting moan escapes my throat as I realize the truth: it's not something that can be pushed aside.

Out of sight, out of mind.

There's no way I'm going to be able to forget.

Not now. Not ever.

Derek Anderson isn't just hotness personified; it's practically his job description. And with every deep conversation, every laugh, every lingering look, I've become drawn into him, ensnared in the trap of an untrappable man who could pick me up or put me down for his pleasure as easily as a child should put away a toy when asked.

Clenching my thighs closed, I reach for the shower gel, squirting a thick glob out and whipping it through my hands before rubbing it into my skin—scrubbing, to get it out of my mind.

But it's impossible.

Thoughts of him wash over me like a waterfall.

What would it be like to feel his hands again? His lips? His tongue?

I squeeze my legs even tighter, slathering my body with soapy suds as I remember Derek's hands, clutching my hips, his stronger fingers roaming my body wherever he felt like it—when he saw fit.

I let out a small cry, letting my head roll back against the shower wall.

My body warming, I let my hand trail down the surface of my belly, moving to the apex of my thighs.

The steam fills the shower stall as my fingers begin to tease and touch.

Encouraging the memories to escape from their cage. Exploring new ones I'd like to make if given the chance.

An image of the two of us—sweaty and panting in tangled sheets—hits me, and I spread my legs, my hand moving to cover my breast with its slippery trail. Rubbing.

My other hand trails down my belly, over the curve of my mound and separates my lips as my fingers find the little nub at the tip.

I whimper softly as I move my fingers, caressing.

I might feel like death.

But this—touching myself to a fantasy of a Derek—makes me feel so alive.

I feel...

I let out a moan, my hips jittering as I imagine Derek's lips on mine. His tongue stroking inside of my mouth. His body pressed against mine. His cock—unlike any man's I've ever had—pressing against my...

My hand drops to my breast, stirring the water around the very tip, and I moan as I fill my hands, squeezing and moving and circling...

"Having trouble sleeping?"

I startle, my fingers dropping from my body. I look to the door.

The steam from the shower masks his face, but I am able to see a shadow of his handsome features. His voice is like gravel. Rough. Deep. "You were moaning," he says. A pause. "What's the deal?"

I can't control myself. My eyes arrow to his crotch.

Derek groans.

He crosses to the shower, stepping inside—his well-defined body still shimmery with showers of water. He lets the shower run, the water soaking his body and dripping down his tan, muscular shoulders.

"I don't know what you're talking about," I manage to say.

"My bathroom wasn't spared. It still has traces of vomit last night," he says. "May I?"

A lightning bolt shoots through me as I watch him step into the shower. My eyes skip down to the erection that the shower water fails to hide.

"May…I?" he repeats. His eyes are focused on my breasts.

I move my hand back to my breast and gently squeeze it, burrowing my fingers into the soft flesh.

The look in his eyes changes.

And I feel it.

Feel the air around us growing denser. Hot.

Lurking.

Thick.

He moves toward me.

I nod, my hand stroking the breast my fingers are hiding.

The shower fills with steam.

And I see a dark shadow slide over his eyes, as he marches toward me, knocking my hand to the wall, pinning my wrists against the marble.

The heat around me is incredible.

I tighten my eyes, and I feel him lean in. His breath against my ear. The low rumble of his voice. "Don't," he says. His voice is hoarse. Thick. "Don't move."

A moan escapes my throat.

Derek reaches for the knob to the shower stream, tilting his head down to the top of my head.

My eyes are glued open as he leans toward me.

His lips brush mine. He kisses me.

Softly.

I gasp as his mouth, strong and demanding, finds mine willing and waiting.

He leans into me, entering my mouth, his tongue delving forward, meeting mine as if it has a will of its own.

Suddenly he releases me, dropping his hands from me, leaving them to hover at my shoulders as he leans away from me, to the flat surface on the wall.

I shake my head. I can't get enough air.

"Lean against the wall," he says sharply.

I blink at him.

"Lean up against the wall. And stay there."

I remain in place, confused. I lean up against the hard surface with a gasp, and he shakes his head.

"Good girl," he says. "Don't move."

I nod.

The water continues to pour.

Derek grabs the shampoo, squirting it in his hands.

I relax, hating how much I love being at the mercy of his hands.

The scent of the shampoo fills the air.

He begins to rub his hands together.

His eyes are locked on mine. He's staring at me intently, to the point of pain.

I watch him. Take him in.

My eyes follow his movements as he grabs my hair, lathering his hands with the thick, white liquid and then gently urging my head back.

I lean back...

I hear him move.

Strumming through his body.

His hands slip behind my back, and he begins to massage a kneading motion into the tense muscles that flex there.

I sigh deeply, my eyes closed, leaning against the wall.

"Do you have any idea," Derek begins, "how good it feels to be able to touch you?"

I don't respond as I nod.

I don't even want to.

His hands continue on my back, moving down, his finger swirling down the column of my spine.

His lips press against my neck.

"You make me want to eviscerate any man who's ever touched you," he whispers. "Every inch of your skin has my name written all over it."

My eyes widen.

Then I squint.

I realize my head is resting against the wall, my face curled into the curve of the marble, my eyes clamped shut. Heat rushes through my body. Wetness.

"What are you doing?" I breathe.

My breasts are naked against the shower wall, and Derek is kneeling on the floor, with his hands on my waist. Kneeling behind me.

His hot breath skims the small of my back as his hands slide up.

The feel of his knuckles grazing my skin makes me want to lie down.

I want to curl into a ball.

I squeeze my eyes closed.

I can't hear his voice over the sound of the falling water. "You make me crazy, Mia."

Then he places his hands on my thighs, claws penetrating against my skin. I jerk back.

"Don't," I breathe, not knowing what I'm saying, but knowing I need to say something.

His eyes lift to my face as his hands run shower gel and shampoo over my ass.

"I've never met anyone like you," he whispers.

My chest tightens.

"I...I...I'm–"

His index finger traces the line of my spine.

"I'm what?" he asks.

He leans closer.

And then his lips nuzzle between my cheeks.

My head snaps back, as if hit by a bullet.

"I never thought I'd be here," he says, his breath on my skin.

I can hear him.

Feel his hot breath.

I close my eyes. I can't hold it in.

"I'm holding you like this, my Mia," he whispers. "And I have no idea what I'll do next."

I gasp as his hands run down my leg.

"But what I do know," he says, his fingers on my skin, "is that I don't plan on sharing you."

"No," I breathe.

"I know what you mean to me."

"I...I...I...you don't know."

His fingers reach the top of my feet, the warm water streaking up my bare legs, and I tighten my fists, feeling the steam on my skin.

I press my face against the wall, my eyes open, staring at the tile, at the steam permeating the air.

"I feel you when you're not with me," he says. "I feel you."

I turn my face to the tiles, my eyes burning.

"I...I...feel you too," I whisper, "more than you know."

He leans up, his hands detangling the dark mass of my hair, his mouth moving to the back of my neck, his tongue sliding along as if tasting my skin. Grabbing the washcloth from my hand, he stands.

I hear his feet.

The washcloth attacking my back.

Even the water, pouring from the spout in the wall, feels hot.

His hands against my body.

His mouth.

A moan escapes my throat.

"Mia," he says, breathing my name as he lowers the cloth, sliding it until it reaches a place where no man has gone before. "Mia."

I gasp, leaning back, the water pelting my skin as Derek washes the most intimate part of me, his hand sliding between my legs as he again lowers to his knees, his fingers finding the puckering of my ass.

"I can't—" I can't breathe.

And then he's on me.

His lips on me.

His hands, gripping my sides and pulling me to him.

I moan as his tongue finds the opening of my bottom...and licks.

I can't believe this is happening.

He's...

His.

Mouth.

His tongue.

Tasting.

This.

Can't be happening.

I grab the wall, my hands wrapped around the marble, my fingers curling, my knuckles white.

His mouth leaves me and then teases me again.

And again.

And then again.

Until I can't hold it any longer.

I should stop him, my mind screams, but nothing else comes out.

I can't speak.

I cry out.

My back arches as I thrust my chest forward, my hand reaching down, burying itself in his hair.

And Derek doesn't stop. His tongue moves faster, the water streaming around him like a shower of shimmering diamonds.

I'm falling.

I'm hooked.

I'm...

He sweeps his tongue against the opening of my ass and my knees buckle, every ounce of embarrassment leaving my body and burning into the shower floor.

And I fall into a sea of pleasure, the steam wrapping around me, the wet, hot water trickling down my shoulders.

Derek.

I lean against the walls, my head falling forward, my body shaking.

I'm falling.

And nothing but Derek is there.

I gasp deeply, my hands shaking, my body going limp against the wall, the warm water raining down on me. As Derek licks me from behind, I feel as if he's my only lifeline. Without him, I feel as if I'll sink.

Dissolve.

Disappear.

In a sea of desires.

Needs.

Leaving everything behind.

Leaving only Derek. And me.

As my body starts to convulse, my limbs jerking into a full seizure, I come, his name on my lips, my heart cluttered with cravings for a man I can never have.

Because I'm a mess.

Because, as great as this is, I know he won't stay.

His mouth pulls away from my body, his arms wrapping around my waist, and pulling me to him.

His mouth continues up the indentation of my back, along my neck, above my earlobe.

His tongue never ceases running along the surface of my skin.

"Jesus, I can't get enough of you," he whispers into my ear. "I scare myself with how many things I want do with you. Do to you. All the time."

I lean back, my hands leaving the wall, my legs splayed out, Derek's arms holding me.

I choke. On a laugh or a sob, I'm not sure. Maybe both.

It's hard to tell with Derek hard behind me, enclosing me against the tile, his bare feet on either side of mine.

With the water as camouflage, I let go of a small laugh that is laced with sadness, my head falling back onto his shoulder, his lips running up my cheek, his nose resting just under my eye.

"I know," I whisper, "I want you to do more things to me." I exhale. "Including getting me that coffee."

He laughs, his arms holding me tight. "Cocky as ever."

"I thought you said you liked your assistants ballsy."

"And I meant it," he says, his finger tapping against my lip. "I just didn't know ballsy like this."

I smile, using my tongue to tickle his finger before wrapping my lips around it. "Everything is more intense when I'm here with you."

"Then you're not sick of me yet?"

I squeeze my eyes closed, dreading what I'm going to say next. "I can't get enough of you," I confess, swallowing as Derek's lips move to my neck.

I open my eyes.

He's staring at me.

I wiggle away.

"But," I say, "that doesn't mean I trust myself around you."

He grins. "True. I know the feeling. Let me get you that coffee...before I do other things to you that will make us late." He slides out of the shower, grabbing me a towel, which I wrap myself in once I step out.

"I'll be right back?" Derek asks, holding the towel out.

I nod, accepting the towel. He kisses my forehead, his fingers caressing my back, and it is all I can do not to melt in front of him, not to reach and grab him when he turns around and walks out of the bathroom.

I lean against the bathroom counter and sigh. I'm a mess.

Fuck being in the process of falling for Derek Anderson. I've already fallen for the man I'm working for.

And I know it won't work out.

He'd already made it a point to keep his distance when shit hit the fan with Scott Disrick. How long before that distance comes back? Before he gets tired of smelling me on his clothes and opts to change? Before he does what my ex-fiance Jason did?

Sleeping with me once more, only to wake up and tell me...

No. I'm not putting myself through that.

I run my fingers through my hair, shaking my head.

I dry off, my body still shaking, my visions pure, delicious euphoria. For a second, I let my mind drift, envisioning a world and a future completely with Derek.

I let myself hold onto that vision for a minute...before letting it go.

With a final look in the foggy bathroom mirror, I finish drying myself and leave the bathroom, searching for the nearest clothes.

Once I've wiped the tears from my face, I find a pair of sweatpants and an old sweatshirt within minutes and begin dressing.

Chapter Twenty-One

DEREK

The coffee quickly brewing in the dual-burner is the perfect balance between sweet and dark. There's a basket of muffins done already, and I take a quick step back, admiring my work as I try to fight the immediate yearning that covers my chest like a warm blanket.

The thought of Mia, and the way she submitted to me in my shower...it stirs me.

And I know this is going to be the only time I'm going to get some time with her.

We sure as shit can't do what we're doing now, once we step into the office. Among hundreds of other employees.

God, just one more night, please.

I find my thoughts drifting...before deciding to get some eggs and bacon from the fridge. It's not closed for half a second before I suddenly hear someone scream.

"Mon dieu!"

I glance up. "Shit! June."

My housekeeper.

The retired Frenchwoman, who came to work for me

almost two years ago, clasps a hand over her mouth. It takes several seconds before I realize what she's screaming at.

I'm naked.

In all my Mia delirium, I forgot to get dressed.

"Oh non oh non, non!" she exclaims, still in French as she shakes her head and covers her eyes on the other side of the kitchen.

"June, I couldn't...the coffee...I didn't want to disturb you..."

I can hear her mumbling something again in French, her eyes covered, her hand in an upraised position as I cup my balls in my hand, balancing the bacon and eggs with the other.

"I was going to...I was coming to...I just..." I clear my throat, my voice much more confident, "I'm so sorry, June. I was just trying to make breakfast. For once."

Her hands lower, and even though I can tell she's still blushing, her green eyes look me straight in the eye. "Like that, Mr. Anderson?"

"I didn't know you were home."

"I was...but I wanted to try to get an early start. On the cleaning...and cooking."

I glance at the clock, then back at June. "I kinda wanted to do that myself this morning, June. I don't have that much time, and I..." I glance at the doorway leading to the second floor. "I, uh, sort of have company."

June's eyes widen once more, her blushing growing. "Ah, I see." She squints her eyes at me. "She must be a very special woman. Though cooking like…this is very odd."

I laugh. "Yeah, it is." I place the food on the stove and switch it on, my back turned to June as she continues to mutter something in French.

I turn around. "I'll just be a minute, okay?"

She smiles, nodding, her eyes on the bacon and eggs. She clears her throat, I'm guessing for the courage to say what she's about to say. "I don't mean to invade your personal space, but..." She holds up my cell phone in her hand. "This was ringing a minute ago in the foyer." She grins. "I'm guessing you didn't have any pockets to stow this in this morning."

I glance at my cell phone, then back at her. "Oh, uh...thanks."

"It stopped. But you might want to see who it was. It seemed to be important."

"Thanks, June. I'll get it."

I dart my eyes to the clock, then to the message window that's been showing up all morning.

The message is a simple "Call me" in bold letters. From Ryder.

I sigh, wondering what he wants. With a click of a button, I turn on the stove before finally pressing Ryder's call button.

"Anderson," he answers.

"Hey, Ry." I place the pan on the stove. "I got your message. So...what's up?"

"Jesus, man." I hear Ryder's voice crack. "Where the hell were you? You never miss a call. You usually answer your phone on the first ring. And you're always up earlier than I am, working or stressing out about work or probably trying to pull that perpetual stick out of your ass, I dunno."

"I was trimming my shrubbery," I say, placing some bacon in the pan. "And...I had to get an early start."

"That's it? You were trimming your shrubbery?"

"And I was...eating." I pause, adding in the eggs. "Muffins. Yes. I was eating muffins."

"You were eating muffins and not answering your phone?" He snorts. "Man, those must be some good ass muffins."

I think of Mia. "Ahem. They certainly were."

"Thought so."

I turn around, adding some of the scrambled eggs to the

plate where the bacon lays. "What's up? You mind telling me what you're calling so early for in the first place?

Ryder sighs. "I guess I just wanted to make sure you had a good morning...before I fucked it all up with my terrible news."

"Terrible news?" I glance behind me to find June heading out of the kitchen with a mop in her hand. "Can't get any worse than what's already gone down."

"Oh, yes, it can. I'm sure of it."

I roll my eyes. "Ah, yes. Saving up the suspense again...The oldest Ryder trick in the book. Why don't you just tell me flat-out whatever's got you up this early and save the drama for your girlfriend fanbase, huh?"

A pause follows. For a moment, my brother gets quiet and then says, "This can't get out."

I blink as soon as I hear this, red alert bells going off. "Okay, obviously something's going on. You have my attention."

"Well...It's like this...We got a break in the case on the leak for the Mandy story."

I grab the spatula. "That's good news, right?"

"Yes. It's good news...but...it's also bad news."

I frown, scraping the eggs and bacon onto one of June's exquisite, hand-painted place settings. "Why? What's the mystery? Our leak turn out to be the dude in Accounting? Or...perhaps it was the guy in Legal with the toupee? You know, I never did like him."

"No." A heavy sigh can be heard in the other end. "It's not any of them..."

"Well, who is it, Ry? I've been preparing for this. So, tell me: Which employee is responsible for the leak? And don't leave out any details. I want to hear who it is. I've decided I want every single juicy morsel."

My brother sighs, and it's as if the words are coming out of his mouth in slow motion. "...It's..."

"Just for the love of all things holy, spit it out already."

"It's your assistant...Mia Kamaka."

I don't know what I expected. But in all the universes in all of the time, I never thought my brother would say those two words.

The air seems to instantly suck every available oxygen from my lungs.

It's as if my whole body is frozen in place. Nothing moves —not a single muscle, not an eyelid.

My brain is screaming, but there's no sound coming out of my mouth.

Dumbly, I stare at the plate in my hand.

"What...? What did you just say?"

The world has suddenly stopped. Along with my heart.

Ryder clears his throat. "I said that it's Mia Kamaka. That she was the one responsible for the leak. Look, man...I'm sorry. I know you've had a hard time finding assistants you can trust, and then there was the whole, uh, situation with Mandy, but—"

I drop the plate. "You're lying. That can't be true. No fucking way. That's..." I stop, shaking my head. I turn around and grab for the pan on the stove, but I knock it aside in my clumsiness.

The pan crashes to the kitchen floor, rattling and rolling under the table. The smell of sizzling bacon fills my nostrils. The plate I'd been holding falls to the floor and cracks apart on one of the sharp shards.

I ignore it. "I don't believe that. I don't. It can't be her. She hadn't even started at Hare & Holeton when the Mandy news came out."

Ryder's voice comes in, sounding as if it's coming from another universe. "True...but we think she may be working with an accomplice at the company. We're trying to figure out who, but—" He stops. "I'm so sorry, man. But it is her. And it's not a joke. There are impartial witnesses to this. The guy I hired has all the evidence."

"No." I shove the table aside. "That...That can't be true. I guarantee you it's not true."

"I know, but it is."

I grip the counter so tightly my fingers ache. "No. It's not true. I won't believe it."

"Like I said, there are impartial witnesses, and it's all recorded for purposes of the investigation. The writing was on the wall. Seems it was a setup from the beginning, I guess. Her getting the job, trying to befriend you..."

Memory flashes flood my mind in a torrent.

The way she looked. Her smile. Her flushed cheeks when she gave me the whiskey at Sopra. Her hands. Her hair. Her eyes.

The way she'd wrapped her pretty hands around the bottle, accidentally brushing against my fingers.

Her teasing comments, her laughter, her touch.

The way she looked at me, like she was seeing me. Unmasking me.

The way she'd told me to take what I wanted.

The way she'd stepped forward, closer, into me.

The way she'd felt when I kissed her.

I swallow heavily, her face dancing in my mind. How could it have been her?

Ryder's voice cuts back through again, his words carrying over the speaker like a buzzing in my ears. "...I know you think it's some horrible plot, but it's probably for the best, I think. You don't need any extra drama in your personal life right now with everything you're going through."

"No." I stare at the shard of plate that's resting innocently on my kitchen floor. Once more, the world starts to close in on me. "It's a fucking lie, Ry..."

"Look, man. I know you're upset. I get it—"

"But you don't get it. Because that can't be right..."

"But if you would just listen—"

"I'm telling you: You've got it wrong, and—"

"Dude, I'm not fucking lying here!" Ryder snaps, like I haven't heard in years. "It's true, okay? I don't know any other way to say it. And, man...I'm sorry. I'm sorry that you've been having so much difficulty finding people you can trust."

"Don't you dare patronize me." It's hard to form words through the block in my throat. I ache, searing pain in my chest. Everything seems to be closing in on me—the counter, the table, the plate, the kitchen, the house, and everything else. "I don't care about that at the moment. I just want you to tell me you're mistaken about this. Say you're mistaken. Tell me you've got a bad feeling about it or that it's some type of weird coincidence. Say anything, but don't tell me that it's her."

"I'm sorry." Ryder's tone is neutral, somber.

I try to swallow, but there's a lump in my throat. "It can't be right."

"It...I—" He exhales harshly, his voice low. "Look, I didn't want to say it, but it's the truth: Mia Kamaka is the one responsible for the leak."

"Oh, come on, Ry! That's goddamned absurd. Ridiculous."

"It was her, man. It was her." Ryder's voice is now full of desperation. "She was hired by some private eye guy to follow you. We don't know who hired her. We're still working on that piece of it. But the PI in question is solid. It's all recorded in his files."

A wave of nausea rolls over me. "It can't be true," I whisper, shaking my head.

"It is."

No.

I can feel the blood drain from my face. I can barely hold the phone.

I sit on the edge of the kitchen table. I can feel the tension mounting. I can hardly breathe.

"Dammit, man," Ryder says. "Dammit, this is awful. I'm sorry. I just can't..."

"It's her." I choke back something that feels like a roar. My lungs clench so tightly I think they might shatter. "And you're sure? You're positive?"

"Yes, I'm positive."

I squeeze my eyes shut, let out a heavy breath.

But that makes no sense. I think of that daisy chain smile. The one she wore on her face when she walked by my booth in the corner of the restaurant. That smile.

But that can't be right.

"I'll call you back in a minute." I hang up before he can even reply.

It can't be right.

The phone feels heavy in my hand.

My legs start carrying me before I can stop them. And before I know it, I'm storming towards my bedroom. My steps are quick and jerky, solid. Mentally, I'm already halfway to Hell.

But when I get there, I slam open the door like a white-hot flame.

I don't know what I want.

I don't know what I'm doing.

My heart's in my throat.

Stress is coursing through my veins, burning me up from the inside out. I push open the door to the bedroom, slamming it so hard behind me that it bounces in its frame.

"Mia!" I yell to the room in general and the air in particular. My voice echoes like a gunshot. "Mia!"

I can still feel her warmth in the room, chaotic and intoxicating.

But there's no her.

"Mia!" The raw and thick emotion in my voice echoes again and again.

I'm baring my teeth, practically breathing fire.

Everything's red. All the walls and windows and doorways.

I take a deep breath, but I exhale as if it's a hiss. I take another breath, counting to ten.

She's not there. There's no trace of her.

In fact, it's just my stuff.

The quilt on the bed where she slept last night. The robe she wore, draped over the desk chair. The traces of her perfume on my dresser. The proof of her there. How she was, what she did, how she handled all of it.

I can feel the rip in my soul.

I clench my fists at my sides, staring at the robe that bears her scent. I can feel the blood pounding in my ears, filling my ears.

All those memories...

All those feelings.

And it's all for nothing.

I hear footsteps, a rustle of fabric.

I turn around and find my housekeeper June standing in my doorway, her face void of expression. "Uh, Mr. Anderson?" June asks hesitantly, her lilting voice subdued. "Um, did you still want your breakfast, sir?"

My insides clench painfully. I can barely speak. "No, June. I...don't think so."

"Okay, sir. I understand. I'll be just outside in case you change your mind. By the way, sir..."

"Yeah?"

"You're still unclothed, sir. In case you were wondering..."

"Yeah, June. Thanks. I'll take care of it."

June backs out of the doorway, hesitating when she runs into the doorframe.

I turn away, facing the bathroom door again. The bathroom where just a half an hour ago I brought her to her climax.

I clutch the smooth plastic of my cell phone in my hand, squeezing it so hard it almost snaps.

The truth of it all hits me like a fist to the gut. I start to shake, can barely control the tremors. All the feelings, all the feelings she stirred up in me.

All that she offered and gave me...

And everything about it...it was all a lie.

Steeling my jaw, I head to my bedroom closet, rifling through the many suits there with one hand as the other places my cell back near my ear, dialing Jenny's number.

She picks up in two rings.

"Morning, Derek. And to what do I owe the pleasure of this call?"

"This call isn't really about pleasure, Jen."

"Aw shit, is this about Mia getting drunk last night?" She exhales. "Look, I know we probably shouldn't have invited her out and let her get drunk like that. It's just it had been a tough—"

"Jen, that's not why I'm calling. I—" I pause. "Actually, it kinda is. I want everything you have on her."

"On who?"

"Mia. My new...assistant."

I've known Jenny long enough to know that she's frowning over the phone, those fiery-tinged eyebrows of hers practically sewing together. "Oh, Jesus. Not another assistant...You're not writing her up, are you?"

I take a moment, my jaw still continuing to work. "No. I'm not." I grab the suit I was looking for in the closet off the hanger. "I have something much better in mind."

Chapter Twenty-Two

MIA

Sneaking back into my own apartment isn't easy as I expected it would be.

The building were Tina and I live used to be an old factory. Everything in it makes a sound—small or big. And there are a symphony of them as I try to squeeze in the door just before eight AM after spending the night at Derek's.

It's as if the exposed brick walls, the wooden floors and tight hallways, and the neighbors' clattering all have something to say. "She's back! Mia's back! She's back."

And they're right: I am back.

But a different me is walking back through those damned halls.

Breathing out a sigh tinged with relief and a million other things, I close the front door with a soft click when I hear the sound of a solid footstep.

"Caught you, ya ho."

I spin to find Tina behind me, brown eyes curious and amused, her thin arms crossed across her camisole.

"Babe, sneaking back in after staying out all night..." She

shakes her head with a soft laugh. "Never thought I'd see the day."

I frown, a thousand excuses running through my mind.

"I, uh, went to Happy Hour with some coworkers," I say in a soft half whisper.

"Yah. And then spent the night with that gorgeous, semi-asshole boss of yours." I start to gape but close my mouth when Tina continues. "He texted me."

Okay, now it's my turn to gape. "He what?"

"Your boss. Last night. I'm guessing he grabbed my number from your phone. He just wanted to let me know that he was..." Her gaze roams over me proudly. "…taking good care of you."

Kicking off. my sensible high heels, I clutch my coat around my shoulders, walking farther into the living room. "Uh, yeah, he did."

"Uh huh," Tina says behind me. "I'm sure he did." I hear her footsteps follow. "You didn't even have to break out one of your crystals for serenity or prosperity or whatever. In fact, you haven't broken out any of your funny little rocks since that hard-bodied billionaire came into your life. Coincidence?"

I move towards my bedroom, shucking off clothes as I go, but Tina continues to hover.

I sigh. "I don't know...Maybe...?"

"You're being awfully vague for someone who looks she's been profoundly fucked."

I look up, shocked. And instantly realize my mistake when Tia points at my face. "Ah-ha! So, he did fuck you? Details! Now!"

I start unbuttoning my blouse, stopping when I realize my hands are shaking. I fall back on my bed, face-up, not bothering to hide the turmoil on my face. "Oh God..."

Tina flounces on the bed-top beside me. "I'm sure you said a lot of 'Oh God's' last night, huh?"

I stare at the ceiling, gnawing on my bottom lip. "We didn't...fuck, Tina."

"You didn't?" Her tone is skeptical.

"No, we didn't. But we did do some, um, other things."

"Okay, don't Monica Lewinksy-semantics me. What things?"

I start playing with my hands. "A lot of other...amazing, incredible...mind-blowing things."

"Wow."

"I know." I sit up, swinging my legs over the side of the bed. "But—"

Tina raises a hand. "'But'? Okay, there is no 'but' when you're talking about a man doing amazing, incredible, mind-blowing things to you." She looks at me expectantly. "Please tell me you didn't anything stupid, like..."

"I left," I blurt out.

"Left?!" Tina's brown eyes nearly bulge out of her head. Her dark hair sways as she sits up straight. "After the amazing, incredible, mind-blowing things? What? Why?"

I stand up, running a hand through my wild hair. "Because..." I close my eyes. "'Because I've been through this song and dance before, Tina. I know this song by heart, okay?" I exhale, shoulders sagging as I face her. "Because Derek is an honest-to-goodness billionaire, Tina. And I'm a server without a pot to piss in in Seattle. Without any kind of future."

"Mia, I don't believe that."

"You don't have to. It's been proven already. It's why Jason left me. It's why my parents took his side. I mean, for God's sake, they attended his engagement party to the women he left me for." I shake my head, noticing the cracks in the ceiling, the fractures in the foundation of our apartment building—a reminder of the cracks in the foundation of my relationship with my ex-fiancé, Jason.

Cracks I had ignored until the entire relationship collapsed.

Tina grabs my arm, pulling me towards her. Her gaze searches for mine. "Are you kidding me? You're seriously blaming yourself for what Jason did?"

"I mean, not all of it, but—"

"There are no buts, Mia. You are not at fault for a man making a promise to you and then betraying that promise the second you didn't fall into his little plans. Your parents' plans. You didn't want to be an architect. You want to be a photographer. And if they can't understand and support your wishes, then to hell with them." She blows out a long breath that fills the air in my tiny bedroom. "Look, you want to hear the truth? Jason left you for a bobble-head Barbie-wannabe because he's an insecure man who was threatened by your dreams and your 'out of your league' love. And your parents were so upset that you opted out of attaching yourself to Jason's 'wealth' and 'security' that they abandoned you in times of need. You're not at fault, Mia. You're a better person than they are."

I blink back tears, staring at Tina. "Thank you."

"You're welcome," she says, biting her lip. "Now, give me a little more about the billionaire."

I draw back, the world around me seeming to swim. The tiny room feels denser, the air thicker. "Um, the long and short of it is that I got really drunk last night at Happy Hour. And he was...there. He took me home. Cleaned me up. Put me to bed." A nervous laugh leaves my throat. "And in return, I threw up on him."

"Threw up on him? The same uptight jackass in a suit that you usually seated at Sopra?"

I shake my head with another low laugh. "He's not a jackass. I mean, he was... But I think it's been a front of sorts. He's inquisitive. Introspective. Creative. He-" I scoff softly, shaking my head. "He wanted to be a comic book artist. That's why he got into the publishing industry. He's a fan of spoken word and other arts. He's considerate. Thoughtful. Surprisingly tender..." I trail off.

Tina watches me. "Uh huh. Okay. Wow. Sounds a lot like Jason...not." She stands to gaze down at me. "Mia...Good God, girl. This man sounds made-up."

"He does..." I finish unbuttoning my blouse as I imagine Derek's face.

His ice-blue eyes melting when he looks at me. His lopsided grin and white smile. The hard lines of his body and face, belying his gentle hands.

And touch. And kiss. And mouth.

"He does sound unreal." I stare into space, realizing. "He really is. He's incredible, Tina. Really, he is."

Tina stares at me, a knowing smile on her face. "Then pray-tell, why on Earth did you leave a man like that?"

I look at her, waiting.

"Ah-huh." She smiles widely. "Exactly. I say, go get your man, baby. This one's made for you."

I roll my eyes. "Shut up."

"I love you, girlfriend. But if I can't tell you the truth, who will? You're going to pass up on a man who sounds like a man written in a novel? The ones that make you all hot and bothered and get those little panties of yours wet and—"

"Tina!"

"I'm just saying! You're not going to pass up on this man, are you? He sounds too good to be true!"

He is too good to be true.

"No. I just have to figure some things out." I close my eyes and sigh. "I just...I can't get over what he did after the dinner at Fellows. The way he was acting...the way he just kinda dismissed me after he dropped me off."

"But then he showed up last night to Happy Hour and sorta rescued you? Picked your drunk ass up and cleaned up your vomit and, ultimately, made you orgasm until you passed out?"

I wince. "Uh yeah. That was pretty much the gist of it. Though, it didn't happen exactly in that order."

Tina crosses her arms, a scowl on her adorable face. "He's a man. A stubborn man. A rich man. A complicated man, wanted by the press and women all across the city. He'd be a miracle if he got everything right the first time. Cut him slack, why don't ya? He clearly cares about you. And if he's showing up for you like this, he clearly wants whatever you two have got going to work. Look, I know you, Mia. You're a tough nut to crack. You're a tough cookie to break. But if you keep closing your heart to love, you'll just keep repeating the same fucked-up patterns because of Jason. You're not going to escape this heart-breaking pain you're living in...unless you break down that wall. And trust me: Jason Doughty isn't fucking worth it. So, please...Stop being so stubborn. And let this rich and not-so-uptight bloke in."

I groan, sinking my face into my hands. "I know you're right. I just...I can't handle another betrayal like I had with Jason."

"I get it. But, sweets, I've never seen you like this. So conflicted and torn. Squeezing your heart so tight until you practically can't breathe." Tina slips her hands into my own. She looks in my eyes. "You've been fighting your way out of what happened with Jason for two years now. Don't you want to move on with your life? Find out if the life you dream of, the love you deserve really is out there for you? Don't you think you've earned your own happy ending? Don't you think?"

My eyes snap to hers and I don't know if I can speak, I don't know if I can breathe.

But I know she's right. Tears slip down my face as I nod and choke out, "I deserve better. And I'm..." I pause, swallowing as I look into her eyes. "I'm ready to try. I really am."

"Good. That's what I want to hear." She slaps my knee. "Now, get dressed and get out of here! Hopefully, you can continue some of those amazing, incredible, mind-blowing things with your possible happy-ending man on his office desk."

I swat at her, a giggle bubbling up. "Okay, okay. Office sex aside, I do need to be in the office shortly."

I check the time on my phone before rushing to the bathroom as Tina calls out, "G'head! Wash all those amazing, incredible, mind-blowing things off your beautiful skin. Start with a clean slate, baby."

I laugh, turning on the water and stepping into the steam-filled bathroom.

'Go get my man.'

I was starting to think, that maybe—just maybe—I was liking the sound of that.

Chapter Twenty-Three

MIA

Arriving to work in record time, I make my way towards the tall glass behemoth of a building that is the downtown Seattle headquarters of Hare & Holeton, Derek's publishing company.

Dressed in a new set of clothes, a black-trimmed, fitted skirt with a sexy, low-back blouse, I can still feel remnants of this morning's shower session with Derek still lingering in my hair and on my skin, and I smile.

Despite the nerves in my belly, I throw my shoulders back as I take the elevators up to the top floor, more determined than ever to make amends after my talk with Tina.

I owe Derek an apology. Or three.

I may have some deep-rooted issues to work through, but in the light of a new morning, I'm hoping I can push past one or two.

When I reach the floor for Hare & Holeton, I head for the break room first instead of my cubicle, needing the coffee more than a moment of peace.

I place my laptop case on top of the counter, turning to grab a new mug when my hand hits someone else's.

I glance up and into a face almost identical to Derek's, except for the darker hair and amber-colored eyes, his cheekbones and jaw even more pronounced.

He smiles, the hint of a dimple appearing. "Good morning."

"Uh, good morning to you, too. Sorry about that. I wasn't watching—"

The man shakes his head a little, his dark silky, full hair brushing his collar. "No, my fault. I snuck up on you." He smiles. "I was trying to snag some of the simple syrup for my coffee there at the counter."

"I don't blame you." I move a few feet to give him room, jerking my chin in the direction of the box. "This break room has better add-ons than Starbucks. And seeing as how we're in the birthplace of overpriced coffee, that says something."

He laughs softly, sexy and low. "Ah. So, you're not a fan of the giant coffee chain, I take it?"

"I prefer better quality coffee."

"'Quality coffee'? Are you actually dissing Starbucks to a man born and raised in The 206?" he teases.

I cock my hip and put my arms across my chest. "I gotta call it like I see it. Where I'm from, we have the best coffee in the world. It's called Kona coffee, and if I hadn't moved out of the area, I'd still be drinking it every morning...and doing everything in my power to avoid that brown-water you all call coffee here in this city."

"Now, that brings up an intriguing quality about you, Miss Beautiful and Smart Businesswoman who doesn't like giant bean-brewed coffee. Where exactly is 'where you're from,' might I ask?"

"Originally from Maui. When I say Maui, I mean...the actual Maui, the island itself. Wailuku, specifically. I moved to Seattle only about six months ago after leaving my first job out of undergrad. All to wind up in a city with second-rate coffee where it rains most days." I shrug. "I'm not as used to it as you East Coasters."

"'East Coasters'?" He laughs hard, his deep voice echoing. "I've never heard a single soul call Seattle the East Coast." He opens the coffee pot and grabs himself a few tablespoons of the pale-brown liquid, placing it on the counter.

"I'm from Hawaii. All you mainlanders are the 'East Coasters.'" I pretend to glare at him.

He grins, opening the pack of sweetener, then dumping a few heaping teaspoons into the cup. "What if I took offense to the term 'Mainlander'?"

"You can take offense to whatever you want. That's the name this side of the Pacific has given you."

He slaps his hand on the counter and pretends to cringe, eyeing me. "So, a vagabond and a coffee snob who's not the biggest fan of the cynical, overpriced, service-driven monster that is Starbucks in Seattle..." He shakes his head. "We'll make a convert out of you yet. I, on the other hand, am a firm believer in the monster that is Starbucks. But only if it's in Manhattan."

I laugh out loud. "Wow. Mainland snobbery isn't just a myth. It's actually an actual thing."

"Har har." He turns back to the case containing the sugar, grabbing a few more spoonfuls of the white powder. "As I was saying, a woman so completely conflicted about her coffee preferences is a woman who I must know more about. But alas, I've got a meeting to hurry to." He turns, his blue eyes twinkling as he looks over his shoulder at me. "Nice meeting you, Coffee Snob."

"Nice meeting you too, Mainland Snob."

He chuckles, heading out of the break room and jogging down the hallway to the elevator.

Likeable. Handsome. Flirtatious.

Yup. I was sure I officially met one of Derek's brothers.

Jenny was right; if they're anything like Derek, each one of them must be a walking wet dream.

And still, well-mannered coffee guy is no match for the man I kissed this morning. The man who tore down barriers inside me I didn't even know were there.

The man I might just be falling in love with.

At the thought of him, I turn and grab the laptop case and my coffee, heading for my cubicle to scrounge up some courage to do what's needed.

I take a deep breath.

Rounding the corner and stepping inside my cubicle, I stand rooted to the spot, coming face-to-face with a woman I've only met once.

A woman with distinct strawberry blonde hair who I instantly recognize from last night.

"Well, look who finally showed up."

Seated in my office chair, Alexa Bullock warmly smiles, staring at me a beat too long through her glasses, one hand on the armrest of my desk chair, the other gesturing her finger in the air. "I guess all that talk about how you were a hard worker is not as correct as I heard. You barely made it to your desk on time."

I swallow, feeling a curl of alarm snake down my spine. "Well, yes, that's almost true. It's only a few minutes till nine." I turn to glance at the clock on the wall before turning back. "But you were certainly right about something else...This is my desk." I look over her shoulder. "And now I'm left to wonder why you're sitting at it."

"Your desk?" She scoffs. "Sweetie...you haven't even been here two full weeks, and already you've claimed it as yours. Cute."

Her blonde hair is in a tight bun. Her clothing is impeccable, her makeup precisely done. And her attitude toward me is that of a true snob.

I knew this woman was not my ally the moment we met. I was right.

But what scares me more is how comfortable she feels in my seat. She has the look of a person who knows something I don't.

I try to brush off the nagging sensation that comes over me. "Yes, my desk." I rest the laptop backpack on the desk, close the pack and then slide open my laptop. "Now, if you'll excuse me, I have to get back to work. I complete tasks better sitting up. From what I hear, you work better off the floor."

"Rawr!" she chuckles. "Kitten's got claws. I bet you thought those claws had a good hold in Derek. Fortunately, for me, that's not the case."

I stiffen, my body tightening, the hairs on the nape of my neck standing up. "What? What do you mean that's not the case? What-what's going on? Did I miss something?"

"Hmm, you might want to take this up with Mr. Anderson when he gets back to his office. He'll be delighted to explain things to you. You know...this being your last day and all."

"What?" The word barely comes out. My mouth is that of a fish.

I can't think. I can't move.

I can't breathe.

I can only stare.

My chest is tight with dread.

Eyes wide, I can feel my mouth move, but each syllable stutters out like a car out of fuel. "Last day?? Last day what? Why am I—what are you saying?"

The woman smirks, tapping on the armrest of my desk chair. "Oh, c'mon. Don't make this any more difficult than it has to be, honey. You're already done here..." She shrugs. "Sorry. So, you might as well just slink back to where you came from and let me take my place. Now, be a doll and pull that chair over to your desk so I can sit down. I have a meeting on the other side at ten."

My chest is pounding.

My stomach is twisting.

I have to force my brain to focus, to think.

I quickly close my laptop and grab the case, ignoring Alexa as I turn. I'm down the hallway in seconds, moving fast.

Coffee mug in hand, I don't slow down until I'm at the front of his office. And even then, I barely have enough time to compose myself.

I push in, slamming the door behind me.

I have to swallow to pull in a deep breath of air as I wait for Derek to look my way, his eyes locked onto his tablet, focused on whatever he's doing.

I drop the bag on my desk, my voice barely above a whisper as I seethe, "You mind telling me what the hell is going on?"

He finally looks up, eyes innocent and inexplicably cold. He sets his tablet down.

"Hey, come in. Have a seat. Don't mind knocking, I guess. Well, it doesn't really matter at this point, now, does it? You're not going to be here very long anyway."

My head spins. "Have you gone mentally insane in the last few hours? You're firing me right now? For—for walking out of your house without saying goodbye? Are you that petty, Mr. Anderson? Or are just that much of an ass that you don't care how stupid you look?"

Derek's icy gaze is unwavering as he looks me over from head to toe. He doesn't even offer a response.

"Playing Mr. Non-Talkative Jackass isn't going to work this time, Derek." I throw down my mug. "I know you better than that...Tell me: What the hell is going on? Why are you doing this to me?" I swallow. "To us?"

Derek's nostrils flare, his large fingers flex. His voice is a dangerous growl from where he sits. "I could ask you the same question, Ms. Kamaka. And technically, I'm not firing you. Alexa is. And by the way you stormed in my office, I'm gathering that that's exactly what she already did." He stands, and not a single wrinkle shows in the tailored suit he's wearing. "Let me rephrase. I could ask you why you felt the need to come here and make a scene, hmm? When you were never really an employee here..." His stare hardens at me. "Just a spy, sent to follow my every move."

I'm breathing hard, my pulse pounding. Blinking in surprise, I swallow again, what I'm about to say sticking in my mouth. "I...don't know what you're talking about," I finally manage.

"Bullshit." He takes a step closer, a hand coming down on his desk. "Tell me: When did you decide to completely fuck me over?" He takes another step closer to me, his demeanor turning frigid, making the room even smaller than it already was. "Was it the first time we had a real conversation in Sopra? Was it the first time you kissed me? Or was it when spread your legs for me and you rode my face like a stallion after dinner at Fellows?"

He pauses, a sneer coming to his face as he stares down at me. "Tell me when you decided that I was an easy mark, Ms. Kamaka." He keeps walking, strands of his caramel-brown hair falling over his face.

With the city of Seattle as his backdrop, he stands tall in the center of the room behind the wood inlaid desk his company's logo—an eagle hovering over a book—carved into it. His voice is steady when he speaks, each word echoing with an ominous pressure.

And he's so beautiful that it nearly breaks my heart.

The pain in his blue eyes is palpable from this distance.

I stare back at him, my body trembling from his cold gaze and tone.

And despite the fact that his voice is nothing but venom, all I want to do is run to him and hold him close.

I open my mouth to speak, and my heart falters. "I was never going to follow through with it," I choke out. And then I remember. "That photo contest I told you about. It—I needed...I was just looking for a job. And this was an opportunity. I swear I didn't know it would be you..."

He raises an eyebrow, the fire in his eyes burning through the distance between us.

His chest is heaving as he stops about ten feet from me.

"Short of finding another reason to slither your way into my life, Ms. Kamaka, I'm afraid the answer to that is clear: I'm a very easy mark. You're right. You played me. You showed me that I was right to be the person I've been all these years. Distant...Cold..." Derek turns, the color of his eyes darkening, turning almost cerulean with his rage. "Did you know that you had my attention, Mia?" His head cocks to the side. "That you'd become the touchstone I needed to make me see a future better than the one I envisioned for myself? Did you know that I was falling for you...the way I thought you were falling for me?"

His stare stays fixed on my face, singeing me with a blue, blazing flame.

I'm holding my breath in my chest, my stomach hurting—as much from the hurt in his voice as the coldness in his expression.

"Did you know anything about me at all?" he growls.

My voice is tiny. "I do...And you know me too. That's why I need you to believe me...I know why you're doing this."

"And why is that, Ms. Kamaka?"

I wipe my hands down my skirt, stopping at my thighs. My bottom lip quivers. "It's because it's easier to believe the worst about people. It's easier to never let your guard down. It's easier to keep them at a distance because you're afraid to get hurt." My hands find hips, my voice trailing off. I swallow hard, fighting the tears pricking at the backs of my eyes. "It's much easier to do all of that...than to admit that you might actually need a person you can't control. It's much easier than admitting that you can't breathe, can't function, can't think at all without them. Because if you admit that, then you…you're admitting that they own you now. And you hate being owned." I take a deep breath. "The way you own me. The way you've owned me from the very second we met."

The words fall out of me, my eyes squeezing closed as I move toward him. He doesn't move. And when I finally breach the distance between us, I dare a look up at him, my eyes blurry with unshed tears. "You're inside of me, Derek Anderson. You've been inside of me, in my head, in my body..." My lip wobbles. "In my heart since the minute I saw you."

Biting my lip until I taste blood, I look up at him. "I don't know how to do any of that—breathe, function, think—without you. I don't want to do it without you." I raise a hand to cup his jaw. He's like a stone statue, his face harsh as I brush my thumb against his cheek. His eyes are wet.

"I don't want…I can't…"

His focus drops to my fingers, and I find myself anticipating his touch, his skin against mine. When it never comes, my throat goes dry. God. I squeeze my eyes and shake my head, my vision blurring with tears. "I don't want you to hurt like this. I don't want to lose you."

A silence draws to a standstill, the heated air between us desperate.

And then his eyes drop to mine, heavy and perfect. I lean in, my lips just below the warmth of his. They are trembling.

"What would you have me do?" he whispers.

My stomach flutters at his touch. Flutters at the need in his voice.

And I'm sobbing as I nod my head. "Please...Please fuck me. Please just…"

His eyes are still cold—still angry, but it makes no difference as he pulls me before I can say another word, and my knees turn to butter as Derek lifts me in his arms.

Chapter Twenty-Four

EREK

I don't think. I don't hesitate.

I just grab her. My arms wrap around Mia's body, and I pull her to my chest. I crash my mouth down against hers, pushing her curvy body against my desk.

I kiss her...like I feel. Deep and desperate. Hungry.

My hands tangle in her hair, and with Mia Kamaka's lips on mine…It's the first thing I've ever experienced that can compete for the world's Sexiest Moment title.

I've been with my share of women...despite what my brothers think.

Beautiful women. Intellectual women.

Women who dressed the "right way." Talked the "right way." Walked the "right way."

And none of them can hold a candle to this woman.

Mia.

A woman, who to the naked eye, is wrong for me in every way. A threat to my business, to my company, to my sanity, to my…everything.

And yet I need her more than I've ever needed anything.

My parents had abandoned me and my brothers long

before the car crash that took their lives. And as the second eldest, all my life, I've done everything to keep us afloat, to keep the family together, to keep the company from crashing and burning from the inside.

And in doing it all, I convinced myself that I didn't need anybody else. That I never wanted anybody.

Until her.

My hands are surprisingly steady as I slowly pull them down to her waist. Around her sides. Her breasts. Her thighs beneath the floaty skirt she's wearing.

I raise my eyes to hers, my lungs seizing as I stare down into their depths.

Her mouth is red from my kiss, her chin and cheeks wet from tears that have fallen down her beautiful face.

I kiss them. I kiss them all.

With Mia's ass in my hands, I carry her over to my office desk. Placing her down, I lean forward and kiss her again before knocking aside the stacks of contracts, pens and papers.

I pull back, a heat forming under my hands.

"Spread your legs, Mia."

Her eyes fall to the space between our bodies. She licks her lips and underneath her skirt, her beautiful thighs come into view.

I reach down between them, my eyes drinking in the sight of her. Her lips are glistening, her face is flushed as I grab a hold of her underwear.

"Keep your eyes on me, baby." I lift my gaze, locking it on hers. "And don't move. If you move, I won't be able to control myself." I narrow my eyes, my mouth a firm line. "And that would be a shame."

Her eyes blink, but they don't leave mine until they fall to the fabric in my hand.

She backs up against the desk, her arms braced on either side of her. Her head cocks to the side, her gaze flicking across my body, burning a path of goosebumps down my chest and arms.

"Derek…" she says softly.

"I told you to keep your eyes on me."

Her gaze comes back to mine, her lips spreading softly under her breath. "I am...I will."

"You will what?"

She swallows. Her gaze falls to my crotch, slowly traveling up to mine again. "Keep my eyes on you, that's all."

I smile. "That's smart, Mia."

I don't have time to contemplate my response before she drops her eyes, her hands coming to my hips. I raise an eyebrow. "What are you doing?"

"I…" She swallows, licking her lips and losing her train of thought. "I can't…I can't wait. I'm going to…I want to…"

I wait.

"I want to touch you," she breathes.

I shake my head. "I haven't yet given you that right. And you agreed not to move."

My fingers tangling in the fabric of my suit, I roll onto my knees and come up over her, something dark and deep and sinfully delicious rolling through my veins.

Flicking her skirt forward, I gaze at her pussy, already so wet and warm. I take one finger and lace it down the edge of her folds until she gasps.

I place my fingers squarely against her flesh. "Do you remember what I told you was forbidden?"

She bites her lip. "To touch?" she whispers.

I nod.

"You were very clear."

I take my finger and slide it up and down her wet, delicious flesh. "Do you want to touch?"

She shivers, her lips parting as she closes her eyes. "Please, Derek. I wasn't trying to...I swear it. I was just…I was…"

I lean in, tracing my lips over her jaw, down over her neck.

My teeth scrape against her throat, drawing a moan from her lips.

"Did you want to touch me?"

Her head tilts backward. Her lips are parted, her eyes fluttering shut as her hips undulate. "Yes…I was just…"

"Shhh…no excuses. Just your admission." I put my finger to her lips. "I want to hear it. I want to hear you admit that you want to touch me."

She nods, closing her eyes. "I do…I do want to touch you. Please, Derek. Please let me. I promise, I won't move."

I smile, moving my finger to her mouth. Her legs folding around my arm, I let her suck my finger inside her mouth as her lips come to rest on the sensitive skin of my palm.

Her eyes flutter open, locking on mine. Every part of her body is limp and still. Her shoulders fall forward, her eyelids heavy and sated as I pull my tailored suit pants down along with my boxer-briefs. Her arms are tight around the edge, her knees hitched up, legs strewn wide as I step between them.

"Hold onto the desk, baby," I growl, my fingers enclosing around my already-hard cock. "You wanted me to fuck you. And now you're getting your wish."

Her eyelashes flutter open, and she raises her arms over the desk, gripping the metal edge. Her jaw and lips are parted, her expression completely open and surrendered.

I stop, only for a second, before pulling back and plunging deeply into the absolute heaven that is Mia.

She arches and gasps, her hands moving over the desk.

Nothing is slow about this fucking. Nothing is tender.

Nothing is gentle.

It's the fucking we know we both need. The only kind that comes from the raw hunger that has savaged the two of us, every second of every day, since the moment we met.

It is a fucking of possession. Of ownership. Of need.

Of desperation.

"Yes..." she breathes, her eyes closed, her hands gripping the desk tightly. "Derek..."

My mouth meets hers, the kiss the necessary fuel we both need to keep moving against the friction of her body against mine. The heat of our skin, the slickness of my body against hers, the way our bodies completely meld and lock together drives me wild.

Being inside of Mia...

It's home.

And I take her there. I take us both there.

The sound of my body slapping against hers, the way she cries out in need and desire, the way her nails scratch against the desk, the way her hips rise against mine.

It's everything I was missing.

And everything I know I'll never have again.

"Derek..." she whimpers, her fingers gripping the edge of the dark wood like a lifeline. "Oh, God. You feel so good."

I can't look at her. I can't stare at her face.

It's too much.

Her eyes beg me for more. Her body seeks release and satisfaction.

And mine...mine is crying.

It's telling me to grab her tight. It's telling me to claim her.

To make her mine.

But I can't.

"Oh my God...Derek..."

With my name coming off her lips so softly, I almost come undone.

It's a cry of longing, a cry of need.

And it sets the sensation in my body on fire. Especially when I feel Mia come, giving herself over to me in only the way that she can – the only way she would ever give herself over to me.

With complete abandon.

With complete trust.

With complete loving.

It's enough to push me over my own edge, and I shudder, my body rocking against hers, completely undone with the last few thrusts of my hips – the last few thrusts of my heat against her pussy, the last few thrusts of my body within her.

I'm done.

I know it.

I feel it.

I know I won't be able to get out without ripping my heart out of my chest and leaving it behind to bleed.

And I do.

I can't take Mia with me. Not after...this.

Instead, I grab her face and stare down at her as I finally come down from our insatiable high, pulling her into my arms and claiming every part of her.

She snuggles against my chest, and I trace my finger over her lips before pushing a lock of hair off her eyes.

"Aargh…" she exhales, her eyes fluttering closed as she reaches upwards. "I could kiss you…but I know the rules." She trembles. "You feel so…" she exhales. "And that—that was amazing…"

I run my hands up her trembling arms, bringing her hands down and untangling her fingers from my hair. "I thought you were supposed to follow the rules," I whisper, kissing her knuckles.

She nods, pulling her lips away from my stained hand, licking her own. "I was. But then you pushed me to a place where there are no rules. Where if it's right, it feels right. So..." She searches my face. "Should we…take this to my apartment?"

And there it is.

The question after sex.

The question no one wants to know the answer to.

The question that means she's interested in something more.

I know this question.

And I know what it would have been...

Until now.

I bring her hands to my lips. I kiss them before holding against my chest, my body nearly failing me as I straighten and take a step back.

"I'm...sorry, Mia. I can't. I can't go to your apartment."

"Why?" She laughs lightly. "Has no one at Hare & Holeton ever heard of remote work?"

She reaches for me, her hands curling around the back of my neck, before I break away. Her hands freeze as soon as she sees the look on my face.

"No," I say, my voice gritty as I pull away from her grip, my body screaming not to. "I can't...because you're still fired."

She blanches. "What? But… this... We..."

"Said goodbye," I interject, my throat nearly squeezing my chest as I pull my pants up, hastily tucking myself back in. "And goodbye is not easy, Mia. But it's…best." I break off. "It's best for both of us, of course."

I can see her processing the words, but I can't watch.

I can't watch the pain and the raw devastation that comes with the replay of what just happened.

"Best for both of us?" she repeats, her panic obvious.

I straighten the collar of my shirt, my shirt that smells like her skin...and I can't help but wince.

I nod, unable to speak. Because the truth is that it's not best for either of us.

It's the absolute worst. And so is the timing when I hear a knock on the opaque glass door.

"Mr. Anderson?"

I stiffen, my eyes darting over to Mia. She's no longer leaning against the desk. "Yes?" I call out.

"Your meeting is about to start, sir. Do you want me to let them in the conference room?"

"Yes," I grit out, my chest tightening. "I'll be there in a moment. Thank you, Alexa."

"Yes, sir."

As soon as she's gone, Mia speaks up, her voice weak. "I guess that's my cue to go."

"I think…" I look at her. "I think you should. We should. We just… I just don't know what to say right now."

"You don't have to say anything. You've said enough already." She straightens her skirt, before fixing her blouse. "I appreciate your honesty. But fuck you for not lying to me instead."

I don't say anything else. I don't need to.

Mia's already gathering her stuff, her body shaking as she gathers her belongings and puts them in her bag. "I'll see myself out." Her voice cracks. "Have a nice life, Derek."

I open my mouth to respond, but there's nothing more I can say.

Especially when she opens the door.

"Goodbye, Mia," I say, after a beat.

But she's already gone.

The facade I've put on fades the minute she's out of my sight.

Dizziness rolls over me, and I reach for the desk.

Sitting heavily in my chair, I steady myself, my heartbeat slowing as it breaks apart into pieces.

It's the first time in my life that I'm not sure I can put it back together.

Chapter Twenty-Five

MIA

The next few days without Derek feel like an eternity.

A mix of emotions rage within me every time I hear his name, which seems to be a lot with the publicity around his ex-escort girlfriend still making headlines in the media—the frenzy only heightened by his Tyson-like punch to Scott Disrick, another one of the biggest names in local publishing.

A small severance package—courtesy of Jenny and Hare & Holeton—arrive two days after my firing, and still I can't pull myself out of the craptastic funk that has come over me ever since I left Derek's office, heartbroken, confused and completely in pieces.

Aside from spending time on Shelly's portfolio like I promised, I spend most of the time home alone, taking nothing but sleeping in as an answer.

On the morning of Derek-less day number four, Christina bursts into my bedroom to the tune of "Show Me the Meaning of Being Lonely" by the Backstreet Boys playing in the background. She lumbers in as if entering a nuclear waste zone, stepping over the piles of calming crystals and discarded Doritos bags, a huge smile on her face.

"I've found it!"

"What?" I ask, rolling over to find more foiled bags next to me in bed. I groan.

"A beach photo shoot location for Shelly."

I blink, pressing the palm of my hand on my forehead. "I'm sorry, what? You found a beach photo shoot?"

She whips out a sheaf of papers in front of my face. "Here. I've found more than ten venues that are interested in shooting her portfolio."

I grab the papers from her and skim through them, my eyes glazing over. "It looks like…" I glance over the first few lines, taking in the words. I sigh, shaking my head as I look up at my best friend. "It looks like you're taking pity on me."

Christina frowns. "What? Why?"

"Because my heart's been shattered all week. And you know I need a do-over."

"Oh… oh." Christina's frown deepens. "I'm sorry! I wasn't thinking." I stare at her, and Tina gives up. "Okay, so yes, that's exactly what I'm doing. But you just look so...so sad. I felt like I had to do something," she explains.

I let my gaze drift over to the window where I see a chunk of the Seattle skyline peeking through the grape vines surrounding the building opposite my apartment. "Would it be terrible if I came to the shoot in this?" I glance down at my outfit—the same t-shirt and yoga pants I've been wearing for three days straight.

"That's better than what I was planning for you to show up in, which is a cat lover sweatshirt and sweatpants." She pauses, staring at me like she's trying to figure me out. "But yeah, you should maybe make an effort. Look at you. You're skin and bone."

I mumble a 'thank you' and start rearranging the paperwork Christina brought over before snatching a Dorito bag, shaking my head when she hands me her now-empty cup of Starbucks.

"Okay, well...enough of this. We've got a photo session to plan," she says, crouching to perch on the edge of my bed.

"I am so sorry. I've been a crappy best friend lately."

"Hey. What happened to that optimism I used to know and love?"

"It's all trapped in one of my fluorite crystals." I crack a smile. "Anyway, I've got some time before I'm supposed to pick up my camera from the store."

Tina gasps. "The camera? That Canon EOS you wanted to help you win The Visions Collective photo contest?"

"Yup." I fling the covers back from my bed. "The one that's due in three days." I exhale. "That severance package from Derek's company was enough to cover the deposit and the rest of the monthly payment."

"So…I guess this means you're officially a fully-funded photographer now. You've got all of the gear and the perfect camera to shoot with. Looks like you got everything you wanted after all."

"Yep. I guess so." I try to smile but can't.

"That's great, Mia. Seriously great. I'm so happy for you," she says, tossing an arm around my shoulders. "You're going to win that damn contest, I know it. And when you do, you'll come back to Sopra to tell our dumb-ass manager Jerry to stick his job where the sun don't shine."

"I will. I promise. As soon as I win," I say with more gusto than I feel, trying to sound as optimistic as she is.

"Okay, deal. I'll keep my fingers crossed while we're in between shoots," she says, leading me to my door. "Now, let's get you to the beach. Then you can kick your feet up and work on a seductive series of shots for your portfolio. Oh, or maybe—"

"Let's just go. I could use a break from this apartment. You know, to stop being reminded that I've been living off cheesy snacks and leftover beer in my fridge for the past few days."

"I wasn't going to remind you of that," she says, pausing in the doorway to my apartment.

I roll my eyes. "Try not to think too hard about it. Anyway, I'm gonna go pack up my camera and get ready."

"Yes! Oh, and please, for the love of Aaron Carter, turn off that music and get your butt in the shower first. You've got orange Doritos dust all over your hands and fingers and, quite frankly, nobody wants to see it."

"I don't."

"That's exactly what I mean, Mia. Now go pack. I'll see you in twenty. Oh, and Mia?" she says, turning back to face me. "It's good to see you smile again. I think you're going to have a great time today."

"I know, I know."

I wave goodbye, closing the door behind me.

Heading back to my bedroom, I snap off the lights and flop down on my bed.

But my thoughts and heart are elsewhere.

I stare up at the ceiling, my eyes wide, and my mind and heart lost in the wreckage of where I used to be.

I can't find a place for them anymore.

I can't remember who I used to be.

The universe has thrown all of its cards in the air, and there's no one for me to point a finger at but myself. Navigating to the Chamber of the Arts event site, I try to remember that feeling I had while ensconced in those four walls.

I try to remember the joy, the passion, the driving hunger for my art that had flowed through my veins.

And I almost manage to...

Until I see a photo of him.

The picture gallery from the night of the CoTA event

Scowling, I try to stop my eyes from lingering on the

picture, but each time I'm unsuccessful. Derek is just as gorgeous in the flesh and blood as he is in a high-res image. And every time I see his face, my heart breaks a little more.

Tina's right.

I've got to snap out of this. It's all I can think. Snap out of this. And move on.

Forcing myself to tear my eyes away from Derek's handsome face, I drag myself out of bed, heading to my bathroom.

I stand under the stream of water.

And keep standing there.

I lean away from the spray, watching the steam overtake me, giving me the sense of a misty, intangible shroud.

The water trickles down my arms, over my shoulders, across my chest and back.

I run my hands over my face, hoping to wash his picture, his face, his hands, and our time together off my skin, but it doesn't work.

His scent is so deeply ingrained into every cell of my being, it's under every one of my nails, behind my eyelids, and woven into the heartbeats he's been stealing over the past few months.

Stealing right out of my chest.

The water's almost cold by the time I turn the faucet off, my body shivering from inside out as I wrap a towel around my body and slowly walk to my bedroom.

Drying off, I don't bother to look at my reflection in the mirror.

It will only be a reminder of what I've lost…of what was never really mine to begin with.

I throw on clothes, make-up and quickly dry my hair before throwing it up into a ponytail.

A knock sounds on the apartment front door.

With no energy to go to the living room and open it, I yell "Come in!"

I hear the door creak open, and I fully expect Tina to

come barging in, telling me that I look like a drenched zombie and ask if I'm looking for brains.

But I hear nothing.

No feet pad across the hardwood floor.

No human voices inside my apartment.

No movement of any kind.

No sound of the door clattering against the wall.

Curious, I clutch my towel tighter, and head towards my bedroom door, turning the corner, only to find someone that's not Tina on the other side.

The woman standing at my apartment threshold with her hand still on the doorknob is instantly recognizable.

She's not the one I expected to find, but I can't say I'm the least bit surprised.

With thick dark hair and long legs and a face that can make angels weep with jealousy, the woman is a sight to behold, more so in the flesh than any image on a screen.

And there she stands, before me, at my door…obviously waiting for me.

A woman whose face, from all the articles and social media posts, is nearly impossible to forget.

"Mia," she says in a throaty, husky voice. “Are you Mia Kamaka?”

Her voice ignites an avalanche of memory and heartache and insecurity…all tumbling through me, one after another.

"Hello," I say dumbly. "It's...Mandy, isn't it?"

Derek's ex-girlfriend Mandy walks towards me, a coy smile lighting up her face.

Chapter Twenty-Six

EREK

"Mr. Anderson...Mr. Anderson!"

I look up.

"Is there anything else I can get for you, sir?" The waitress waits patiently for me to give her my order.

It's the first time I've been back at Sopra since that night I walked out with Mia.

Since she walked out of her server job and right into my life, fucking it up...and making it marvelous at the same time.

A round of mused, tender laughter echoes around the restaurant, and I dip my head, hoping no one will notice me.

I shake my head, taking in the mug of coffee she's holding in front of me. "Just this, thanks," I say as I take a sip of it, wishing it were whiskey.

She's young and pretty, with a mass of curly blond hair.

She seems to be the only waitress actually working in this place. I'm pretty sure she was brought in to replace Mia.

It would be a nice evening...if everything didn't remind me of her.

The January Seattle evening weather tonight was hotter than usual, and I've been sitting inside the restaurant, taking the air conditioning. Rocks, blues and reds are playing in the background, and the candlelit tablecloths only make the fact that I've been eating alone at the table that much more apparent.

I glance at my watch, groaning at myself.

"I'll take your food order in a couple of minutes."

I look up when the waitress nods, catching the way she checks out the scene.

I wouldn't even be here if Scott Disrick's people didn't call my office, setting up a surprise meeting with their boss.

I still can't believe he wants a re-do after that punch.

I guess I should be grateful.

Despite recent events, business at Hare & Holeton is booming. And the extra publicity from the Mandy scandal isn't hurting any.

Our IPO has been delayed a month or so, but we have every intention of being ready for the market by the end of this year, with record-breaking profits.

The company's never been better.

So why does it feel like none of it matters anymore? Why do I feel like my life is in a downward spiral?

"Can I get you anything else?" the waitress asks, causing me to look up.

"Nah, thanks. This is perfect for now."

She smiles at me, then turns and walks to the front of the restaurant. I watch her go, wondering if she's half as clumsy or as witty as a waitress as Mia once was.

The thought causes me to frown.

I shake my head. Even thinking about her makes me want to drink.

I take another sip of the coffee, an irk of self-pity attacking me when a hand sits a glass on my table. I glance up ready to stand and greet Scott, only to realize I'm not looking into the face of the CEO of Bella Publishing.

I'm looking into the face of the COO...

Of my own company.

In a suit the color of used coal, my cousin Killian stares back at me.

His broad arms tense by his sides as he takes a large seat, not saying a word to me.

I set my coffee mug down hard, the clink of porcelain against porcelain and the resulting echo making him tip his chin in my direction.

It's the face-to-face I've been avoiding for weeks. And I guess I can't avoid it any longer.

I sit. "Killian..."

He raises a chocolate-colored brow. "Derek. Good to see you. Been a while."

"I guess so. I didn't realize I'd just run into you."

Conversation flits around us, the smell of tomato sauce and cinnamon wafting by our table.

"Looks like you've been here awhile, though. I used to see you in here a couple of times when I've come in for lunch. Haven't seen you in a while. Guess you go out for dinner."

I look him over.

I guess he's here to do damage control.

"Perhaps. Or maybe I just don't like frequenting places where known liars like to congregate."

Killian smiles, a sad, slight grin pulling at his lips. "As good a reason as any."

I lift my brow in response, not saying anything back for a moment, then dip my chin. "What are you doing here?"

"I came here to see you."

I narrow my brow, trying not to get angry. "Well, as you can see, I'm in the middle of a business meeting that's about to start."

"You are." Killian looks at me, his voice as stern as his expression is hard. "With me."

I cross my arms over my chest, glancing all around. He's not making a lot of sense. "I don't get it."

"Scott's not coming, Der. I mean, c'mon. Did you really think he was going to meet back up with the guy who punched him before he could even dig into his sea scallops and the roasted duck?"

I nod, glancing down at the table. "Shit. I should have known." I fix my tie, reaching for my coffee at the same time. "Who helped you set this up? Was it Jenny? Bet it was Jenny." I shake my head. "She's been getting in my business since I was seven years old."

"The year you finally stopped eating glue." He smirks.

"Lies and fallacies. I've never stopped." My own lips curve into a smile as my head lifts, scanning around me. "So, tell me: What the hell are you doing here, Killian? What's going on this time?" I lean forward. "Did you find me another escort to trick me into dating? Or was Mandy really such a good ride, and you want a go of your own?"

Killian's eyes narrow. "So, you figured out Mandy was a fake. That means you're not as hopeless as I thought."

I lift a brow, not believing what I'm hearing. Heat builds under my collar as I point a finger at my COO's face. "I'm starting to think you have no idea who I am, Killian. For as much as we've grown up together, you would think you of all know people know how much I've gone through for the company—for you. For all of us. So, so much. And now that the company is rolling in dough, you don't have to worry about the money anymore. Me, I am in over my head. You don't know what I've been through. I mean, did you get the laugh you wanted out of all this? Knowing that I was dating someone paid to date me? That was really the end-goal?"

Center to center, our eyes meet. He stares at me. "Let me tell you a story, Derek. About how life can change in a second. I was just down there, looking at the spread of our IPO. We're in a good position. We're ready to move forward. The IPO is a tad behind schedule because of problems in the markets, but it's still happening. The big publishers are already buying in.

And we're getting bids from the other retailers to buy us out already, though we're not even poised to sell." He pauses, giving me the serious look that made him my second in command. "And yet with all this success, our CEO had no intention to accept the IPO because he has a score to settle."

"Me? I have a score to settle?"

He shakes his head. "Of course you do. With yourself. That control freak who holds the fate of your company in his hand to bastardize every step of our IPO as much as he possibly can."

I stare at him, knowing what's coming.

This is the part I hate. The part where Killian drops a few bombs and drops me back into my nightmares.

Where he tells me I'm overcompensating for my absentee parents. Where I'm not really that angry—it's just that I had a bad childhood and want to make my own rules now.

Where my need to control my life gets to me and makes me react the way I do.

I look around the restaurant, suddenly wishing I were anywhere—anywhere but here. Not wanting to hear what I'm going to hear next.

"Derek, you've lost your way. I mean, look at yourself. You're drinking coffee because you can't be bothered to eat. You're sniping at someone who is only trying to help you. You have skills. Real people skills, that kind that made you our CEO. And you're not using them. You're sabotaging yourself with your own insecurities and self-defeating behavior. I mean, Jesus, I know you mean well...but...That Scott Dirick deal? Acquiring Bella Publishing?" He blows out air. "It was a shit move from the beginning. But you've been so determined, so focused on the money that you've lost the human part out of all this. Hare & Holeton is a company built on us...on our ideals, on the people. And we've lost so much of that."

I nod, my stare thinning. “We’re gaining too much money, then? Is that it?"

"No... But we're losing our souls. We need to keep up that personal touch so we maintain our values, what we stand for. That's how we can keep our edge, for the long haul. It's what made us better than everyone else. Better than all our competitors. It's what made us strong and we're losing it."

I lean forward, my voice rising. "Yeah? Is that why you hired Mandy?"

Killian doesn't blink. "Yes. I was hoping you'd find the fun again. Become that Derek we all knew and loved. The charming one, the carefree and happy one. The one you forgot exists..." He shrugs. "But in the end, I don't know. It didn't have the desired effect."

I open my mouth to say something, then close it again, knowing it'll be a waste of breath, but I have no other choice.

I knot my hands on the table. "So, I'm not happy? That's what you're saying?"

"That's an understatement. I mean, you've effectively turned the company into nothing more than a corporate machine that's losing its core. It's not about the money. It's about the people." His jaw clenches. "But the week prior...I don't know. Everyone had started to see a change in you. For the better. You were a hit at the CoTA event. Apparently, all the reporters, the attendees loved you." He gives me a large smile. "You became the nice guy again. You were charming. You were funny. You were making women swoon around you again. The fire, the sparkle was back in your eyes."

"And no one else saw it?"

"No. You had a few who recognized it in you, and I didn't need the reviews to know it was true."

"So what's the point?" I snort. "You're not exactly over-joyed with me either."

Killian exhales, then sits back in his chair, his eyes some-where behind me. "Well, it's easy not to be happy with you when you're being a grade-A dick. The minute the Seattle Post released the news of Mandy being an escort, you went into robotic mode. Snapping at everyone. Lashing out at people. Keeping everyone at an arm's length. It was easy to stay the hell out of your way. But now that you're showing the old Der again, I'm not going to stand by and watch you self-destruct." He shakes his head, his amber eyes lifting to mine once more. "Derek, like it or not, you are my family. Despite how fucked our childhoods were, it's what your parents, what Harriet and Holeton, would want us to do for each other." Killian sighs. "And I want you to be happy. I want to see you get that happily-ever-after every one of us deserves. You can't do it on your own, Derek. You can't do it alone. You have a lot of work to do if you want to make things right with yourself."

I frown, my fists tightening. "So what exactly is it you want me to do?"

"Hold onto whatever it was that made you happy and stop the insanity. It's not too late." His eyes dart to my hands. "Come back from your madness. Make things right."

"Is this your way of an intervention?"

Killian nods sternly. "And I'm not giving up. Now more than ever. You're the only one who can figure out the path forward. We're here to support you."

"I don't think it's possible to fix this mess, Killian."

"I think you can."

My mind goes immediately to Mia. To her sweet lips. To her selfless behavior.

To the warm laughs and even warmer conversation. To her creativity and the way she saw things in the world outside of the box.

To her impulsiveness.

To her mouth, her taste, her giving nature...

Her smile.

Killian pours more water in his glass, his eyes glinting with concern. He gives me a look. "So, why don't you tell me about her?"

My eyes dart to his. "Mandy?"

"Mandy..." He laughs loud and hard. "Hell no. I'm talking about the woman who captured your heart. The one that has you swinging at rich, suited assholes in fancy restaurants."

"I didn't say I had..." My mind skids to a halt, then my eyes snap to him again. "You really think...?"

He nods. "I most definitely do."

I swallow, my skin warming slightly. "And...?"

"And...I know what you like."

I snort, taking a deep breath, glancing away, my mind playing with it all right now.

Killian's brow furrows. "Derek, look at me."

I do.

"I met her. I met Mia. In the break room, at the office. And she's fearless. She's everything I knew she'd be. She's funny. Shit-talking." He laughs. "She's incredible..." He inhales deeply. "And she's your match. You'd be a damned fool to let her go."

"She doesn't want to see me anymore."

"How do you know?"

I look away. And Killian sees it all.

"Because you thought she leaked the Mandy story, didn't you? Yeah, Ryder almost had me going with that one...until he found out who the real leak was."

I sit up straight. "Who was it?"

"Oliver Blare. Ryder found out tonight...Turns out Ryder's assistant was working for Scott Disrick on the low. He hired a PI to dig up even more dirt on Hare & Holeton. That bastard Scotty never intended to sell his company. The whole deal was part of his plan to corner the market on this city. And to punish Quentin for stealing his girl. And now he's planning to expand his business portfolio onto a national scale...leaving us, Fortune, and all the other newspapers out in the cold. Basically, he wanted to ruin us once and for all..."

My eyes widen. "All because of a high school fling?"

"Yeah. Some things never change. Looks like Disrick's still

holding a vengeance flame because of Quentin pulling a romantic robbery."

I snort, gaze sliding away to the windows, my mind playing over all of it.

Killian pauses. "It wasn't her. Mia was never a part of this. The PI offer, apparently, was just a weird coincidence, and it turns out that she never accepted the job at all."

"Yeah...I think I knew that."

Killian shifts in his seat again, giving me a concerned look. "So, I'm going to ask you. Call me crazy. I know it's only been, what, a week or so. But...is Mia the one?"

"The one?"

He nods. "The one who'll change your fate. Who'll complete you. Make you whole again?"

I look away again, my hands clenching into fists on top of the table. My head stays down, my throat feeling too tight to speak. But it loosens. "She's...of my ilk. She has a good heart. And she isn't like Mandy."

"Is that a good thing or a bad thing?"

"The best. The best thing." I take a deep breath. "My only problem is...she doesn't want to be with me. She spoke the truth. I was a horrible person to her. And I know there's no way she can get over that. So... it's probably better if I forget about her. Move on."

Killian stares at me. "Kinda like what you did with Mandy?"

I nod. "Yeah, but with Mandy...I actually wanted to move on. I enjoyed seeing her, but I never actually wanted to be with her. With Mia..."

"Yeah, well, it doesn't sound like you want the same from this woman."

My eyes shift to his. "No. I don't think I do. Not at all. I can't. Not with Mia. It's...it's just different with her."

"She isn't going to let you off that easily, man. She's not like anyone you've ever known. Especially not Mandy."

"I know. Which is why..." I clear my throat. "We're better off just being friends."

But my mind...my body...my memories...they all recall something else. A thought that carries weight. A little too much weight. A little too much pull. I swallow, glancing over at him. "Have you ever seen a person...someone you couldn't forget? Who got under your skin and into your blood?"

He gives me a long and scrutinizing stare. "Yeah. I have."

I blink. "But...you've never mentioned it."

He shakes his head and looks away. "Never wanted to. Not with anyone."

"But you've...?"

He nods, taking a deep breath, then glances back to me again. "Yeah." He glances away. "And I've always regretted it since then, too." He takes another breath, his eyes looking back to mine. His stare is hard—stern, his expression flat. "So, if you think Mia's your match. And you think you can fix the damage you caused. Then fix it. Don't let your fear be more than your needs." He pokes a finger at my chest, pointing. "I've seen you fall. I've seen you fail. I've never seen you fail like this. I've never seen you like this. I've never seen you so..." He clears his throat. "Completely miserable."

I swallow, eyes shifting away. But Killian is right.

I need something more. Something different than my own uncertainty. More than my doubts. I need a woman like Mia. Which is why...

"And if your fears keep you from diving in," Killian says. "you're going to regret it every day for the rest of your Pearl Jam-loving life, I'm telling you. And I'm talking not just regret, but life-wasting-crying-in-the-rain-never-mind-the-twenty-pairs-of-underwear-in-the-bathroom regret. Because that's what it's going to be like."

I swallow, glancing back to him. "I know." My mouth twitches. I shake my head. "I'm not going to regret it, Killian."

"Then what are you going to do?"

Finishing my cup of coffee, I put it down as I stand up from the table.

I take a deep breath, my words a quick, low response. "Whatever it takes." I reach for my suit jacket, slipping it on. "Whatever the hell it takes."

Chapter Twenty-Seven

MIA

Three days after my spontaneous meeting with Derek's ex-girlfriend Mandy, I sit back in my chair and close my laptop.

The submission is in.

The Visions Collective photo contest is officially over.

And I still can't believe it. All the work leading up to the submission, all the sleepless hours, the cold hard floors of my apartment...and now it's over.

With Mandy's permission, I've submitted my electronic copy of my photo submission to the Visions Collective website with her title attached to it.

Changing the title to anything else just felt...wrong. I didn't want to exploit Mandy's actions or the situation in any way. I just wanted to make it right.

So I did.

I just hope it'll be worth it.

I've been thinking.

And I've been praying.

And I've been debating.

But...I'm finally settling on a plan.

I just wish I had it figured it all out much sooner.

I lean back in my chair as my laptop gives me a soft beep. I jump a little as I look up at a knock at my bedroom door, then stand up and walk to it. "Come in."

The door swings open to reveal Tina standing there.

"Hey," she says, pushing the door closed, her back to the door. "You all dressed?"

I nod, giving her a small smile. "Yup. I'm ready to begin my first shift back at Sopra."

Her face lights up. "You're excited."

"About Jerry being fired?" I finish taking off my sweater. "Well...partially. I'm a bit nervous. I mean, as a manager, Jerry was a big sleaze-ball, but...I guess, with him, I knew what to expect. I knew that he was just sucking up to his boss in order to get what he wanted out of him. All I can hope is that this new manager will be less..."

"Of a breast-ogler?"

I snort. "Yeah. And that this new guy won't get too touchy-feely with every waitress, either." I tilt my head to the side, gazing in my full-length mirror. "Though there's really no telling what he'll—or she'll—do."

Tina moves to my side and starts fussing with my hair.

I look over at her. "You're here early. You usually don't even start prepping for a shift at Sopra until five."

She nods. "Well, I wanted to be here to help you get ready. And welcome you back." She pushes back a lock of my hair. "I know it's not the ideal situation for you right now. But," she stresses, "I have no doubt that it'll get better. You're going to win that damn photo contest. And in the absurd event that those jackasses at Visions Collective choose someone's else photo, then you've still won." She gives me a sweet smile. "Even if you're a back-up."

I give her a nod, glancing to my reflection in the mirror. "Gee, thanks."

Tina leans over to my dresser, taking out a small bottle of

perfume. "I mean it. You've worked hard on your submission. Spent the last three days and nights of your life working on it. And I've got no doubt that all of your hard work paid off. And if that wasn't enough," she pauses dramatically, spritzing me with the perfume before flopping on the edge of my bed, "you actually had the balls to agree to a rendezvous with your beloved's ex-escort-slash-fling-slash-girlfriend. I mean, those are unbelievable balls."

"Well, you've made your point. I guess that was pretty huevos-grande of me. Tell you the truth?" I reach for my lipstick. "Mandy had some pretty grande huevos of her own to seek me out like that. She tried to contact Derek on her own. And when that didn't work, she reached out to Derek's Chief of Staff and then his old assistant...and then she found out about me."

"What do you mean 'found about you'? You mean, she knows that you and Derek, you know...?"

I shake my head, pressing the lipstick to my mouth. "Uh, no. Definitely not. Not at first..." I sigh. "She found out about me from Derek's cousin, Killian, actually. She discovered that I was working for Derek. Thought I might reach out to him and get them in contact. You know, so she could apologize." I scoff, tutting softly. "She didn't realize that I was actually in love with Derek until we sat down and—"

"Wait," Tina interrupts, her brown eyes sending off alarms in every direction. I fall silent.

"Did you say 'in love,' Mia? Are you saying that you're in love with Derek Anderson?!"

I feel my cheeks warm, my blush color adding to the color already there. "I didn't mean...I wasn't looking for—"

"Yes, you did," she cuts me off with a firm nod. Tina gets off my bed, pulling up the hem of her black leggings. "You're in love with Derek Anderson?!" Her eyes get all big and her mouth falls open as she moves toward me, her words clear as a bell as she shouts them in my face. "You're in love with Derek Anderson!"

I pause, my lips catching on each other as I blink, my eyes staring upward in shock.

My heart thuds as I look at her, noticing the tone and expression in her voice as she shouts. She isn't really asking me if I'm in love with Derek.

No.

She's telling me. Loudly, proudly.

She knows.

Just as I've known. Known on some small level from the night we walked out of Sopra together.

Known that there was something there that wasn't there with any other man.

Known that I've never been freer, more me than when I was with him.

Tina's right…

I'm in love with Derek Anderson.

I feel like I'm falling as it hits me, knocking the very air out of my lungs. I glance up.

"Tina..." I'm breathing hard, fresh tears springing to my eyes.

She shakes her head, walking over to my side. Grabbing my hand, she gives it a squeeze, her thumb caressing my knuckles. "Don't cry, Mia." Her voice is low now. "Every time you cry, it makes me cry. I don't want to cry. I want to celebrate with you."

I blink, shaking my head. "Wh—wait, what? You want to—"

She stands up, pivoting on her heel, her hands flying towards the sky and then down. "Celebrate. Because this is huge." She pauses, taking a deep breath and closing her eyes, her hands resting on her hips. Her entire body sags a little and when she opens her eyes, they're watering. "I'm sorry. It's just...You've had a wall of ice around your heart since Jason 'Jackass of the Century' Hamilton. And-and Derek's blanking that wall in one fell swoop. I know how Jason made you feel, Mia. He chipped away at your heart. He stole pieces of you, then scrunched them up and threw them away after he was done with them. He made you question yourself, your worth, your potential..."

I watch her talking, feeling the sincerity in her words. I think back over everything that's happened, from the moment I met Derek to the moment I fell so hard for him.

I realize that Tina is right. So right.

It's true.

About Jason, about my parents, about me.

Jason's betrayal was a catalyst—a real ass one—that flipped a switch in my head, switching off that inner voice that confirms my worth and potential, leaving me spinning.

I've always been so sure of myself, but after that, I started to question everything and I started to doubt every decision I made.

Until Derek.

"Jason stole my confidence," I whisper, looking at her as she gives one more turn. "He used my fears against me and I fell apart. But Derek...Derek has never made me question myself. He didn't damage me. He didn't chip away. He just saw something in me that I didn't see in myself. And that was enough to make me realize how good I was. He made me feel good. He made me feel like I was more than I thought I was. He made me feel like I was lovable, even if I couldn't love myself. He made me feel like I wasn't worthless. Like I wasn't broken. He made me see my strength. Made me realize that I did have the power of choice. On my own, I didn't have that. I hate to say it…" I exhale, my body suddenly lighter than it's been all week. "But I kinda… needed him to give it back to me." I take a deep breath. "God...He's already helped me put the pieces back in place." I smile tearfully. "He's already made me feel free."

Tina comes to me, pulling me into a hug.

My heart sinks as I think of my parents...of their choices, of their reasons for backing Jason when we broke up, of their emotional abuse.

I hug Tina tight, my emotions already a mess from so much. "God, I'm a fucking softy." I shake my head, a laugh escaping me. "Who knew?"

Tina's arms slip around my back, her cheek pressed against my shoulder. "Welcome to the team, my sweet. You'll totally love it." Her voice is fading. She sniffles a little. "I'm just so in shock. You loving Derek..." She stops. "And Mandy, she—"

"I think she might love him, too...still. But...it was over for her."

"Yeah?"

"Yeah." I exhale. "She said she could recognize that look in my eyes. And from the way Killian mentioned my name, she was sure that Derek felt the same way about me."

"Wow." Tina shakes her head. "I still can't believe it. The woman is a kick-ass detective."

"I actually found myself opening up to her. About the contest, my thoughts on what I wanted to do for it, on Derek. I seriously don't know if it was her or her own guilt or what, but...she made me promise that I'd show Derek the photo that I was submitting." I shrug. "She wanted me to make him see it. She—" I pause, my gut twisting into serval knots. "—she really wanted to prove to him that he was making a huge mistake, if he were to let me go."

"So...are you going to let him?"

"Let him what?"

"Let you go," Tina clarifies.

"I...I—" I sigh, grabbing onto my hands. "I don't know."

"I mean, you love him...so why not?"

I take a deep breath, leaning in closer to Tina as I speak. "Because I still haven't gotten a response from him. I've been sending him short messages non-stop for the last three days...and I haven't gotten a single response in return." I bite my lip. "I don't know what to do. I think he's mad, but...I really don't know. Maybe I should think about it more before making a decision. I mean, I...I don't want to let him go unless he wants me to."

"That's not much of a plan, sweetie."

"I know." I put my head back down, sighing in frustration. "But I mean, it's a plan, right? I just...I don't want to make a rush decision based on emotional feelings, you know? I hope he loves me, but if he doesn't...and never will...then I don't want to get my hopes up before he can tell me himself."

Tina nods. "Well, you know what they say. It is better to have tried and failed than to have never tried at all."

I smile, nodding again as I move to the closet and take out my shift dress, along with my heels, then sit down on my bed, taking off my socks.

"I think it's in the movies," I say. "The Princess Bride. Where Vizzini said it."

Tina rolls her eyes.

I shrug, wiping the last of my tears from the corners of my eyes. I stand. "Anyway...I've got to go finish getting ready. I'm the first one on today. And—with my luck—I'll be the last one off." I grab my purse and move to the door. I open it, turning around. "Tina, thanks. For everything. For helping me out with...this." I shrug. "For everything."

She takes a step forward, reaches out, and squeezes my hand. "Want anything? Coffee? Hot Croissant?"

I shake my head. "I'll be fine. I'd—um, I'd like to think. And I'll go grab something on my way in." I swallow. "I'll be fine."

Tina nods. "You know you can call me for anything, right?"

I nod as I take a step outside. "Yeah. I'll call you later."

"I'm meant to start my shift at seven-thirty. So, if you need anything before then, just call me."

"I will." I walk down the hall and into the elevator, pressing the button for the lobby. The usually-broken lift comes to life, allowing me on board. I press the lobby button again and keep adding in random numbers as the lift continues to register that I'm indeed there, before finally letting me on and to the lobby and out of the building.

The bus stop is only a few blocks away, and I walk there fast, my mind whirling in circles, my hands clenching, my heart racing with anticipation.

And worry.

I mean—I want to see Derek again.

More than anything.

I want to feel the connection between us, to feel him safe and secure in my arms once again.

But...I don't want to force myself on him.

I want him to want me.

Still.

Before...I want him to know that—despite my feelings for him—that he is the one who has the choice.

I love him enough...to let him go, if that's what he wants.

The bus ride to Sopra is quick. I'm so lost in thought, I barely register the buildings that I pass, the streets and the cars, the busy Seattle sidewalks or the thick, wet, messy Seattle rain dripping down on me in sheets, my lashes clinging to my skin, my hair dripping against my shoulders.

I move out of the bus, turning my face up to the early evening rain, letting my tears mingle with the cold drops as they slip down my cheeks and drip along my chin.

I let the rain drench my blouse and skirt and my coat, my purse and my hair, soaking everything in with the shards of my shattered heart and soul.

When I finally make it to the front doors of Sopra, my face is damp from both the rain and my tears, my body soaked from it all. My soaked-through clothes are clinging to my body and my hair is a huge tangled mess.

But I don't care.

At least I'm on time for my shift.

At least I'm here.

At least I made it out on-time.

Reaching for the door handle, I step inside and look around.

The front of the restaurant is empty—completely empty—of customers and employees alike.

"Hello?" I call out, my voice echoing.

Silence.

"Hello?" I call again.

I let go of the handle and look over to the right, seeing a light on in the back, behind the office.

I tiptoe over, slowly and quietly, my heels making no sound as I try to step lightly, slowly, carefully.

And I watch as the kitchen doors slowly open, inch by inch, slowly revealing the inside of the kitchen as they do.

And standing there, looking out, his eyes, his face, his arms, his tuxedo-covered body all lit up with the light from the rarefied kitchen within, is Derek Anderson.

And he's looking straight at me.

Like he's been expecting me all along.

Like he's been waiting for me.

Like my world has finally come full-circle.

My heart jumps in my chest, my throat swells tight, and my brain goes blank for a split-second, unable to register what's happening,

Unable to stop my hand from raising and covering my mouth. Unable to stop the tears from welling up behind my eyes as I gasp softly.

"Hello, beautiful," he says softly and with his eyes. His deep, sensual, soulful blue eyes. "I've been waiting for you."

I don't hesitate.

I don't even breathe. Or think.

Even if I could, it wouldn't be about anything other than the man right in front of me.

Heart racing, stomach doing somersaults, I break into a sprint, up the steps to the kitchen, through the door, and straight into his arms.

Chapter Twenty-Eight

DEREK

The last word barely leaves my lips before our mouths are on each other. The distance between us disappears in the blink of an eye.

My arms come to life, finding their way around Mia and wrapping her close. Her soft body colliding with my suited one, I press myself to her, feeling the warmth of her perfect skin, knowing nothing about this embrace will be normal.

Because there's nothing "normal" about how I feel right now.

Nothing normal about how hard I am.

Nothing normal about what's burning inside me, just below my chest.

And nothing...normal...about how much I missed Mia.

My arms tighten around her, my fingers pressing in tight.

I try to pull her even closer...but she withdraws, out of reach.

My voice is thick. "Mia?"

I watch her chest rising and falling.

All I want to do is take it one step further.

One step.

"Are you okay?" I ask.

"No." She shakes her head. "No. No, I'm not okay...after how we left things the other day."

My throat burns. "You mean how I left things. How I left you." I pause for a second. "After what I did to you."

She nods. "That's exactly what I mean."

I take a deep breath, and I speak, my voice barely recognizable to my own ears. "Mia, I'm so fucking sorry."

"Are you?"

"I am. More than I can ever say. I was only thinking about myself. About my own pain. My own bullshit, Mia...not yours. And I never even thought about how I'd hurt you. I never thought stopped to think...what would happen when I lost you."

Her face twists. "Lose me? You didn't lose me, Derek. You gave me up." She swallows hard. "And I know why you did it." Mia takes a breath. "But I'm still not sure it should matter. You ended it...before we even had a chance to get started."

"Mia. More than anything in this world...I don't ever want to lose you again."

It's a struggle to utter the words, but I do my best to get them out. To share my feelings. "I didn't know how to...deal...with the feelings I had for you. The feelings I *have* for you." I try another breath. "I thought I knew what was best...but I know better now. And I know that it was all wrong. All wrong. I'm here to prove it to you. To prove it to you now."

She swallows hard, her brown eyes bearing a hole through me.

"Mia," I continue, "I have never felt this way before. And you were right, the other day. I was...I was lying to myself. About my feelings. About being ready. About you owning me." Emotion fills my throat, weighing on my words. "Because you do. You own me, Mia. Every inch of me. From the top of my head down to my soles." Without thinking, I lower to one knee, one hand still holding hers. "I belong to you, Mia

Kamaka. Only you." I stare at our intertwined fingers. "And I promise to never hurt you like that again. No words can express how much I fucking hate myself for the way I've behaved, the way I hurt you. I am truly sorry. And I promise, if you'll have me—me and all my fuck-ups and baggage, you and yours—that I will do my best to be worthy of you."

"Derek. I..."

"Let me finish, Mia," I interrupt. "I know I have no rights over you. I know that you have your own life...And you don't have to forgive me. Or come back to me. But I want you to know that wherever you are, whatever you do, however you live and breathe, know that...I'll never be far from you. From your thoughts and memories and your heart." I squeeze her hand. "But I have no issues with begging. I'm pleading with you…to trust me again, Mia. To give me another chance. To give us another chance. And I promise that I will spend every waking minute of every single day making it up to you. If you'll be mine, Mia...if you'll be mine like I am truly, wholly, completely and without question yours. For as long as you want me."

She shifts, then slides her hand out of mine and brings both her hands to my face. Placing her free hand on my head, warm and soft, smooth and moist with rain, she glances down at me, her voice husky, her eyes glassy as she stares. "You're on your knees. On Sopra's floor. In a suit."

I blink. "I know."

"You're going to ruin the suit."

"Fuck the suit." I exhale, love swelling through me. "Mia, the only thing I care about right now is you." I take her hand and press it to my chest. "I'm on my knees. For you." The warmth of her hand shoots through me. "Because I want you to accept me. The real me. Not the guy who pretends he can do everything. But the man who can't do anything but love you."

She brings a hand to my cheek, running her soft palm across my face.

"Say yes, Mia. Please. Tell me you forgive me for what I did. For what I said. For hurting you. For leaving you." I pause, sucking in a breath. "Because the truth is, I can't live without you."

Mia stares at me, her eyes streaming tears, her lower lip shaking as she whispers, "Derek Anderson," she says, her voice a whisper, slow and soft. "I've never stopped loving you. For a moment..." She swallows. "I've thought of nothing but you. And I forgive you. For everything." She swallows hard, moves in, slides her arms around my neck and pulls me to her. "I forgive you. And I forgive myself. For everything that's happened. I just need you, Derek. I need you. The real you. The one I've gotten to know all this time."

I wrap my arms around her waist, holding her tight, her hair streaming rain onto me. "I need you, Mia. More than I've ever needed anything. And I promise that...I'll try to be worthy of you. I'll try to be..." I take a deep breath. "I'll try to be good enough for you. Every day."

She leans back, then cups my face in her hands. "I love you, Derek." She kisses my cheek, then my nose. "So much. So much I can't breathe."

"I love you, Mia. I love you." I kiss her, hard, deep and infinite moments pass, both of us lost in the kiss for a lifetime, the two of us electricity, both of us burning bright and intense. I pull back, breathless, and smile. "I love you so much. I love you, I love you, I love you!" We both laugh, deep and long, grinning, pressing against each other, never wanting this moment to end.

Mia pulls back, her shoulders shaking as she laughs, a tear streaming down her cheek. "My, my, Mr. Anderson. You picked a hell of a day to be honest with yourself."

"I did, didn't I?"

She shakes her head, softly smiling. "And on my first day back at work."

"In front of your boss."

She shrugs. "But you're no longer my boss."

"No, I'm no longer Alexa's boss. I let her go after I heard about the way she spoke to you."

"She spoke to me like that because I was fired by you."

"Yeah." I shrug. "I know. She's already taken a job at another publishing company...and me? Well, I flogged my own guts out for what I'd done to you. And then after moping into my whiskey for hours on end, I decided to find a new position to fill—one that's a lot closer to you."

"Uh, what does that mean?"

I breathe out. No more running from my feelings, from my heart. "You're here to start your shift, right? To meet the new managerial team, correct?"

Her hands cup my face as she peers closely at me, eyebrows knitted in confusion. "Uh, yes. That is correct."

I pull Mia even closer as I stand. "Well, you're looking at the new executive team right now."

"You're the new manager at Sopra?"

"Of course not," I say firmly. "I am not the new manager."

"Oh, because I was—"

"I'm the new owner," I reply softly, shifting my hand under her hair.

Her eyes open wide and she stares up at me. "I'm sorry?" she whispers.

"I'm the new owner."

She's still staring at me, still not understanding. "The...new owner?"

I arch a brow. "Yes. The new owner. One who owns the organization. The owner is always the one who...employs. Or buys." I look down, seeing her eyes are now focused on my lips.

"I purchased Sopra Italian Ristorante this morning. It's mine now. Well, it will be, officially, after the paperwork goes through. I just wanted to be here to show my face and help with this latest transition. My advisors have been working day and night for the last three days on the due diligence and to prepare the building for ownership transfer. I'm only here to make sure it goes smoothly and to personally to give my staff time off for their dedication and for the quality of their service."

I release a breath, looking down at her. "And to make sure this is a new day for Sopra. And for you," I add sweetly, pressing a tender kiss to her lips once more.

A breath. A blink. A smile.

The smile grows.

"But what about Danny Macpherson?" she asks, pulling back from me to look up at me.

"I outbid that overgrown penis by five million. Then I talked to your manager, Jerry—"

"Jerry?"

"Yes. Also known as the sleaziest guy I've met in a long time. Him. I fired him."

She's speechless for the first time I've known her. I've rendered her speechless and she looks at me with unbridled shock. "You-fir-fired-him?"

"Yes, Mia. I fired Jerry. No hard feelings though."

Her eyes light up, a spark of hope shining in them. "But why? W—why did you do this?"

"Because I wanted to."

The corners of her mouth curl up in a smile that sends a shockwave down to my core. "You wanted to?"

"Well, I mean, yes. I wanted Sopra Ristorante, sure. It's one of my favorite restaurants in this city. I appreciate the lines of whiskey they keep, and you won't find a better cup of coffee anywhere else in the city. Plus, I really enjoy the dinner plates. Nice and hearty. The chicken ravioli is my favorite. I could eat that every night." My gaze burns into Mia's. "Amongst other things, of course."

I watch as her smile grows bigger, her teeth on her lips, still wet from mine. "So you knew I worked here again, right?"

"Of course."

"Okay, but...how?"

I arch a brow and my voice lowers to a husky, sensual whisper. "Because, Mia, you're my angel. Because you are mine. Because I know you better than anyone...And because your roommate Tina told me."

"Tina told you I was coming?"

"I asked her. We've been talking."

"Talking...?"

"For the last few days. Talking about you. About how I feel. About how I've been a prized prick, even more than usual. About why I've been unable to stop thinking about you."

I sigh, looking down at my feet. "It killed me not to be able to talk to you, to share this with you. Hell, I have no fucking clue how I'm still keeping it together, even as my own damn legs are threatening to give out. It's a good thing I work better with you when I'm on my knees." I grin, gripping Mia harder.

"Me, too," she whispers. "Me, too."

I let the moment linger, enjoying the look of contentment on her face.

She smiles and looks up at me, her dark hair hanging down over shoulders. Her nose is still red, her cheeks still tinged with the cold. She's still beautiful.

Stunningly beautiful.

"I'm going to do better. I'm going to be better. For you," I whisper, touching my forehead to hers again, seeing the fear and hope in her eyes. "For us. No matter what."

"You've got that right." She briefly squeezes my hand. "That's the Derek Anderson I've come to know."

"You're the one who taught me how to be him." I stroke

her hair. For an interminable amount of time, all I can do is gaze at my beautiful Mia, peering hopelessly into her brown eyes—eyes the color of a deep brown taffy just pulled from the long and hard till. Eyes the color of coffee and milk, and light from a dip into a cauldron of flames.

Her eyes are filled with tears, but I can't tell if they're tears of sadness or tears of joy. Her face is beaming with hope and rapture. But she has a look of shock on her face, and a look of disbelief.

"Wait a second." She looks at me, her eyes fluttering, the skin rising and falling on her throat. "And the future?" Her sweet brows pull together in a frown. "What about all our rules? All our lists? Are those going to change?"

"What rules?"

"The ones about 'any intra-office fraternization being strictly professional' and 'any romantic relationships being strictly non-disclosable within the scope of employment.' Going to be kinda hard to avoid those when you're now my boss again."

I smile and run my nose from hers to her cheek, inhaling her perfume, her perfume mixed with her faintly minty breath and the scent of her skin.

Urging her closer to me, I whisper into her ear, "Outdated regulations that no longer serve us. Outdated rules that I only kept to avoid getting caught with my pants down. And since I know how fond you are of what's in my pants...I'm removing all of our rules for you this time around." I whisper, "For both of us."

And I let my lips graze the side of her neck, on the sensitive and delicious skin just behind her ear.

"I'm not sure if I should be touched or offended," she laughs softly.

I reach down low and lightly stroke her thigh, below the hem of her short dress, then up her body. My palm is gliding along her thigh, then under the hem of the short skirt.

"Oh, if you'd like to be touched..." I whisper. "I can accommodate that."

I continue to lightly stroke her skin and I hear her breathing hard. She's trembling, trying to breathe and swallow. I pull the hem of her skirt up and continue to inhale her scent and to stroke her skin. I hear her gasps and she is breathing quicker.

"Ah...I think it's supposed to be touch, not—"

I drag us backwards and into the nearest booth before she can finish. Pulling Mia into my lap, I capture her face in my hands and I look into her eyes.

My eyes are locked on her face. I'm breathing her in, my heart is beating rapidly again, but for a different reason.

"Slower?" I whisper, smiling.

"It's...Well, I just...Yeah, I'm not sure I'm the best judge of what is 'careful' right now."

"Don't worry about those rules right now," I tell her, my eyes combing her face. "Just go with it. Just feel it. Let's go a little higher on the 'careful' scale."

I cover her mouth with my own. I inhale her scent, her lips, and the sweetness of her mouth.

I gently stroke her lips with my tongue, until she opens her lips and takes it in full. "So let me ask you something. If you're working, are you not allowed to flirt with customers?"

She laughs. "Nope. Not allowed. Especially suit-wearing, whiskey-stealing handsome men," her lips jump to my own in a peck, "who are now my direct employer."

"And what about telling me you want to rip my clothes off?"

"Definitely not allowed."

"Well, I think it's only right that you should be able to have some benefits."

She rolls her eyes and smiles. I swivel my gaze from her eyes, down her body, and I watch as her nipples become hard, pressing against the soft fabric of her dress, pushing and straining against the sensual amount of cleavage.

"Hmmm. I'll get to work on that benefit package right away. So tell me..." I draw my eyes back to hers, my fingers lightly trailing her chin, and my hands lightly drawing down her neck and along her dress, inching it up. "...tell me Mia..." I whisper, my lips to her ear, my thumbs lightly gliding along her mouth, "what is the policy regarding part-time waitresses who sleep with their bosses?"

"Um...I don't know. Is my paycheck gonna be docked for that?"

"Oh, it'll be docked alright. I'll have to...deduct your clothing, for sure."

"My clothing?"

"That's right. I'll deduct piece by piece..." I unzip her dress in the back and push it down. I watch as it slowly slides down inch by inch, so slowly on her beautiful body. I am breathing her, drinking her, inhaling her all in.

I un-shoulder and then unzip the halter top of her dress. I hear her breathe, hear her gasp and watch as the dress slides down and off, onto the floor.

Her eyes follow the dress, then they drop back down to my lips, to my neck, down to my chest, and lower, until they fall on my pants.

"You know..." Her breath is so close to mine, it almost feels as if we're breathing in unison. "I think you should deduct my underwear, too. Just to be thorough."

"They are definitely not work appropriate."

She's standing and her eyes are on my pants. She watches as I unbutton the top.

And I put my hand in my back pocket and pull out a foil packet. I glance at her and smile. She smiles back.

I toss the foil packet to her, and she reaches and catches it in her palm. Her eyes are wide.

"I may need a hand putting that on. I was wondering if

you—as my employee—might be interested in helping me out?"

She holds out her hand toward me. "I better receive a bonus for this, right?"

"Oh yes, a thick, hefty one will be in your pay envelope in the next few minutes."

Her fingers lace with mine. Her eyes lock onto mine. We're both smiling as Mia unzips my pants with her other hand.

She whispers, her voice shaking, her breaths shallow and quick, "That bonus better be pretty big."

"Oh, it will be, Ms. Kamaka. I can assure you. Big enough for you to remember for many nights to come."

With a laugh, a few quick adjustments and a moan, we melt into one another. I can feel Mia's hips against mine, where she's riding me. I can feel the vinyl of the booth. The air-conditioned heat inside the restaurant.

But more importantly, I can feel that this—us—is where I belong, where I've always needed to be.

I can feel her heat as her hands softly caress my skin. I can feel my heart rate begin to increase. Her face inches from mine.

Our own little world, away from anything else.

In Mia, I've found my fit. My mate. My match.

In her, I'm anchored. In her, I'm found. In her, I'm home.

And I know this is just the start.

"I love you," I murmur.

"I love you too," she replies.

I stroke inside Mia's soft heat until, at last, I can feel her muscles ripple around me, my name on her lips a signal of a new beginning...

Chapter Twenty-Nine

Two weeks later

MIA

I pull up to Derek's condo with a dozen giant bags of food and a giant box of desserts and stuff.

And I can't wait.

Derek was right. Hosting a Happy Hour is very different than attending one.

We're all supposed to be meeting here to eat as much Tamsung Fusion food as we can fit in our mouths, and we've bought the mee goreng sin (a fusion of western and Chinese cuisines), the babi guling kek (chicken in red curry with cashews), and the rendang, which is a beef stew cooked in coconut. We've got all the stuff for faarofushi, too.

I'm bursting out at the seams.

I run inside with the stuff, bags in hand, and Derek looks at my load, then the food and laughs.

"You might have bought too much stuff."

"Oh, hush. It's a reason to celebrate. And it's going to take a long time for me to eat all of this. And I have to have something to drink with it."

"Mmm, I can definitely see that."

"Alright, let's begin, then. The sooner we get started, the quicker I can begin eating."

Derek grins and puts out some bowls and plates. Eggrolls come out on the table, and I inhale two of those.

"Mmm...oh, that's good," I mumble through a mouthful. "I'm almost ready to begin, but I've got until at least Ryder and Jenny arrive."

Derek looks over the massive kitchen counter. "You mean 'Frick' and 'Frack'?"

"Ugh," I say, taking out more food containers and placing them on the counters. "They're still going at it like cats and dogs?"

"Yep. They have been ever since I shared the news that Jenny was up for the CIO role at Hare & Holeton." He turns, leaning against the countertops, blue eyes bright. "Truth is: I couldn't hold it off any longer. And hell, the rest of us agreed. Jenny's the best pick for the position. She knows the business, its infrastructure, its budgets like the back of her hand, on top of being the most qualified, beyond a doubt."

"Well, I don't think that's the problem, honey. The problem is that the CIO and CTO are supposed to work closely together."

"Right."

"And your brother is the CTO. And, well...y'know the relationship between Jenny and him...being..."

"Mortal, sexually-frustrated enemies?" he asks.

"Yeah," I say, sighing. "It'll make for a really strange co-working dynamic."

"Trust me: There won't be a co-working dynamic. There will be Jenny making the decisions and telling Ryder what to do, and then there'll be Ryder, frowning and telling Jenny what to do, and Jenny sighing and telling him she already knows everything and dismissing him. It'll be great."

I do my best to stifle my laughter. "Well, I hope they work it out...whatever that means for two people who shouldn't be armed around each other. In the meantime, Mr. Anderson, before our guests arrive, I have a message for you. A private message for you. It's coming from my end of things."

"Hm?"

"First of all...this is our first rule of hosting Happy Hour for fellow Hare & Holeton employees here: No business talk. Leave that for the office. We're here to drink, eat, and have a good time. Going over financial projections is not a good time...Well, it isn't for anyone but you. And maybe your brother, Alton. Got it?"

"Okay, I think I can manage that."

"You can also not criticize people's food choices. Now, I know you and I didn't do much, um, eating the last time we went to Tamsung for lunch. But you cannot make people eat what you want. I've put out a lot of non-Fusion food, and just because you're a Seattle foodie does not mean you get to lord your food choices over others and make them do what you want."

"Got it. Tuck my inner food snob..." He grins. "Among other things safely away. Of course."

"You'll also have to make sure that your body language and your personal expressions do not intimidate people. I know that's hard for you because you're technically the boss." I reach over to him, adjusting his collar, and he stands up straight. "But I want you to be your let-loose self. The charming, funny, sophisticated man who's no longer hiding behind a frown and those five-thousand dollar suits, capisce?"

His hands close over mine as our gazes clash. His voice is a deep rumble that sears my skin. "I 'capisce' just fine, baby. Relax. I've got this."

I grin, brushing my lips over his. "Good. You may find

yourself in situations that you don't like. People chatting you up. Someone wanting to turn the music we've got playing from 'Sound Garden' to...I don't know...maybe the extended version of Everybody (Backstreet's Back)..."

"And by every 'someone' you mean you?" My man smirks, sliding his hands under my shirt.

"Maybe. And, under normal circumstances, you can stop this whenever you want. But you cannot pull out of this now."

"I wouldn't dream of it."

"Good. That's fine, then. That's all I needed. Now I just have to keep an eye on you. I'll be watching you."

"Closely, I hope," Derek answers darkly, his hands going lower, pushing my skirt up. "I'd like to be watched closely, Ms. Kamaka."

"Oh, honey, you know you will be." I lean in for a kiss—one that starts slow and starts to deepen, letting his hands roam beneath the hem.

"And you know where I'll be," he says, pulling back and letting our foreheads touch as I look into his eyes. "Right here, watching you watch me. You know, surveillance doesn't have to be a bad thing," he says, smirk widening.

I laugh. "I should hope so. You're a handful."

Derek decides to grab his own handful, reaching underneath my skirt to cup my ass. I gasp as he says, "And you like it."

I definitely do.

And I'm just about to let his hands venture even farther, when we hear someone at the door. He groans, but I just chuckle.

His swear is brusque. "Damn it."

"They're our friends, love," I say as we step apart, zipping back up and hiding the evidence of what we were doing. "And now the festivities have officially begun."

Heading to the door, I smile as Derek reaches over and

grabs a bag off the counter. "Right. So, while they're at the door, I'll take care of the food. You keep watch."

"Okay. I'll be right behind you."

I open the door thinking it'll be our first guest. But what I see behind the threshold has me stunned.

Standing there is my best friend Tina with a group of Hare & Holeton employees—Ryder, Jenny, Shelly and a man I know now as Shelly's husband, Zane. And they yell out as soon as they see Derek and I.

"SURPRISE!"

Holding bottles of champagne and plastic cups, they shout "Congratulations!" as they burst in past me and Derek. And I turn around, looking for Derek as we've barely had time to catch our breaths before they all attack us.

Tina comes first, kissing my face and practically garroting my neck with her arms.

Derek jumps over the little barrier we have, and his brother Ryder comes at him like a shot, giving him a hug. Jenny and Shelly surround me and give me hugs too, and Zane says "Congratulations, Mia. That's definitely a win for the good guys."

I laugh as Zane and Derek give each other a man-hug. "Thanks for the help, bro," Derek says, squeezing him.

Everyone's all smiles, hugging and kissing and making unnecessary noises. And I have no earthly idea just what the hell is going on.

"Um, hello?" I shout over the commotion. "Anyone wanna tell me exactly why this is a surprise party?"

I look to Derek first as he steps away from the others and his eyebrows waggle.

I have the feeling I've been had. Especially when Tina steps forward, clearing her throat like she's about to speak a secret. "What? Derek didn't tell you?"

I gape at the man.

Oh shit. Oh my Lord.

He's not going to...

He wouldn't...

Would he?

I look over at him and he just... He just looks so sweet. So smug. So filled with mischief.

I realize what the mischief is all about when Shelly whips out a large square in her hands I hadn't seen until now.

It's a picture blown up.

My picture. Of Shelly and her husband.

It's the picture I submitted to the Visions Collective contest. Taken in the early evening on a rooftop lounge in West Seattle, it's of a couple sitting and watching the sunset over the Puget Sound together.

The scene is filled with rich, golden light, and the couple is illuminated by it, a soft and mellow glow in their faces.

I called it "Fearless" because that's what Derek called me the night we met.

Because that's the way he makes me feel on a daily basis. Because that's what it takes to fall in love—to give it all your fears up and just throw yourself into it. To fall into something that has no guarantees. That has no safety net.

And this picture... it did that for me.

I am so, so proud of it. It's a beautiful portrait of romance and light, framed by the setting sun.

I'm even more proud when I see the ribbon attached to the corner of the frame.

As Shelly takes the ribbon, I smile as she turns it in her hands. "Second place, Mia. You won second place."

"I did?" I ask, surprised.

"Yes, you did." Derek steadies me as I hug Shelly and I remember that, in all the commotion of the last weeks, I forgot about the contest.

I forgot about winning.

Being with Derek in all these recent weeks, I'd already felt as if I'd won.

"So, I guess this wasn't a Happy Hour after all?"

He grins. "No. It was an important event to celebrate." He bends down to me, wiping a strand a hair off my forehead. "Congratulations, Mia. I'm proud of you, my constant temptation."

I turn my eyes to the picture, seeing the sunset reflected in Shelly's eyes and the glow of happiness on her husband's face.

And I realize I'm trembling.

I honestly don't know what to say.

But I know what I can do.

I yank Derek down and kiss him, hard and needy.

I don't let him up until he's teary-eyed, pleading and overtaken by my kiss.

I smile, looking up into his eyes, a tear hanging from the edge of my eye. "Thank you, Mr. Anderson."

Then I tuck the ribbon into his breast pocket and I turn my back on the lot, swallowing the concerto of hoots and hollers and "get a room's" and thanks and congratulations.

They're calling to me. I know they are.

But Derek is yelling at me. "And where do you think you're going, lady? You don't get up and go. We're not done yet."

He's right. We are not. Not by a long shot.

He grabs my wrist and spins me around, lifting me off the ground and holding me against his chest.

"You're not escaping that easily. Get used to being the spotlight, baby."

I smile and reach up, wrapping my arms around his neck. "I was going to the cellar to get a bottle of the really good champagne, but... maybe I'll just make do with you."

"You know what? I think you'd have better luck right here. I highly doubt that bottle I chill for you will come close to what you'll find hard and absolutely ready for you in my pants. And believe me, Ms. Kamaka, it does a body good."

I laugh hard, slapping at him to set him down, and when

he does, he looks at me with so much love in his eyes it almost hurt to see it.

"I love you, baby," he says, his forehead resting on mine.

"And I love you, Mr. Anderson."

His grin widens as he takes my hand. "Tell me something I don't know, beautiful."

I kick off my heels and let him lead me to the cellar of his gigantic home. "You are absolutely every bit of perfect," he tells me, eyes wide with awe.

I kiss him again and as we descend into his dark and hidden room for his best wines, I think he might be too perfect for me.

But I could make that work.

A girl can hope.

And she does, I think to myself.

Bolder. Better. Braver than she ever has before.

And I'll just call this my second place win. Nothing wrong with a little second place when you've already got first.

THIRTY

Epilogue

Two months later

DEREK

As the thick, dark door swings open that day, I know that Mia is at the top of the stairs.

I feel her.

I sense her.

I know her, and now... she is going to know me.

She is going to know what I have been doing here. She is going to know the deepest, most embarrassing parts of me.

And she is going to love me no matter what—no matter what comes out of my mouth, which I'm pretty sure will be mush.

I am the king of this castle, the sovereign of the kingdom I have created.

And I am more nervous than a hooker in church.

The butterflies in my stomach are threatening to burst out and make a run for freedom anytime now.

The private room in the back of Sopra Italian ristorante—the place I now own, the place that serves pasta like a mother would serve her children any day, any time of the day—has been turned into a decadent dining parlor like I've never seen before in my life.

Candles, dripping with wax, have been placed on every solid surface.

White sheets slide across the stark, cold, marble expanse of the room to take the place of confining curtains, bringing the white-washed, simple elegance inside to life with subtle light and the soft, rich smell of burning spices.

I had Chef Sorrentino back here over two weeks ago and the room was transformed to the wood of my heart.

Now sitting at the sole table pushed back into the center of the room, I am ravenous.

Not just my stomach, that is.

I wait, listening for the footsteps. My heart beats harder as they come closer to the room.

Until the person the footsteps belong to walks into sight.

Mia's best friend Christina is the first to step into the door, strolling in the customary white Sopra button-down shirt and black skirt.

"Damn it. Thought you were Mia."

"Um, I was," she answers. "Or she is. She's here. She's upstairs, being gushed over by Mr. and Mrs. Harker."

I sigh. "It's the Visions Collective contest that's got the patrons all riled up. The second Mia placed in the contest, her picture was splashed nearly everywhere. She's been on the cover of every magazine in town at every newsstand I've been to in the last two weeks. She's become a celebrity overnight. She's got potential clients ringing our phone off the hook, begging for her to photograph their wedding. All the local modeling and public relations agencies are begging for her to shoot for them."

Christina shakes her head. "She's always been super talented. Now everybody's singing her praises and trying to beg her to work with them. You did good, Anderson." She grins. "You did real good here. Mia's one of a kind..." She glances down. "And so is that massive rock you bought her. I've only seen one other thing that was that big. And I'm pretty sure it sunk the Titanic."

I pat the ring box in the pocket of the dark suit I'm wearing, nerves ripping through my body. "You think she knows?"

"Not a clue, Blue Eyes. She's completely in the dark. I told her I was leaving her behind to check up on tonight's menu. With me being the manager and you being the owner, she didn't suspect a thing."

Both of us are quiet for moment, listening for the soft, rhythmic sounds of Mia's footsteps. When we hear nothing, I take a deep breath.

"I'm going to go get her," Tina tells me. "Before the Harkers talk her pretty head right off."

I nod, watching her go.

The room falls silent again, and, I swear, there's not a heartbeat in the world that's as loud as mine.

Suddenly, my phone rings.

I nearly jump out of my skin.

It's my brother Ryder calling. Normally, I would ignore it, but today's Jenny's first day in her new role as Chief Information Officer.

I briefly wonder whether she and Ryder have buried the hatchet that exists between them, but when I pick up Ryder's call, I realize that that's the last thing that's happened.

I swipe my screen to answer it, and his voice is tense, sharp.

"Please tell me we have a back-up CIO, in case something happens to our current one..."

"What?"

"I mean, in the event that our current Chief Information Officer 'mysteriously' disappears, I just wanna know if we have a back-up CIO waiting in the wings."

"Ryder..."

"She's insufferable, Der. I mean it. Insufferable. The woman is insufferable. She's hell bent on bringing every bit of Hare & Holeton into the 'twenty-first century', as she calls it. Even going so far as to offer her services without charge. She's hacked into every department's operation, trying to centralize them all in a very obvious, and very public way. She thinks she's Darth Vader reincarnate, here to take over the universe."

"Look, I—"

"The woman kicks puppies, I'm telling you."

"She doesn't even own a puppy."

"Well, then, she rents them out to kick them."

I exhale. "Ryder, I don't know what to tell you. We're fine. We've handled the transition. We're fine. Everything is fine. Jenny knows what she's doing. She's good at her job. She fits the company perfectly. She's just like you."

"I've never met a more difficult person in my life, Der."

"After listening to you just now, I beg to differ," I answer, not even bothering to put on my best management voice. "Now that that rant's out of your system, you mind calling me back some other time? I'm kinda busy right now..."

He stops. "Oh shit. You mean..."

"Yes, I mean. If you'll excuse me, Ry, I have to ask the most beautiful woman I've ever seen to marry me...Is that alright with you? If it is, I'll get back to you."

I end the call with an audible sigh of relief.

Jesus, my CTO and CIO are likely to kill each other before the month is up. I can't say I'm not surprised.

But what I am surprised by is the woman standing thirty feet from me.

She pauses, her hand at her throat, looking as vulnerable as I have built this place to be.

Her dress is gorgeous. Stunning. Like her.

I can't take my eyes off her, her beauty hitting me in the chest.

Her dark hair dances around her in a wild ring, echoing

the cocoa color of her eyes. Her peanut butter skin looks polished and flawless, like the buttery down comforter I'm gonna prepare her to sleep on every single night of our lives.

I can't breathe.

I can't move.

And I can't look away.

Mia smiles, tentative.

And I want her more than I ever wanted anything in my life.

"Well?" she asks, softly, moving toward me.

I stand, heart beating the congas against my rib. I inhale. Loudly. "How much of that conversation did you actually hear?"

She keeps smiling. "Just enough to know that your brother's still got a lot of... issues to work out within him."

I stare at her.

Then, I laugh.

She keeps moving toward me.

She stops at the landing. "You ready?"

"Ms. Kamaka, right now, I'm ready for anything you are. I've dreamt about you for way too long to waste another minute."

"Is that right?"

"Yes, it is." I take a step closer to her. "Someone in this room is about to become a very happy man, Mia."

She smiles, emotional. "That's good to know. I've always wanted to be a happy man," she laughs, "and... I don't know, but I've never been all that happy in my whole life, until I met you, Derek. I've dreamed about this, too. And I think what we're about to do might just be crazy enough to work."

I reach out for her. We're standing five feet apart, but I can feel the electricity. She reaches out, too, our hands touching.

She takes a breath and I can't wait another second.

I pick her up, carry her over the threshold and lay her

down on the cream couch. I smile at the enthusiasm she possesses.

She kicks her shoes off and pulls her dress off, laying back against the soft plush cushion, showing off a lacy bra and a hint of some luscious, luscious fabric sitting at the apex of her thighs.

I groan.

"I know I said I didn't want to waste another minute," I exhale, running a finger along the swell of her breasts just above the sexy lace. "But I need to feel you right now."

She pants, reaching frantically for my pants. "I know the feeling. I want you more than you can imagine, too."

I take the fabric from above her thighs and tear at my own belt. "I guess this is the only way to really find out if you really do know that feeling. Because...I'm not sure I can wait one more minute to find out if you know what I'm talking about."

She raises her hips, helping me remove her tiny fabric.

I groan at the sight of her.

No woman's ever looked more beautiful.

The contours of her are putty in my hands, the softness of her skin almost makes me forget the need to feel her everywhere.

I unbutton my pants and pull my shirt over my head quickly.

I part her thighs and slide my hands deeper between them, inhaling.

"God, you are marvelous," I exhale, "A goddess in lingerie... I think you might be too damn good to be true, Ms. Kamaka."

She raises her hips, joining me. We move together, and she cries out as my fingers find her center. I look into her eyes and can see the pure passion in her.

"You can call me the future Mrs. Anderson," she pants, "and you'll have to, if this is going to work..."

I lay her back on the couch and press my body on hers, laughing.

"The future Mr. Anderson loves it when you talk dirty," I growl into her ear.

We stay on the couch a long time, laughing and kissing, my fingers exploring her from head to foot.

Then with us both half-naked, I stand and pull her up with me.

This is far and beyond not the way I planned to do this.

But it's better than anything I could have ever imagined.

Kicking a chair out of the way, I drop down to one knee. I grab for the box in my pants pocket, determinate to consummate at least one task…before finishing the other.

Mia looks down at me, wide-eyed.

I take her tiny trembling hand in mine, my heart pounding strongly in the hollows of my chest.

"Mia," I say, "I don't want to lose you. I want to make love to you, forever and always. Will you let me keep you just this way? For the rest of our lives? I love you so much. And I know it's a lot to say, but I love you more than you can imagine. You are my everything. And I want to make you safe in my world...forever."

I open the box.

Mia gasps, rising up on tiptoe to see the ring.

She looks up at me, her eyes brimming with tears of joy.

And I know what she's thinking.

Every single word in that sentence is a promise...and I intend to keep them all.

I actually love the feeling.

"Yes," she says, breathlessly, hugging me.

I slip the ring on her finger, and, to no shock, it's a perfect fit. Gifts from the heart always are.

She looks at the ring, staring at the gorgeous sparkle. "You know, you did promise to leave me, then asked me to move in, now, proposing like this..."

I laugh. "It's just been a very long couple of months. I owe you for making our first few weeks together a rollercoaster. Next weekend, we'll go ring shopping and get you something even better than this."

Her eyes light up at that.

"Wow, only a man... who's in love...could think of something like that. But I'll settle for forever and always."

I kiss her, deeply.

Longest few minutes I've ever waited for.

At the same moment, she kisses me back for an eternity.

But the kiss is nowhere near long enough.

"But first," she says, laughing, "you should probably see this. Just to be sure."

I smile, knowing she's talking about the couch where we just removed most of each other's clothes.

She backs up and jumps onto the couch, landing with a bounce.

She turns to me, raising an eyebrow. "You know you want to, don't you?"

No woman has ever teased me like this before.

And now none ever will again.

I raise an eyebrow at her, crossing my arms. "And if I do? What will you do to me?"

"Whatever you want."

I grin. "Well, I have a few ideas. Most of them involve repeating all of the things we just did."

"Oh, really? Did you want to go for round two, now?"

"Or three, four, seven...ten."

"I'm down for all of that."

She skips back over to me, laughing.

She starts by taking off my belt with a devilish grin on her face. Her hands slide down the length of my bare chest, slowly, and she smiles.

"I'm sorry if I took too long getting here," she says,

pinching the waist of my pants and pulling them down slowly. "But I can promise it'll be worth the wait."

"If you think that's enough to take the edge off, you really don't know me as well as you think you do."

She laughs, kissing me, followed by a deep, passionate exchange. She tastes like the Hawaiian sunset. I inhale, grabbing at her hips, pulling her back to me.

I take my time with this. Making love to her doesn't just feel good. It feels...necessary.

I plunge my hands into her hair and bury my face in her neck.

This is where I want to be forever. Standing like this, eventually in our forever home. Falling asleep beside her over and over, feeling her skin to skin. Because I already know if I can't hold Mia, I'm not alive.

I feel all of her every time she's close to me. I crave her touch and her gaze, her laugh and her kindness, her warmth, her sense of humor and the way she looks when she comes.

But most of all, I crave her, just this way.

I roll onto my back on the couch, Mia giggling and falling on me, straddling me. I hold her in my arms, her chin on my chest, right where she belongs.

Want more Seattle CEOs and the women that love them?

Corporate sabotage, spicy romance, and the smart women who just might be able to tame these Seattle Billionaires are what you'll get in the rest of this heart-tugging romance series...

The next book is Ryder Anderson and Jenny Forde's in **Rival to the Billionaire.**

Sparks fly in this steamy workplace romance when this sexy, stubborn publishing exec meets his match in his new coworker.

Start THE RIVAL now to storm through the Seattle's hottest billionaires together!

Rival to the Billionaire

RYDER

I'm used to getting what I want—in bed and out of it.

And I sure as hell am going to get what I want this time.

The new project I'm about to pitch will launch our company into the big leagues...

If only my nightmare of a colleague would stay out of it.

Knowing Jenny Forde practically all of my life hasn't made it any easier to be forced to work alongside her.

Determined to be my rival, she'll do anything to sabotage my plans.

She's stubborn, uncooperative, and in need of a good hard screw in order to loosen her up.

Problem is: I need her to sign off on my project, and I'll stop at nothing to get her to say yes. Yes to my proposal. Yes to me.

And yes to realizing that she might just be the thing my life's been missing all along.

JENNY

Ever since Ryder Anderson and I were kids, I've hated him with every fiber of my being.

And he knows it.

But getting an excellent job at his big Seattle publishing company has allowed me to put our past behind me.

Firmly.

I'm going to succeed at my job. And rise beyond my rivalry with Ryder for good.

If only he would stop driving me crazy.

With his arrogance. With his dark, devastatingly good looks. With how he can make me feel with just the slightest touch.

I need to stay focused. I can't let this insufferable jerk break down my resolve.

But what if he's not the arrogant jerk I've always thought him to be...?

Could the man beneath all that arrogance be the one to finally make me understand what I've been missing?

—

Head to evemadisonbooks.com for more banter, billionaire news and steamy scenes to come!

About the Author

Eve Madison is a Billionaire Romance author who has a passion for crafting steamy stories that will make your heart race faster than a Ferrari on the Autobahn.

When she's not writing about tall suited men with tattoos, you can find her indulging in her two favorite vices: chocolate 🍫 and tequila (but not at the same time. That would be messy).

Printed in Great Britain
by Amazon

22285485R00178